BOOK BOYFRIEND

Kris Ripper

carina
press

carina
press®

Recycling programs
for this product may
not exist in your area.

ISBN-13: 978-1-335-51717-3

Book Boyfriend

Carina Press
22 Adelaide St. West, 41st Floor
Toronto, Ontario M5H 4E3, Canada
www.CarinaPress.com

Printed in U.S.A.

BOOK BOYFRIEND

Chapter One

It all started when Art—Art's, like, my best friend or whatever—turned up on my doorstep, in the rain, crying. Well, not exactly my doorstep. The doorman called me because there was a person crying in the lobby.

I mean, I didn't know it was Art immediately, it was more just *incoherent crying person for you in the lobby* with an undercurrent of *it's slightly disruptive to have an incoherent crying person in the lobby so maybe take care of it ASAP thanks*. Since I don't have a lot of positive experiences with crying people I was a little *eek emoji* about it on my way down. Were they even my crying person? If they were incoherent maybe they belonged to someone else in the building and when asked who they were there to see they somehow slurred their words and the doorman misheard "Preston Kingsley Harrington (the third)" instead of whatever the crying person had actually been trying to say.

I was all set to suggest this as a likely event when I saw them—him—Art, incoherently crying in the lobby. His bangs were darker than usual and dripping rainwater down his face, his normally cheerful fuzzy pink unicorn backpack was looking soggy and morose, and he was holding on to—was that—a computer tower in a trash bag? Which was dripping a steady puddle onto the cracked marble tiles of the lobby.

"Art, oh my god." The thing is, Art's my best friend, and

he's also like, okay, he's also something else, something that doesn't really have a name, a word for it, so when I saw him in the lobby, eyes puffy, pink unicorn sagging, my heart kind of tripped all over itself like something was *wrong*, really wrong, something was actually terribly, horrifically wrong. And I had to fix it, whatever it was, whatever was wrong, because Art should never, ever look that sad. For real, he never *did* look that sad. What could be that awful? Had something happened to his parents? His brother? The family dog, a big, drooly mutt with a deep bark and basically no instinct to kill you even if you were actively hauling off the TV?

He looked up at me, his mouth opening. I thought he might be saying *help*, so I stumbled forward and reached out for him. "Is everyone okay? What about Rolf?"

"Rolf?" His eyes were so bloodshot. "Of course Rolf's okay."

Which, if something really awful had happened, he probably wouldn't have said it like that. "Oh. Right. Okay. Good. So like...'sup?" Because obviously whatever had happened wasn't that big a deal, since the dog was all right.

He stared back at me with big, tragic eyes. "I broke up with Roman."

Fuck yes. This wasn't a crisis at all. Cue the marching band, this was a cause for celebration. "Oh no," I said, trying to sound...not as happy as I felt. Roman and I hadn't liked each other, which meant that I'd barely seen Art, my *best friend*, since he'd moved in with that jackhole. I tried to muster something else to say that wouldn't sound cheerful AF. "Uh...that sucks."

"It doesn't suck." His chin lifted slightly. "It's awesome. Because I'm amazing. And that guy's a dick."

"Hells yeah he is. I mean. *Roman.* Like he's Madonna or something. When we all know his real name is Austin. And what's with that scarf? I bet he even wore it when you were banging. Also, someone seriously needs to tell him there's no such thing as a casual blazer. And there's nothing cool about living in Red Hook. In a loft. Just because you think you're an *artist*."

Apparently this wasn't the amazingly supportive speech I thought it was. Because now Art was scowling.

But, hey, he wasn't crying, right? So that was good.

"Oh, you should talk. At least Roman is doing something with his life. He's super passionate about his work—"

"You mean, carving scented candles into political figures and then selling them for fifty bucks so people can 'burn down the establishment'?"

"—and he's got a *future*, okay? What do you have other than an apartment your folks gave you and a phone full of hookup apps?" Oh god, was he crying again? "Roman was an *adult*. And he cared about me."

"You just said he was a dick!"

"So what? He's a dick, you're a dick, I'm a dick, everyone's a dick, PK." He brushed angrily at his face. "Just some dicks you fall in love with."

This seemed like a really good time to point out that I could be the kind of dick he fell in love with—I mean, not like with my actual dick—with me as a human who happened to be a dick. I wasn't going to bring my dick up in a conversation with a crying post-breakup person who was huddled around his computer like it was the only thing keeping him from falling apart. Except suddenly Joey Cagliari was standing there looking like he was torn between laughing and laying down the law. "Think you can take it upstairs, Mr. Harrington? Mrs. Vanderplibble is threatening to call the police if you don't stop shouting about dicks in the lobby."

"Uh, yeah." I shuffled. "Sorry."

For this way-too-long moment, both of us just stood there. Art's hair was curling slightly from the rain and I couldn't stop thinking about how much I wanted to touch it, twine it around my fingers, just like I wanted Art to be entwined around me. Uh, not in a creepy "welcome to my basement" way. In a...*please never leave me again* way.

He hefted his computer tower a bit more firmly under his arm. "Um, PK?"

Oh shit. I was so busy daydreaming about having Art in my life I hadn't even invited him into my apartment. But this was totally my moment. My moment to show Art that I was there for him. That he was safe and welcome and important to me. Even if the world was a nuclear wasteland overrun with feral zombies and all I had was a bunker, a teaspoon and a tin of baked beans I couldn't open, my bunker would be his bunker, my teaspoon his teaspoon, and my tin of baked beans I couldn't open his tin of baked beans he couldn't open.

"So you wanna come up?" In my head I was escorting him toward the elevator all gentlemanlike, but in reality I was arm-flopping at the hall. "Also, why are you holding your computer like a puppy?"

"You know that thing where people say 'If your house was on fire, what would you take?'"

"Please tell me you lit Roman's place on fire." I imagined his half-burned scarf lying amongst the ashes like a limp dick.

My eagerness to see Roman's studio in ruins fell flat at the devastation in Art's eyes.

"Sorry," I mumbled.

We got in the elevator, standing decorously side by side like we were at a funeral for someone neither of us had known that well but whose funeral both of us felt obligated to attend. While we rose with agonizing slowness to the third floor, I wracked my brain for something to say. Something smart.

Something sensitive. Something appropriate to the situation of my best friend showing up super sad because he broke up with his loser (quite successful artist jerk guy) boyfriend.

"Uh, do you want to get drunk?"

Art did this tearful chortle thing. I'm not sure if it was actual amusement, or more like *I can't believe that's all you got.* "No. Thank you. I think I just want to sit. Or lie down? Actually, I probably don't want to lie down. I definitely couldn't sleep right now."

Sit! I could do that. I flung open the door to my apartment, rushed over to the sofa and triumphantly shoved a stack of fancy literary magazines my parents had gotten me an annual subscription for but I hardly ever actually looked at to the floor.

Art sort of trailed in after me. Then he frowned at the magazine avalanche, which I immediately stacked more, uh, respectfully, because Art was a book lover, a short story lover, a *word* lover, and didn't like to see fancy literary magazines disrespected like that. He was the one who used to read them back in college. I'd dump my mail in a pile next to my bed and he'd rescue the magazines, which he'd go through from cover to cover and talk about with my parents the next time he saw them. In his extended absence, they'd gone largely unread and unloved.

But all that was over now! Art was back! Sans that jerk Roman! I gestured—*please have a seat on this luxurious sofa I have cleared for you*—but he just kept standing there, clutching his computer tower, staring off into space but at least not lecturing me on the proper way to stack magazines I didn't care about. Which, I'm not joking, was definitely a topic on which he could wax poetic for way too long. He'd been working at the same bookstore since he was eighteen and he takes that stuff *for serious.*

Okay. Right. Focus. He was sad. He was clearly sad. From the crying and telling me he was sad. Obviously he didn't know yet what I totally knew, which was that Roman had never appreciated him, never deserved him, but I *did* appreciate him, I totally *saw* him, and he deserved someone way better than Roman had ever been. Yeah. It was time to do something really special. To make all that clear.

Art blinked at me—and it was so weird, seeing his eyes without glasses, or glitter, or little stars dancing at the corners. Like seeing him naked. Or like that time we kissed.

What, didn't I mention that?

It started when Art kissed me after a party our second year of college. Or I kissed Art. Or however it happened, we were kissing.

Except we were also, like, *wasted.*

And while Art kissing me was the best fucking thing that had happened in my life, there'd been kegs earlier, and also Jägerbombs, and also hard lemonade.

So it was like *oh, this is what everything is supposed to feel like,* but also *I'm gonna throw up,* and those two things were majorly not compatible. I had to tell him, *Hold that thought,* and Art said, *Sure,* and his eyes were a bit bloodshot (because kegs and Jägerbombs and hard lemonade) but they were beautiful. Sort of greeny-browny-gray but all at once.

And then I ran out of the room and puked my guts up.

By the time I'd snorted mouthwash and had a shower and gotten back to our room, Art was passed out on his bed. He'd thrown an arm half across his face, eyelashes all gummed up with glitter from earlier, and he was drooling, and somehow he was still beautiful.

But obviously I couldn't kiss him because…kinda assault and shit?

So I waited all night.

And then the next day Art woke up and was like, *Holy hell, what did we do last night? I have suffered a minus two penalty to my constitution.*

And I was like, *Art.*

And he was like, *And we kissed hahahahahaha.*

I mean, he didn't say hahahahaha. But he made a noise that was totally hahahahaha.

And then he said, *Oh, my head. No more laughing. Ever. And no more kissing. Jesus. What we were thinking?*

And then he went *hahahaha* again and took a shower.

I'd never forgotten that night. And now, here we were five years later, and Art was standing in my apartment with his hair plastered to his face and all I could think was, *Yes, please, yes, stay forever, we should kiss again, I hope that puddle isn't going to stain, I should probably clean it up.*

And my heart did this *thing*. Like it was this shiny silver birthday balloon expanding to fill all the spaces inside me, this thing that made me want to tell him everything right then, in that clearly not-right moment, because I hated that he was sad but I was so, so happy that he was *here* and I needed to do something, anything, to prove it.

"Hey," I said. "I totally have a monitor I'm not using."

Wait, what? No. No. PK. No.

"It's in the junk room," I added, starting to back down the hallway. "Hang on, I'll be right back."

The spare bedroom in my place (and it's not like my parents *gave* it to me, just the renters moved out right before I graduated so it made sense for me to, you know, move in) was supposed to be a guest room, but I also had workout stuff in there and my old computer and random junk I hadn't gotten rid of yet.

Like this second monitor I'd picked up when the computer lab at school was revamping, because I had this great vision of myself at a desk with two monitors looking SUPER SRS. Or also maybe because Art had two monitors and I thought that was cool.

Anyway, I had this monitor, which I brought out into the living room and plopped on the coffee table, moving some dirty dishes covertly to the floor, my shoe kind of nudddddddging them under the table itself. "Uhhh, so…lemme see your tower."

He surrendered it without comment, his eyes following my movements in this glazed, lost way. I'd felt a lot more comfortable when he was shouting about dicks.

I hooked everything up and turned it on, waving my hand like a magician—*please enjoy the computer I have brought to life for you*. "There! You can play games. Or watch Netflix. Or, um, porn or whatever." *Why did I just say that? Why did I just say "porn" out loud?* "I mean, not porn. Or porn! Like, I'll leave that up to you. Whether you porn or not."

Art blinked at me, his eyelashes brushing the skin beneath his eyes, making me think of wings. "Roman said I liked my computer more than I liked him."

I wish. Actually, I wished he liked *me* more than he liked Roman. Which he should have, because bros before gender-neutral-in-no-way-sex-shaming hos, right? But in the bro vs ho battle, I'd lost hard. "That just proves my point that you're way better off without him. Time to move on, Arty."

He sighed. Heavily. The kind of sigh that sounds like the dramatic dying gasp of someone in an old movie. "It's not that easy."

"I'm pretty sure it is."

"Yes, but." An eon passed while he stood there in my living room gathering his thoughts. And then he came out with: "I have been afflicted with a significant debuff called heartbreak. I wanted a fairy-tale romance and what I got was my prince turning into a toad."

I wanted to tell him he was perfect. That he'd find someone else. That he deserved his prince, someone who'd give him everything he needed without complaint. Someone who wasn't jealous of his computer. Someone who knew what a debuff was, because I was pretty sure that twit Roman didn't.

"Buck up," I said. "What doesn't kill you makes you stronger."

"This is why you're my port in the storm, PK." He sounded exhausted. "Because you're so sensitive."

"I am?" My heart beat quicker, like maybe we were going to have A Moment.

"Ohmygod, no. Sarcasm."

I slumped. "Oh, right."

"You're the only person I know in the city who has a spare bedroom. D'you mind if I crash here for a few days? Just until I figure out what the hell I'm doing with my life?"

"No, of course not. Stay as long as you want." Which was exactly what you'd say if your best friend (or whatever) showed up on your doorstep (slash in your lobby) in the middle of a rainstorm (at least, it was raining) because he'd just dumped his (tool of a) boyfriend. Coincidentally also what you'd say if the guy you'd had feelings for since an ancient history drunken kiss needed a place to stay and you knew you couldn't just come out with *also I'm totes in love with you we should kiss again*. See how sensitive I could be? I knew that this was definitely The Wrong Time to say that.

"Thanks." He started toward the junk room—sorry, *guest* room—which was when I remembered that aside from unused monitors and fitness equipment, I'd also stashed a bunch of, uh, home spa stuff in there. Nothing weird or anything.

Just, like, a neck massaging thing. And a foot bath. And also a manicure set.

Maybe if I skirted around him—

"Hey, watch it!"

"Sorry!" I called, frantically trying to get there first. "Why don't you, um, wait a minute while I clear away some of this crap—"

"Like I haven't seen all your stuff before. We used to live together, you know."

"Yeah, I know." It was no use. The apartment was not that big and Art was right behind me. I started shifting stuff around, hoping to at least cover the box for the neck massager (it was one of those, like, *suggestive* looking things, not that I'd ever used it for anything but my neck, and this one time my thigh, after I'd strained something in a freak coffee machine accident at work).

He didn't see the massager, but he honed in on—

"Is this...*your* manicure kit? It's cute."

I didn't know why my face felt like it was on fire. "Um, yeah, I saw this—I mean, I read this article—about how to be taken seriously in the work world—and it said that personal grooming is an underrated quality. So I bought a thing for my nails but I had no idea how to use it and then I googled but I got really confused about cuticles so I gave up." I'd said it all really fast and Art was just kind of staring at me. "What? Is it that weird? I mean, it's just my nails or whatever."

"I didn't say anything about it being weird. Why are you acting shady about wanting a manicure?"

How did it somehow sound...worse when he said it like that? "I didn't! I mean. I'm not. I was just... I thought... I don't know. I couldn't figure it out anyway so I never managed to actually do it."

His lips twitched up a little on one side and he reached out to pat my arm. "Manicures are nice. I can help if you want. Anyway, I think I'll take a shower if that's okay."

"Yeah, sure, course. My house is your house. I mean, obviously it is. While you're staying here. Not like you need my permission to take a shower." I forced a laugh.

"Could I borrow a towel, though? I didn't exactly pack sensibly."

A towel. One of my towels. Art was going to use one of my towels, you know, after a shower. Umm. "Yeah, right, here." I had exactly three towels: the one I used myself, the one I'd once put down when I'd had an, ahem, plumbing issue, and this super fancy towel my mom gave me when I was in college that was so soft and posh that I'd never dared use it and had stored it up out of the way in a cabinet so I wouldn't accidentally grab it the next time I had a plumbing issue.

"Here," I said, bestowing it upon Art like it was bathed in celestial light and angels were singing or something.

"Ooooh, it's the your-mom towel. I'm super honored. I'm gonna go cry about my dipshit *ex*-boyfriend in the shower now." He blew me a kiss and disappeared into the bathroom.

He…blew me a kiss. And he also touched my arm. And told me he'd help me with a manicure.

And now he was getting naked so he could cry about some asshole dude. Serious downer. *Serious* downer.

Chapter Two

Okay, so maybe I couldn't fix *everything*, but I could give Arty a place to stay for…forever? I mean. You know. As long as he wanted to stay with me. Which seemed like it was going to be longer than a minute once the first morning passed and he was in the kitchen making coffee in his work clothes (black skirt over black jeans with black turtleneck and black vest, so like, I guess he was in a mood or something).

I kept telling myself he might be gone by the time I got home, but he wasn't. At least, his stuff wasn't. And then he buzzed up roughly one commute after he got off work, not that I was staring intently at the time or anything, and definitely not like I skipped into the kitchen and started heating a pot of water after unlocking the door for him, or in any other way tried to act like I was totally being normal and also, hey, did you want some pasta? I was just going to make some…

The whole thing was a weird, not-that-delicious cocktail of old times and new sads, and after pasta Art went to his room/ the guest room/the junk room and stayed there the rest of the night. Which left me a little awkward. We'd been roommates, so I didn't really feel like I was his host, like I should be entertaining him. But also he'd just broken up with his prick boyfriend, so should I really just ignore him in his bedroom all night? That felt a little uncool. On the other hand, what was I supposed to do? Barge in and demand he reassure me that he was okay? Obviously that's what I *wanted*, but it probably wasn't what he *needed*. At least, that's what I told myself while I paced around in my bedroom with the door open for an extended period of time, just in case he came out.

He didn't. So eventually I did what I almost always do at the end of the day: sat in front of my computer and tried to write something brilliant. I'd been playing with an essay about how the landscape of self-discovery had changed in the recent past—it was a lot harder to *eat, pray, love* your way around the globe these days—but it wasn't really going anywhere.

Then I went back to the novel I'd been playing with for years, which I'd managed to "finish" twice without making any actual progress on it. Apparently even if you write THE END on the last page, that doesn't make it a book. I kept thinking I had it, I'd finally figured it out, but then it was just…all middle. I'd been working on the same damn book for what felt like half my life, but it was just this muddled up collection of scenes about things happening without anything actually *happening*. I'm not gonna lie, some of them were really *good* scenes, like I'd shown Art what I had, and a few other friends, back in school, and all of them had said it was good, but it wasn't, y'know, an actual story.

I was way too wound up to write anything decent after stressing about whether Art was going to disappear in the night, then the day, and now the night again, but I reread some old stuff and changed a few commas, swapped out a few over-used words for better ones. It was better than agonizing over how much I was friend-failing my bestie. Right? Probably?

To no one's surprise, I was a *slight* basket case at work the next day. I'd managed to say nothing about the Art thing the day before because I half expected to find he'd cleared out his stuff by the time I got home. But there was no way I could pretend everything was hunky-dory forever.

Art always acts like I don't appreciate my job, like I'm just this rich kid who doesn't get how lucky I am to have it. "Some people would kill to work there and you just kind of *oops*ed your way into a permanent position." Which was only partly true! Okay, yeah, I'd applied as a lark because it was what all the interns were doing and I didn't expect to actually get the job, but what can I say? People like me.

It's a real job, though. Editorial assistant. At a publisher I'm not gonna mention because they're kind of big and you've probably heard of them. Not that I'm flexing! I didn't work with, like, the bestselling authors or anything. Basically I'm the guy who'll read your pitch if you sent in the first twenty pages to our catch-all submissions address. I also, uh, manage two legit editors and all their ongoing projects. Sort of. Anyway, I make sure the spreadsheets are up to date so that *The Mystery of the Murderous Cat Burglar of Knob End* doesn't get confused with *The Cat Burglar Murder: A Knob End Mystery*. These things happen! But not on my watch. Theoretically.

Also this one time I had to send a fax. A *fax*. I mean, not really. In reality faxing involved downloading and installing software, which I needed IT (who was a chick called HAWK, all caps, with bright blue hair) to do for me, and she couldn't do it until I got a requisition form from my boss, who sent it through her boss, who had to run it past accounts payable even though the software itself was free.

It would have made more sense to actually find a fax machine. If that kind of thing even still existed. I saw pictures when I was googling "How to send a fax."

My work bestie Maggie is also an editorial assistant, but she works specifically in romance for a terrifying editor named Adams. And I say "terrifying" with all the affection in the world. She was my supervisor when I was an intern, and apart from being brilliant AF, she's also a good boss. By which I mean she didn't make bullshit demands for coffee or picking up her dry-cleaning. I'd ended up floating a little between romance and mystery and fantasy/spec fic, mostly because I wasn't all that driven so I got plugged in wherever. Mags, on the other hand, has only been around about a year longer than I have, but she'd managed to carve an office out of a store room, and had taken on the care and keeping of the house macaw, Puzo, an actual living bird that had been passed down from person to person for over a decade. Macaws apparently live forever. Anyway, Maggie isn't screwing around on her way to becoming a real editor. Like I daily expect her to roll up and be all, *Yo, I got a grown-up job over here*, only not really like that because that's not how she talks, but the gist of it.

Maybe I wasn't on the same track, since I wanted to write books more than I wanted to edit them, but my job totally counted as a real job. And—since I'd lost touch with most of the people I'd gone to school with—it was also my main social outlet, and Maggie was the person I talked to more than pretty much anyone. Which was why I planned to wait a reasonable amount of time before telling her about Art, you know, so as to not be all like HI LET ME WORD VOMIT TO YOU ABOUT MY FRIEND WHO KIND OF MOVED IN WITH ME AND HAS A BROKEN HEART BUT WHO ALSO I MAYBE HAVE A CRUSH ON IF THAT'S WHAT YOU CALL IT WHEN YOU MIGHT HAVE FALLEN FOR SOMEONE YEARS AGO BUT NEVER MEN-TIONED IT TO THEM.

And, to be fair, I didn't do that. At all. Even a little. More like I opened with, "So, what's your best advice for a guy who's supporting his best friend through a bad breakup?"

She blinked at me in this unimpressed *Do I look like I hand out freebies?* way. "I don't give advice."

Which was a patent lie. Usually she'd tell people exactly

what they were doing wrong and how to fix it. "Uh, really? Because I swear just last week I heard you telling Bobbi-with-an-i in events that if she didn't dump her girlfriend you were going to, and I'm quoting here, 'fill out a sexy Tinder profile, get her laid, and show her what she's been missing.' Well, not actually quoting, because you said all that *to* her, so it was more 'you' than 'her,' but you know what I mean."

"I should have done that, I'm so over Bobbi's girlfriend woes. Is that what you need, PK? A Tinder profile and a good bout in the sack? Or wherever you like doing it?"

"No! I mean. No, I do not need 'a good bout in the sack.' And god no, I don't need a Tinder profile." Full disclosure: I already had one and it sucked. Tinder, not my profile. I mean, maybe my profile too? Outcome murky. Plus, I didn't want someone randomly on Tinder to take notice of me. I wanted Art to take notice of me, to really *see* me, the way I really *saw* him.

Maybe the question I should have asked her was HOW DO YOU GET YOUR BEST FRIEND WHO YOU MAYBE HAVE A CRUSH ON TO REALIZE THAT YOU TO-TALLY *SEE* THEM?

Except that would make me sound ridiculous, so I didn't say it.

"Well?" Maggie demanded. "I'm basically only offering Tinder profiles and kicks in the ass right now, so. Wait, is this an ex of yours? Because the last thing you should be doing is soothing your ex over their new ex. That way lies madness, ice cream, and make-up sex that you only later find out was rebound sex. Ask me how I know."

This time I blinked. "Um. So. Should we like…" I waved my hand ineffectively. "Do you want to process or something? I mean. Are you…having feelings?"

"Oh. My. Dear. God. No, I do not want to *process*. Stick

to looking fit and making coffee, sunshine. What's your deal right now, anyway?"

"Nothing. Just. My best friend? Has been with this idiot artist for like months now. And just dumped him, so my friend came to my place? And now he's super-duper sad all the time and I have no idea what to do about it."

Maggie's forehead creased in an unflattering way. "You mean, you don't know how to fix it."

"Yes! Like. What can I do?" I didn't mean to flap my hands around but it happened without my consent, they did a flop-flap-flop motion like they were trying to fly away.

"You can't do anything."

"Wait. What do you mean?"

She shook out her extraordinarily long hair and started doing something with it behind her head. Braiding it into a rope or weaving it into a basket or something. "You can't fix a breakup. Your friend just has to, y'know, get through it." When I only stared at her, she sighed. "Well, what have you tried?"

"Um. I…hooked up his computer?" Sure, in the living room, so he'd ended up having to unhook it all and pull it into the bedroom, but I *had* hooked it up in the first place. "And I…found him a spare toothbrush." That I'd gotten the last time I went to a dentist. "Um… I got him a towel? Not got-him got him. Like, I already had the towel, but I did find it and give it to him to shower with. Not give-give. Lend. Err."

"You're totally hopeless is what I'm hearing."

"Hey! I'm not! I'm a good friend, right? And he's all kinds of mopey and bummed and staying in his room a lot on his computer except when he's at work, and when he's at home he's in his room and his eyes are all red like he's been crying and it's—it's—" *breaking my heart.* "It's sad," I finished weakly.

"Yes, PK, breakups can be *sad*. Good talk. Maybe you

should tell him that, you know, really share your wisdom there."

"Why are we even work besties again?"

She grinned. "Because I didn't get you fired on your first day when you forgot you were answering a work phone and said, 'Look, I like your penis just fine, I thought we were talking about your feet' to one of our VIP authors—"

"Okay, okay, no one has to ever say that out loud again."

"—and I fixed it. That's why we're work besties. You get yourself into muddles and I come in and clean up after you."

"That's a total mischaracterization. What about that time you couldn't find that spreadsheet and I saved the day?"

"I couldn't find that spreadsheet because you randomly renamed it and saved it to the P drive instead of the G drive."

Which, all right, was technically true. "Okay, first, the file naming taxonomy was a freaking *joke* and I made it better, and second, I think the important thing to remember about that incident was how I executed a single search and managed to find the misplaced file, thus saving the day."

"You fixed what you broke that time. Did you break up your friend and the artist?"

"No. Not for lack of wishing they'd break up, but I didn't actually do anything to make that happen." Though the number of times I'd thought about how much better a boyfriend I'd be, and how shitty that mononymned prick Roman was, and how he was always making Art feel lousy about himself... let's just say if you could *will* people to break up, I'd be guilty, but since you can't, I wasn't.

"Probably not much you can do. Be there for your friend."

"Art. His name. It's Art." Why was that important? Except she was my work bestie, and Art was my...uh...life bestie? Was that a thing? Or did that just sound like a euphemism for "boyfriend" straight out of a seventies movie? Except for the "bestie" thing, which I didn't think they had in the seventies.

"So be there for Art. Honor his needs. Maybe encourage him to, you know, do something other than mope and work if that seems like a thing. But if it seems like moping and working is appropriate for him—even if it makes *you* uncomfortable—suck it up, buttercup."

I wasn't always the most insightful person on the planet, but even I could see she probably had a point. "Is it insensitive if I really hope the moping part goes away soon?"

She patted my shoulder. "Just don't have sex with him thinking you're helping."

I choked.

"Ten-to-one it fucks everything up. Rebound banging works best when you barely know each other or you've banged in the past but neither one of you have feelings for the other. Have you banged him in the past?"

"Oh my *god*, could you *not say things like that so loudly*?"

She eyed me. "Why? Why don't you want me to talk about you banging your best friend? Wait, did you? Spill, PK."

"No! Never! I mean, we kissed once but it was only once and it never went further than that!" I rubbed at my face. "It was only once."

"Uh-huh."

"It was!"

She opened her mouth to say something else but then her phone rang and—to my serious relief—she had to answer it, so I quickly escaped to initiate a round of coffee drinks, which was bound to keep me occupied until Maggie forgot the whole thing where I just accidentally mentioned how Art and I kissed that one time.

It wasn't quite a clean getaway. I really, *really* wanted to fix things for Art. But part of the problem was that he'd gone all in on Roman like the dude was a royal flush, when at best he was a pair of twos. Or, okay, like maybe a pair of threes, but he wasn't better than that. And what did it make *me*, that Art, who'd spent so much time with me over the years, never saw me as a winning hand at all? Wait, I didn't really play poker. Was that the phrase? "Winning hand"? Because that sounded vaguely metaphoric, like you'd see it in Shakespeare and act like you knew what it meant and then go to the bathroom and google it on your phone to make sure you weren't making a fool of yourself.

Anyway.

Why wasn't I obviously a better dude than freaking *Roman*? Just because I wasn't a fancy artist guy with a loft in Red Hook. Except that wasn't the whole story, because Art wasn't materialistic. He was…he was a romantic. He liked stories. Stories about love conquering all, the triumph of the human spirit, people coming together despite everything that kept them apart. Stories about charming artists wooing sweethearts with candlelight and poetry and…ugh. Fine, okay, Roman probably had game. But I could have game! I could—I could woo! Maybe I should google wooing. I mean, who even knew what that meant, really? I could figure it out, was the point. I could woo Art. No one on earth was better suited to wooing Art, because I knew him better than anyone else.

But not, like, right this second. I didn't have to google "should you woo your best friend, who you kissed this one time in college and secretly had a crush on or maybe have been super in love with ever since, right after he broke up with his asshole boyfriend" to know that now was definitively Not The Right Time to woo. I'd start small. We'd mostly texted over the last however-many months it had been when he'd lived with Roman, but we'd spent most of college as roommates, so it wasn't like we were starting over.

Art, my best friend, needed, like, stability and stuff. He needed to feel okay again. And who other than me would be able to make him feel that way, right? So I could provide an upbeat home life that did not incorporate candlelight but also didn't incorporate the way Roman used to low-key dismiss his interests (in computer games and romance novels and nail polish and really anything that Roman didn't care about) and his fashion sense and that super cute way he used to sometimes stick a ribbon clip in his hair just for fun...

The more I thought about Roman, the more I wanted to punch him. I mean metaphorically. I don't actually punch people. In my life, I've never punched anyone. Or been punched by anyone. I mean, pushing, okay, a little, but not punching. But if the dude who made Art feel bad walked up to me randomly in the cereal aisle at Duane Reade, I might have hit him. Or, more likely, I would have been like, "Dude, what the fuck?" and he would have been like, "And who, pray tell, are youuuuu?" and then vanished in a puff of opium smoke because guys like Roman didn't shop in the cereal aisle at Duane Reade.

Whatever. The point was, I could be Art's best friend. And he'd eventually work out that my stellar best friend qualities indicated I would be an ideal boyfriend, and then we'd live happily ever after. Made perfect sense. Except for the way Maggie's *banging your best friend* phrase kept bouncing around in my head like a pinball, distracting me for the rest of the day. The worst part was how if I closed my eyes I could still feel his lips on mine, even though we kissed exactly one time years back. Maybe the kiss was a really long time ago, but having him around brought the memory so much closer.

The memory and the old fingers-clutching-at-vapor sensation of just barely missing the greatest thing that could ever have happened to me.

Chapter Three

Being a good friend-slash-roommate was going pretty well. In fact, it was almost easy to have Art around again. There's something about knowing how another person lives, it's kind of…mundane-intimate? Mundanintimate? Like knowing that he'd kill me for leaving dirty dishes in the living room, but as long as I put them in the sink, he'd forgive me for not immediately washing up. I tried to keep my inclination to drop my dirty clothes in front of the shower and leave them there under control (it's such an obviously correct place for dirty clothes, except for the way they have the tendency to multiply over time and become a sort of…heap), and he only took his nail polish off in front of an open window, mostly when I wasn't home, because the smell of acetone gives me an instant axe-strike of a headache. Arty was a way better roommate than I was, and always had been, but when I said that once, Art had pointed out that he wouldn't really want to live with himself as a roommate, because he knew he had "unreasonably high standards" and we were really just *different* instead of one of us being better than the other.

Art was the kind of person who thought *around* stuff that way, even when it didn't exactly make him look like a saint. Which I appreciated a lot, because I was definitely no saint. And he knew it.

It didn't take long to settle into a routine, was my point. It didn't take long for me to add his usual order to mine at the Ethiopian place between the subway and the apartment, or him long to message me every morning to ask if I'd written "anything extraordinary" the night before. Mostly I hadn't, but every now and then I did, and if I said I had, he'd cheer for me. If I sent him a particularly good line, he'd shoot back how great it was.

Art's praise was for real. When he said he liked a thing, he *liked* a thing. When he said, "Hmm, interesting," he *did not like* a thing. He liked, but did not love, my essay about the changing landscape of self-discovery. He liked the idea of it, but thought most of my examples of self-discovery were "blah." I'm not sure how Jack Kerouac is "blah" but to each their own, right?

Still, despite my best efforts at Home Stability, and all of my trying to be Totes The Normalest Normal in Normy Town, he was, like, bummed. In a seriously ongoing sense. He was still doing a lot of crying? Which, not to be unsympathetic about the plight of amazing people recently out of crappy relationships with assholes, but you'd think it'd be a relief on some level to be done with the asshole. To say nothing of having regained a great roommate with whom you shared a high level of mundanintimacy.

And yet he still looked weepy a lot, answering questions with single syllables, except for every now and then when he was suddenly consumed with rage and would explode in some rant about "that pretentious wanker Roman" that felt like it had been waiting to detonate for a long time.

"I gave up D&D for that asshole!" burst out of him in the middle of us splitting a pizza and watching *Dragula* season one.

I glanced at the screen to see if something there had inspired the exclamation. Then I realized that since my understanding of D&D was basically *Something about dungeons, dragons, and I think maybe wizards except they might be called mages?* I wouldn't know if it had or not. "Um...?"

"Not the game, just the group I was playing with, because he didn't want to have people over, except of course he didn't mind having *his* people over, did he? It was only my people who were a problem because he didn't 'get it.'" The air quotes were vicious little hooks at the ends of his fingers.

"Didn't get what?" I ventured.

"Didn't get why 'grown-ups' would want to 'sit around and play a kids' game.' Which just shows you what he knows."

"Yeah. Those, uh, rulebooks or guidebooks or whatever aren't cheap. No way kids could afford them." I knew immediately that I'd said the wrong thing. "What? They aren't. I looked into it this one time." When we were first roommates in college and I wanted to know what was so cool...or, okay, I wanted to learn how to play really well so I could show off to Art and his nerd friends. Except I realized buying a bunch of books was impractical so I figured I'd just learn online, but five minutes into the first video I tried to watch I got overwhelmed and gave up.

"Why'd you look into it?" His eyes were focused on me so intently that I had to look away.

"Oh, y'know. Curiosity, I guess."

"You could have asked me. Like. At any point during our friendship. Since I have made zero secret of having played D&D for almost my entire life."

"Well, yeah, but, uh..." *I was only interested because you were interested and I wanted to be super good at it so you'd be impressed by my skillz* didn't seem like the smartest answer in the world. "I don't know, you kind of... I mean... I guess I figured you wouldn't want to be bogged down trying to teach me?"

"It's not being *bogged down* if you're enjoying yourself, and it's deceptively easy, or not easy, but you can kind of increase the complexity as you get better at it. You don't have to memorize all the conditions for every ability in your head the first time you sit down."

I blinked at him, feeling that old overwhelming incomprehension rising up again. "Um?"

He smiled. "Sorry, I just mean you can start small, that's all. You should have asked me, silly. We could have made you into a really kick-ass paladin." And he kept looking at me. Like, well, in someone else it would have been a "like he was undressing me with his eyes" expression, but with Art, in this context, it was more a "he was dressing me in paladin cosplay, whatever that was, probably a tunic and a battered leather satchel."

It was a little intense, so I looked back at *Dragula* to stop my brain from imagining Art imagining me naked-and-or-in-a-tunic. "Anyway, why don't you have them here? Your D&D people." I gestured to the living room. "We have the space."

The "we" just sort of slipped out, but he didn't seem to catch it. "Wait, really? You wouldn't mind?"

"No way. Why would I mind?"

Art shrugged, but it was one of those *pretending to be nonchalant while actually mattering a lot* kinds of shrugs. "You really wouldn't? I mean, it'd be for a couple of hours. And I'd clean up after, I promise."

I went for a teasing smile. "Exactly what kind of D&D game is this, huh? Does it double as a sex party?"

"You wish." He batted his eyelashes at me with this so-welcome playfulness that I hadn't seen much of since he'd arrived all crying in the rain, and my stomach fluttered at it, like that slightly airborne moment at the top of a roller coaster. "But no, it's just there's usually snacks and notes and, well, we get kind of into it so sometimes we don't pay attention to what's going on around us."

"That's cool. Uh, if you want, you can do that. No worries." Really I'd be up for anything that made it more likely he'd stay in the apartment. As well as supporting him in this thing I knew he loved (and looking like a good guy compared to Roman, that obnoxious hipster asshat).

"Thanks, PK. Seriously."

I waved an arm like it was the least I could do. Since it was actually pretty close to the least I could do. "It's cool. I was always kind of jealous of your D&D parties, to be honest."

"Oh my god. Said no one in the history of ever."

"What? I was! You seemed to be having a lot of fun. And it was this whole…like, language I didn't understand." I sank deeper into the couch and turned toward the TV again. "Anyway, you can have people over. No big deal."

"Okay. Thanks. You want anything from the fridge?"

"Nope."

"Kay."

Score one for me, and negative one for Roman. Though I couldn't wrap my head around how like…pointlessly mean it had been to make Art feel bad about D&D. Why would you do that to someone you cared about? But the clear takeaway here was that I, PK, was better than Art's ex. The end.

And the other takeaway? When Art came back with a bowl of popcorn, he nestled down next to me a little closer than before. Or maybe I was imagining it?

I really hoped I wasn't imagining it.

Chapter Four

I'm not totally sure how it started. Like. I write at night. It's just…what I do. Sometimes maybe it's only a few paragraphs in a notebook, or I two-thumb something on my phone, or I grab my laptop and get something in at the kitchen counter while waiting for pasta to boil. If you look at all the people whose writing I admired growing up—Ray Bradbury, Stephen King—they all wrote a lot.

Then I got older and read Tolkein, and Kerouac, and F. Scott Fitzgerald, and Edna St. Vincent Millay, and Wilfred Owen, and…wait, what was I saying? Oh right, just that people wrote a lot, when they wrote, which was why when they died Wilfred-Owen-years-old you were like frantic with the sadness of it, because there was so much more for them to do.

I wanted to be that guy. I wanted to be Hamilton, pouring his millions of words on the page in order to make sense of the world. And I wasn't as good as all those people (yet), but you didn't have to start out good. "Good" could be what you were later, as long as in the now, you were *writing*. Since Art had moved in, I'd slacked off a little, or maybe it's just that in some way I didn't really understand, Art showing up in the rain had sort of…changed my life? Or the way I saw my future, anyway. Because now there was *Art again*, where before there was only *Ugh, am I gonna have to be nice to that tool Roman for the rest of our lives ewwwwww.*

Oh, god, no. Roman was gone now. For good. But I still didn't get why Art wouldn't at least look my way? I mean, in terms of dating. Obviously he looked my way for a lot of things, like passing the salt, or whether we could bear watching another episode of *Hoarders*, a show both of us felt was exploitative and problematic, but also we were both totally addicted to that well-edited narrative arc of *then Sue turned a corner and realized her pet poodle Pimpers really was more important than going to the thrift store every day and buying more stuff.* Then we'd talk about how even us laypeople could tell you that a lot of those thrift store addicts were super-duper lonely and going to the same store every day gave them the feeling that people knew them and would miss them if they disappeared off the face of the earth, and how could a show like that fail to ever address loneliness and isolation as, like, massive contributing factors...

Anyway, Art looked at me but didn't *look* at me, a sensation that was intensifying over the days—that feeling of not being seen, or of being overlooked, literally, like it had been so easy for him to hook up with Roman back in our last year of college when I'd been *right there*. It was only a matter of time before that confusing cocktail of emotion made its way into what I was writing.

It was only this kind of...aching longing at first. So I ignored it. I'd write a bit of a scene, and it would be about something else entirely. Maybe it would be a guy who hadn't been able to taste since he was in a car accident fantasizing about dark chocolate, or an artist stuck on a twelve-hour flight with fingers twitching for a paintbrush. Just these little snippets of character, not even story. (The only rule for "write a lot" was "don't judge or try to control what you're writing, just play with it." So that's what I did.)

It wasn't sexy. It was never like that. It was...it was desire in the sense of absence, as if my brain knew that what I needed was in front of me but I couldn't have it. Or, like, something.

It morphed into people, but still not in a sexy way. Desiring to hold a child, desiring to feel a dog sitting on one's feet (Art's family dog Rolf did this to me the only time I ever went home with Art and it was so cute I almost couldn't handle it). Desiring something you've had before but don't have now, or something you know you *could* have, but didn't know how to get.

The writing didn't turn overtly into… Art-flavored longing until the damn party. The terrible, ludicrous, nightmarish party. But before that, there was my mother.

I'd waited to tell my parents that Art was staying in the apartment. First, because he was only supposed to stay a few days. Then, because I didn't want them getting the wrong idea. Yet somehow when I mentioned Art had needed a place to stay and had chosen to stay with me, of everyone he knew, my parents had been so casual about it I was mildly insulted.

"Of course he did, dear," my mom had said. "You have that spare room."

Was that the only thing I had to offer? My spare room? I thought my dad was coming to my rescue, but he only added that we'd also been friends a long time, and it's old friends you need in a time like that. Okay, A) it was kind of a sweet thing to say, but also B) I was more than an "old friend," I was Art's *best* friend! For years!

Still, they'd sent over a sheet set and another super plush, fancy towel for Art to use, which genuinely made him tear up. It was sheets and a towel, so I didn't totally get the undercurrents there, but also he had a tricky relationship with his own parents, so you know: complicated.

Not long after that, because she has like zero self-control, my mom showed up at the apartment (unannounced, as she always did).

"Art! It's so good to see you." Air kiss, air kiss. No one should be fooled by my mother's air kisses. She was just the type of shallow that hid a vast abyss of terrifying strategic thought within. "It's so perfect you're here!" Like, hello, she obviously showed up *knowing* he was going to be there. "You can come with Preston."

"I can come with Preston where? And it's so good to see you too." And the thing was, he meant it. My parents had never totally wrapped their heads around Art's whole...self. But that didn't stop the three of them from genuinely getting along with each other.

"No," I said. "Not going. Already told you."

"Hush, dear." My mother—her hair freshly dressed (because you just *couldn't* get the same service in the suburbs, no matter how much you paid), her dress newly bought (because you just *couldn't* get the same styles in the suburbs no matter how much—you get the picture)—took Art's hands in a way I kind of resented/was jealous of and led him to the couch. "I know it's short notice, but if you could just *nudge* Preston to attend this soiree, it would mean the world to me. And to George too."

"Is it fancy? Do I get to dress him up?"

I cleared my throat with a lot of foreboding. Or maybe I was trying to be forbidding? I always got those two mixed up. "Excuse me, I'm not a Barbie doll."

Art grinned at me in an unfairly melty way before looking back at my mother. "Please tell me it's fancy."

"The *fanciest*, sweetie. And"—she lowered her voice in a way completely guaranteed to freak me out—"this is an important evening because we're introducing Preston—or maybe it's reintroducing him—to a *young man*."

Art, the traitor, leaned in. "Oh, *who*? Tell me everything."

"I'm not marrying some son of your sorority sister's just because he's gay, Mother," I said loudly.

"No one's addressing you, dear." She proceeded to explain in excruciating detail her (and my father's and her sorority sister's and her sorority sister's husband's) plan for world domination. Or at least to join their two businesses as well as melding two political powers into one big, like, Frankenstein's monster of an American dynasty.

You could just tell they were all secretly disappointed when neither of us were girls, and then thrilled again when it turned out both of us were queer. We're basically Disney's *Sleeping Beauty*, but without Maleficent. (Plenty of fairies though, *bu-dum-ching.*)

I attempted to sound deadly serious but not like I was overreacting. "Mo*ther.*"

"Now when you say *reintroduced,*" Art said, ignoring me (traitorously).

"Well, they knew each other when they were children—"

"We hated each other," I put in.

"—but it's been a number of years now, and we thought it was so serendipitous that all of us were going to be in the city at the same time."

"To be clear," I said bitterly, "he and I actually live here and the four of you literally planned a party for when we were free, so it's not serendipitous *at all*. It's the literal opposite of serendipitous."

My mother turned on me, and I always forgot just how forceful her personality was until she aimed it directly at my face and pulled the trigger. "You're acting like this is an arranged marriage, Preston."

"It practically is!"

"Oh, nonsense. Please stop being so dramatic. It's merely—" She waved a hand, but didn't actually finish the thought.

"An arranged reintroduction?" Art suggested.

I shot him a deeply betrayed look, which he spoiled by smiling at me again. Best friends you've had a crush on for years should *not* be allowed to smile like that. It was unsporting.

My mother laughed. "Exactly! Now, be so good as to tell me you're free two weeks from Saturday, Art, and I'll make sure you have the details."

And Art, my friend, my (sorta) roommate, my...thing-there's-not-really-words-for-but-means-a-lot, nodded, still smiling. "I am so totally free. I can't wait to meet the man PK's destined to fall madly in love with."

I slumped over, moaning, and hoped the drama of it hid my blush. Just hearing him say the words *madly in love with* did really unfortunate things to my insides, which reminded me of the unfortunateness of Maggie saying *banging your best friend* and then it was all *in love with your best friend* and *banging your best friend you're madly in love with* and ahhhhh, I had to hide in the bathroom for a few minutes until I could calm down.

It was hardly better when I came back out. My mother continued chatting with the person I secretly wanted to be with about the person she not-so-secretly wanted me to be with and I just sat there squirming. Where's a moderate but not fatal disaster when you need one to save you from a terrible social engagement?

Chapter Five

I lived in a state of abject dread for the next two weeks. Art, in contrast, seemed to have found the only thing that could possibly lift him out of his mourning period for stupid Roman: dressing me up for a party where my parents were trying to set me up with a guy I hadn't seen since we were like fourteen, at which point I was kind of too broad for my height (how can a growth spurt affect your shoulders before your legs? HOW?), and Wade had already settled into his tall softness, looking at least three years older than me.

Oh god. This was horrible. My parents (and Wade's parents) were monsters.

Art disagreed. "I think it's cute. I mean, it wouldn't be cute if they had any power over you at all—like, if they were threatening to disown you or your culture forbade you from saying no—but they totally aren't and you totally can." He was holding up ties to me, having already decided on the dark blue shirt I'd wear.

It was, I swear this is true, like Art was dressing me slowly, only a little at a time, the way some people eat every part of a piece of cake separately, like he was savoring the experience bit by bit.

And, well, it's not like I was putting up a fight about it. More Art time was always good. More Art time that didn't include outbursts about Roman was even better.

"What about that one?" I asked, gesturing to a blocky print I liked.

"It clashes, PK."

"It does? I think I've worn that with this shirt before, though."

"In that case, you were clashing." He tilted his head to the side and studied another tie I liked as he pressed it up against my chest...err, against the shirt. Yeah. Better way to think about it. GULP. "I think I like this one. A little whimsical, with the subtle silver thread running through it. You think?"

I was torn. I did actually like it. But also if I said yes, did that mean this whole thing where he was methodically sorting through my ties and pressing the best ones up against me would come to an end? Because thumbs-down. "You don't think it's too, I don't know, too blue? Isn't that as bad as clashing?"

"It's a complementary shade of blue, or really, it's analogous, if you want to get technical, but I think the important thing is that they go together but are not the same. And yes, to answer your question, if you showed up in one shade of blue for all your clothes, I would consider that as bad or worse than clashing."

"Why worse?"

He began the process of narrowing down his decision, carefully comparing the tie he liked to the other top contenders. "Clashing might mean you just aren't paying attention, or"—meaningful glance—"you just don't know what clashing is. It might also mean you know you're clashing and you're making a statement. But all-matching means you were trying to do something intentional, and it's just awful. Yeah, it's definitely this one. Look." He turned me toward the mirror on the back of my bedroom door, inherited from the last tenant.

And actually? "Huh. You can wear a shirt and tie with jeans like this?"

"If you wanted to marry him, I'd put you in something that wasn't jeans, but in this case? I think the jeans are communicating casualness while the tie is giving you a playful edge so no one takes the jeans too personally."

I blinked at my reflection—our reflection, since he was standing just behind and to the side. "You're sure?"

"That if you wanted to marry the man, I'd be putting you in your best suit? Yes. Now, what are you going to do for shoes? That's the thing of it. Let's see..." So Art went through my shoes and I looked at myself in the mirror, trying to see what he saw, trying to see what the people at this dumb party would see. Not an aspiring beau, anyway. Art was right about the jeans, they were definitely serving up *my parents made me come to this so I wore my jeans because they're not the boss of me* realness.

"Do you *ever* polish your shoes?" Art called from inside the closet.

"Um. I don't think I have shoe polish?"

He laughed. "You can borrow mine."

Fine, maybe I had to go to this stupid party, and make nice with Wade, and pretend I wasn't dying to leave, *but* at least Art would be there with me, and he'd be with me later, when we were at home again, debriefing, probably talking about how boring Wade was (he wasn't), or, no, how annoying Wade was (he absolutely was). Yeah. That was the image I wanted to hold in my mind. While I did this thing my parents made me do because they wanted me to marry a boy with whom the only thing I'd ever had in common was mutual dislike.

I quickly turned my brain back toward the present moment: Art, holding a tie up to my chest-slash-shirt. Art, critiquing the way I took care of my shoes. Art, making me laugh. Art, Art, Art...

★ ★ ★

And then, horror of horrors, it was time. No natural disasters saved me from my destiny. No untimely but ultimately harmless power outages in one specific building on one specific floor affecting only one specific apartment. Nothing.

Yay?

On the appointed evening I found myself in my nicest jeans, wearing shoes Art had actually made me shine, and a pair of sunglasses I refused to surrender.

"I am going to *rip those things off your face*," he said, all low and sexy-threatening as we went up the stairs and into someone-or-other's well-appointed apartment (I hadn't paid any attention to the name or location of because all of this was Art's fault so I figured he could be in charge).

Well, in charge except for the sunglasses, though his tone definitely had a "you better mind me, mister, or else" thing going on, which I was not mad about *at all*.

We were still bickering over my choice of accessory when my mom and her sorority sister swooped in and carried us off to meet...um. So. That was...was that...

This fit, gleaming, silky-haired, long-lashed (as in they were definitely fake, but the classy kind of fake), glitter-vested, younger-brother-on-*Supernatural*-look-alike could not possibly be the kid I once shoved in the mud for getting me in the eye with a water pistol.

"Oh *my*," Art whispered.

"Wade, darling, you remember Preston?"

"Of course I remember Preston!" He air-kissed at me. "Sorry again about shooting on your face without consent!"

Art burst into laughter. "I definitely need to hear *that* story later."

"You didn't—I mean—uh—sorry I pushed you over?" Why

was I blushing? Why had I tacked on a question mark to my apology?

He *gleamed* at me. "My thing sounds *so much* better than your thing." Then he turned to Art and held out his hand. "Your skirt is *everything*. Chanel?"

"Salvation Army on West Eighth Street," Art said without missing a beat.

Wade gasped. "You have *the eye*. Please take me with you! I never find anything in thrift stores and it's not for lack of trying. Well." He glanced at our mothers, who had moved a discreet distance away and were studiously looking engrossed in their own conversation while also clearly spying on us. "Maybe not *nothing*. There was the security guard I encouraged to take a quick but satisfying break with me one time. Which was…" Wade's face assumed a dreamy expression that on the one hand looked too comical to be real, but on the other hand did give off the sincere impression that he was remembering a tryst with a thrift store security guard. He blinked at us. "I never find *clothes* there, though. Preston, aren't you going to introduce us?"

Since it seemed petty to point out that they'd already shaken hands—in fact, Wade had held on to Art's hand way longer than strictly necessary—I said, "Sure, yeah, so Wade, this is Art. Art, Wade."

They shook hands again (why?) and Art shared an anecdote about an illicit dressing room blow job in an upscale department store while I just stood there being awkwardly non-exhibitionist (unless you counted drunkenly streaking the intro to philosophy reading group, which, actually, given my more mature outlook on life, wasn't so much wildly daring and exciting as it was creepy and vaguely gross).

Wade was called off to do something host-y—apparently

it was his grandparents' apartment—and I took a minute to regroup. To recover. To...

"Okay, he's so fab I kind of wish *I* was betrothed to him."

I choked. "I am *not* betrothed to him!"

Art's eyes sparkled in that way where he was also smirking, like his lips had one idea and his eyes had another. "You may as well be. I don't care what your mom says, this is a modern American arranged marriage. Your folks and his folks got together when you were children and decided they wanted to combine their empires and the best way to do that was to marry their sons to each other. And here you are! Hashtag equality!"

"No." Wow, I was shaking my head really emphatically. I forced myself to stop. "I don't have to do anything. I mean, I'm not going to. I can't. They can't make me."

Art patted my arm in a friendly way. The kind of friendly that I'd think about for the rest of the night, this casual, warm touch that sent sparks all the way to my toes. He leaned in. "As the scion of a noble family, *Preston*, it's your responsibility to—"

"Oh my god, *stop it.*" I glanced around and this horrible vision hit me, of all the same people here to celebrate the wedding of two men from wealthy families, two men whose parents (re-)introduced them hoping they'd get married... "No," I said. Decisively. "Not gonna happen. I'm not marrying him just because my parents want me to, no matter how fabulous he is."

"Hmm." Art surveyed Wade again, eyebrows rising just slightly. "If you don't want him, maybe I'll marry him."

I gulped. "Wait—what—but—"

"Doesn't he seem kind of princely? You can imagine him hiring a horse-drawn carriage for the proposal, getting down on one knee at the end of a magical evening, all romantic and sweet…" He sighed.

I tried very hard not to gag on my own tongue. "But… but…"

He patted my arm again. "Don't worry, you can be in the wedding party. It'll be great."

And I knew he was joking but adrenaline surged through me like it was time to run from a lion. Art couldn't marry anyone. He couldn't. I could *not* be his best man. Or actually, Art was more of a bridesmaids type of guy. I could *not* be his maid of honor or whatever. I couldn't watch him, like, put on a tux and beam at some other dude. I'd lose it.

If Art was going to marry anyone, I needed it to be me. I could hire a stupid horse-drawn carriage if I had to! Anyone could do that!

He turned away to charm a colleague of my mother's and I watched helplessly. Why couldn't someone try to set me up with Art? I'd go for that. But how…how were you supposed to ask your best bud out on a date after maybe you kissed that one time when you were drunk but otherwise you'd only been friends?

Chapter Six

I don't know how the fight started. Well. Okay. The fight was probably my fault? But also it wasn't.

It started as a fight about what a good boyfriend Wade would be.

"He'd be awful!" I argued after Art went off on an endless recitation of his good points, including his willingness to go shopping (it's not like I was *against* shopping, but I couldn't pretend I loved it because Art knew better) and also how nice he was to his grandma (which seemed like a weird thing to count as a boyfriend point). "He's—he's—superficial, and dramatic, and—and—and he doesn't even have a job!" I finished triumphantly. Take that, Wade!

"He's a research assistant at the Cloisters." I'd been hoping to inspire Art to, I dunno, passion or something, but instead he just looked confused.

"So? I mean. Isn't that like being an intern? You said internships weren't jobs! I spent a whole semester as an intern and the entire time you told me it wasn't a real job!"

"Uh, I think Wade majored in, like, religious studies or something? His mom was talking about how he did a dissertation on same-sex relationships in sex-segregated religious communities and won an award. Anyway, I think he's got a real job."

I was an assistant! An *editorial* assistant! Like, surely that trumped being a research assistant? Or at least tied? Why was he saying that like it was a big freaking deal?

"Plus, he was funny and didn't take himself too seriously." Art held out the hand he'd been nail polishing.

Even as caught up as I was in trying to prove Wade's unworthiness, I did take a moment to enjoy the sight of Art doing his nails, which I hadn't gotten to watch since we'd lived together, and also which it seemed like he'd mostly stopped doing when he lived with Roman. The way he bent over all intently, and studied each of the colors before deciding on one, and carefully, deliberately, applied it, so completely focused. The little line in his forehead. The angles of his fingers holding the brush thing.

"I just think it'd be nice to date someone who was laid-back for once." He turned his nails so I could see. "What do you think?"

"Cool." I wanted to say it looked like he'd painted his nails with my purest hopes and dreams. But obviously I couldn't say something like that out loud. "Glittery and midnighty and stuff."

"Thanks. Anyway, you might not want to date someone like Wade, but I think maybe I would."

The smile, like, fell off my face. *Crash.* "You want to date a guy whose whole life is basically performance art?"

He shot me *a look*. "I just broke up with *Roman*. Whose idea of a romantic evening actually included scattering rose petals on a bed one time, which is nowhere near as fun when you have to clean up all these wilted flowers. Anyway, apparently I have a type."

No, no, no, *I'm your type, I'm right here!* "Well personally I'd want to date someone who was, like, genuine, and sincere, and, um…" Quick, how could I say it? How could I trump romantically rose petal-ing a bed? "Good at making coffee!"

He shoots, he—definitely does not score. What was wrong with me? Good at making coffee, really?

"I can make my own coffee. And it's not like I want to go out with an insincere person, just that there are other things in life than thinking everything you do is the most important thing on earth."

The injustice of this was incomprehensible. "But—but *I* don't think everything I do is the most important thing on earth!"

He laughed and covered his mouth. With his blue, sparkly nails. "Oh my god, I'm not talking about *you*, PK! Obviously. I'm not going out with *you*!"

"You're not going out with Wade!"

"I was talking, like, theoretically. Not for real. Don't worry, I'm not stealing your man."

"That's—I'm not—he isn't—"

Another giggle.

I had to get control of this situation. "Just, I mean, I'd make a good theoretical boyfriend though. In theory. If someone wanted me to be their boyfriend."

"Uh, okay? But I really feel like that's not so much borne out by your dating history, no offense."

"What are you talking about?" I asked, deeply offended.

"Nothing, nothing. Just, you know, it's not like you were all that tuned in to your partner's needs."

My jaw dropped open. "I was! I'm tuned in!"

"PK, you got Shelly What's-it a car organizer for Christmas that one year."

"She was always complaining about how disorganized her car was!"

"You got, um, Tanner one of those soda-making machines from TV."

"It wasn't! I got it at Bed, Bath, and Beyond!"

He held up his hands. "I just don't associate you with peak romance. Which is fine! Totally fine. It's not a big deal."

"No, but…" I could be peak romance! I could be romantic! "What about that time I took Anthony to that fancy restaurant?"

"You had a *Groupon*."

"So what? It was still romantic! It was a romantic Groupon!"

"It was in New Jersey!"

"What does it matter where it was?"

Art sighed. "It doesn't. It's just, if I'm going out with someone, I want them to like…*want* to have a romantic dinner with me. Not at some steak house two hours away that no one's ever heard of that happens to have a Groupon out the week of my birthday. Like, candles and takeaway would be more romantic than that if it was part of a tradition, or had some meaning to us."

"How can takeaway be more romantic than a fancy restaurant? That makes zero sense."

"I know you don't get it. This is probably why both of us are single: I want too much romance and you don't even know what romance is." There was this horrible pause, this break in his words, almost like he was going to say more but decided it wasn't worth it. That *I* wasn't worth it. "Anyway, I need to get some stuff done. Good night."

And that…was it. He just walked out. Away. Down the hall. Whatever. Leaving me with *You don't even know what romance is* echoing in my head.

That wasn't true. Couldn't be true. I'd had relationships before! No one had ever given me a one star on the romance scale! And those had been really good presents, dammit. Tanner was still using his soda machine! Every now and then he'd Instagram a picture of some new flavor he'd tried, so, you know, so there. I was *good* at presents.

I tried to just forget the whole thing—from Wade, and my mother's significant looks, all the way through to *You don't even know what romance is*—but it was kind of eating away at me. I'd never thought I was…really that bad? I had good intentions. Wasn't it supposed to be the thought that counted?

For a while I found excuses to be in the common areas of the apartment, hoping Art would come back out and I could mount a solid defense about my mad romance skillz, but he stayed holed up in his room and since I couldn't hear his music, that probably meant he had on noise-canceling headphones and couldn't hear me conspicuously walking down the hallway, or washing the dishes, or, uh, moving the couch so I could sweep under it, which I'd never done before and was so gross I might never do again.

There was no point if he wasn't coming out to see what I was doing so I could triumphantly brandish my disgusting dustpan like a…like a very passionate-about-cleaning hero out of a romance novel? That was probably a thing, right? I'd interned under the romance editor, Adams, and I was pretty sure I could sell her on cleaning as a romantic gesture. Well. Maybe. Adams was kinda hard-core. Let's just say, if it was a thing, she'd probably seen it already and could cite every instance of it in every romance novel published in the last fifty years.

I finally gave up and went in my own room, restlessly trolling the internet for Interesting Things To Look At and finding nothing but the usual badly behaved celebrities, sympathetic children either dying of things or fixing world problems, and politicians screwing over everyone.

None of it mattered. Gah. Why couldn't he see that I was totally capable of romance? Okay, maybe in the past I hadn't lived up to my potential or whatever, but it was there! I mean, I probably wouldn't have killed a bunch of roses and then thrown their corpse-petals all over a bed because that sounded kind of messed up, but I could do something just as good. Or better! I *could* be romantic. And if Art wouldn't let me prove that, since apparently even the idea of dating me was too funny for words, I'd just have to find some other way of showing him how wrong he was. And the very second I figured out what that was, I would do it, too.

In fact, I bet I could think something up right now. It was, after all, my writing time. The time of day when I stopped being the person everyone else saw, and started being the person I was in my head, which okay, it sounded slightly sad when I said it like that, but whatever. The larger picture was NEWSFLASH: I could be romantic. I'd read the books. I had taken *many* dates to rom-coms, and not grudgingly. I *liked* rom-coms. Want to know my top five on Netflix right now? I could list them for you.

I opened a Word document and titled it PEAK RO-MANCE.

Yeah. There. Good start.

PEAK ROMANCE
BY PRESTON KINGSLEY HARRINGTON III

After another second I deleted the *III*. Probably not necessary.

And y'know, maybe…maybe I'd just leave it at PEAK RO-MANCE for now. It's not like I was showing anyone, and *I* knew I'd written it, so yeah. Good enough.

I wasn't exactly a novel writer. I had a lot of almost-novels, near-novels, middles-of-novels, beginnings-of-novels. I just didn't have any, y'know, endings-of-novels. I'd written short stories in college, which people liked, and kept plugging away at essays and novelish-type things since then. I'd always sort of assumed eventually I'd write something really good, something that captured people's attention and made them think. An *On the Road* for a new millennium, maybe. Or *The Great Gatsby* but I'd update the style and gender-flip the characters.

Anyway, since I was like fourteen or something, writing had been the place I went when reality let me down, and discovering that in terms of Art dating me, I wasn't just starting at zero, but in the negatives, was *definitely* a letdown. Since haphazardly trolling the web hadn't helped, I might as well funnel some of my frustration into words.

I watched the cursor blink for a few seconds, trying to figure out what I wanted. I wanted… Art. To be with him. To kiss him. I wanted him to understand that I was more than just a guy with a spare room. More even than a friend. How could I put that on paper, though?

You painted your nails with my purest hopes and dreams…

Okay, maybe I was rusty when it came to writing romantic stuff, which I'd sworn off of during The Roman Times because it was too sad.

Ugh, maybe I couldn't do this. "This" being anything remotely resembling, like, something Art could relate to. I could scrap it. Maybe I was in the mood for something all beat-poet-like. Or something very roaring twenties. I could go dark like Vonnegut. Twisty like Heller. If I had some drugs I could really dive into some kind of nutty stream of consciousness Hunter S. Thompson thing, but to tell the truth, I never really found a place in my world for drugs. I know it makes me a square, but I really only did drugs when other people were doing them, and didn't do them when they weren't.

But it wasn't enough to do what I usually did, just stream some stuff off the top of my head into whatever story I was haphazardly working on. I needed to write down all the things I couldn't actually say out loud. A place to put all the ways that I was better than the Romans of the world, and even the Wades of the world (though Wade had actually been a decent guy in the end *I guess*).

NOT AS BAD AS SOME OTHER GUYS BY PRESTON KINGSLEY HARRINGTON

Right, no, scratch that, keep *Peak Romance*.

Except what came out was…something else. This real/not-real thing about being in love. Not that I *was* in love or anything, just, when you're writing you fictionalize people and events and…and things. And I definitely didn't think the idea of me being in love was as hilarious as Art seemed to find it.

The day I saw your nail polish matched your sweater was the day I fell in love with you.

And I thought to myself, how many times have you done that, and how many times haven't I noticed?

And if I'd never met you, I would never have known.

I would never have known about electric tangerine. And raspberry sundae. And cerulean dreams. And electric storm.

There's so much I wouldn't know.

But most of all, I wouldn't know how to be in love.

And you know what? I was pretty happy with that, so I kept going. At first it was just this character, and then it sort of coalesced into a story. About this guy who was in love with his roommate and tells them how amazing they are and the roommate's surprised but also not surprised? Like maybe they sort of knew there was something there and weren't sure how to deal with it.

In walks the guy and he's ready with candles and their favorite Korean takeaway and also a new nail polish he knew his crush would love. And then they kiss and live happily ever after. Or anyway, they go to bed and cuddle because: totes romantic.

When I was done I reread it and it was pretty awesome. Also it was way too close to life (the nail polish and the roommate working at a bookstore and also I'd given them Art's favorite bibimbap dish from the place we used to go to in college). I definitely couldn't actually let him read it.

Who was I kidding? It was like one tiny condensed bite of a much, much bigger meal, a more complicated one, with different courses, and different forks for things, and the kind of dessert that definitely looks delicious but is also super intimidating because how do you even eat it? That's what this scene was. A morsel. I couldn't let anyone read it like this. But I was already wondering what would happen next, and what had happened before. How did they meet? How long had they known each other? How long had the main character known he was in love and how did he figure it out? Was there some kind of checklist? A semi-related Buzzfeed quiz? *Are you in love with your best friend? Take this quiz to find out which of TV's* Friends *you are!*

Maybe I'd give him a quiz. The character. You know. If I was going to write more. Because say a guy—any random guy—did take a quiz. And say the results came back *You are totally bonkers in love with your best friend, dummy.* What would that (random) guy do then? What's the next step after he finds that out? Was there a flow chart?

Whatever. I could be romantic. I had the Romantic Din-

ner bubble on the flow chart all filled out. Actually, just because I didn't want to be creepy about it, I swapped out the
bibimbap for Korean barbecue, which Art never ordered. And
I changed the bookstore to, uh, graphic design. Which (purely
coincidentally) Art might have almost minored in at college.
It's not like I was writing *Art* into the story. Just someone who
kind of related to the main character the way Art kind of related to me. It was an, um, literary analogy, like on the SATs.

ART : PK

LOVE INTEREST : MAIN CHARACTER

Umm. Huh. I don't…that was so…blatant. Maybe it wasn't
that. Maybe I should stop thinking about relationships and
analogies and just…everything.

So instead of thinking, I started working on another chapter. An earlier chapter. A chapter in which the main character searches the internet for a quiz that would let him know if
he was in love. Because: relatable. Not, y'know, that I needed
something like that. But I could see it being a very confusing
thing so it'd be nice if there was an objective way to know
for sure.

I'd laid the groundwork for the eventual romantic takeaway scene and gotten in some good besotted pining before I
realized A) I had to get up for work in five hours and B) this
story was the most fun I'd ever had writing.

I had no idea what to make of that, but as for the first
point—yeah. Time for bed. Plus, you never knew about stuff
you wrote in the middle of the night. When I read it over in
the morning the story might be terrible.

Spoiler alert: it wasn't.

Chapter Seven

Here's the thing—well—okay, one of the things. I didn't mean for it to get so out of hand. I was just writing this…this *story*. About not-Art and not-me and all the real-me feelings I could never express to real-Art. At first it was all over the place, these detached scenes that didn't connect to each other, which is kind of…how I write stuff. And also, not coincidentally, why I've never managed to put a beginning, middle, and ending together in one place. Then I wrote a little about how they met, and how they were roommates, and how not-me would look at not-Art sometimes and just *wonder*. What it would be like to kiss. What it would be like to brush hair back from his face. You know. Just stuff. Like that.

Then, after a couple weeks of adding to it every night, I realized I had a good half a book's worth of chapters sort of… half-assed tossed together like a salad you didn't plan for, so you're chucking in some canned tuna (probably too much) and some bits of broccoli (probably not enough) until you've got this weird collection of things that don't quite go together but maybe could? At least, to my practiced editorial eye, cough cough.

So I started to work on it more, like, seriously. Also I got to a hard part, where I didn't know how to get them to that scene I'd first imagined, where everything was *perfect*, which meant I didn't know what to do, so I just started messing around with the transitions to make it feel a little more polished. And added a new scene to the ending, so it felt a little more finished. Until it had a beginning, half a middle-ish, and an ending.

And that's where I...didn't screw up. Exactly. But I was *proud* of this book I was writing, you know? Like it was saying all this stuff that felt important and necessary and romantic and *good*. I obviously couldn't show Art, and any of our other friends would have immediately known it was us in the sense of being specifically not-us, and anyway, you don't show just anyone a book you're writing.

But there was someone I could show. So I mentioned to Maggie over coffee that I was kinda sorta maybe writing a romance novel, which was like dangling a steak in front of a German shepherd. She didn't have the encyclopedic knowledge of the genre that her current (my former) boss had, but it was definitely her wheelhouse. And, as I'd pretty much guessed she'd do, she asked to see it. (Because: steak is to German shepherd as romance novel is to Maggie.)

The weirdest part was I almost didn't show it to her. I'd mentioned it hoping she'd ask to read it, and then when she did, I got scared. What if it wasn't actually that good? I knew it had problems, but what if it had *unfixable* problems?

Maggie rolled her eyes and said, "Never mind then."

Which was when I realized I didn't just want her to read it, I needed her to read it. "No! I mean yes! Please! Tell me how messed up it is, I think it might be messed up, or maybe not, maybe it's really good but I can't tell and it's not quite finished yet but I do have the end, I just don't know how I get there."

She laughed, but not meanly, just the way you laugh when someone you like is tripping all over their words. "Yeah, yeah, just send me the damn thing, okay?" She clinked her coffee mug to mine. "I gotta get back to work."

"Cool, thanks, like really, thanks a lot, I super appreciate it."

"I *super* look forward to it." A raise of the previously clinked mug and off she went.

I went back to my computer and, y'know, tracked down the file in my cloud storage and…sent it. That was that. Done and done.

I tried to get immediately back to work except the idea that she might even now—no, now—no, she's working—it's been a couple of hours, maybe now—be reading this incomplete story that I'd put so much of myself into…it made me feel naked. Not in a bad way. Not in a great way. Just in a vulnerable, slightly exhilarated way that could tip over into nauseous and sick at any second.

I vowed to totally forget about it. Not think about it. Think about anything *but* it.

I completely failed to do that. Or to not do that. I couldn't stop thinking about whether Maggie was reading my not-me/not-Art story to the point where I almost sent an email to the wrong author about an upcoming promo opportunity, like imagine trying to walk that back: *Remember when I said that HuffPost wanted to interview you for their upcoming feature "Run, Jump, and Climb into These Ten Historical Figures' Trees"? Yeah, sorry, that was actually not for you, that was for the author of* All of Human History As Performed By Eddie Izzard, *so sorry for the mix-up, deep apologies again, please don't tell my boss I did that.*

Thankfully I caught the email and redirected it to the correct person. But I still had the sweaty palms anxiety stink of a person who'd actually hit send. Time for more coffee. Or a snack. Or a walk.

A walk, that's the thing people are supposed to do. In my case, since it took either six flights of stairs or a creaky old elevator that might or might not be on the verge of falling apart to get to the street, I usually took my "walk" down one flight, along the L-shaped corridor to the other stairwell, then back up to the seventh floor. Which was two flights of stairs and thus totally reasonable for a walk.

Except Maggie pounced on me just as I was passing the office she shared with Puzo (the ancient macaw). "Who wrote this? I can't believe you tried to pass it off as yours, like you sit around at night writing achingly lovely romance novels when the other dudebros are"—handwave—"sucking the hearts out of virgins or whatever."

"Excuse me, I'm *queer*. I'm not that kind of dudebro. And you think it's achingly lovely? Ohmygod." She'd said that, right? I wasn't hearing things? She said *achingly lovely.*

Maggie rolled her eyes and tossed her shaggy hair for good measure. "Fess up, buttercup. Who wrote this? It's so not your style. And, no offense, but PK, this is like *really* good. This is—I mean, I know I shouldn't have, but I passed it on to Adams, and you can tell your friend to thank me later, but I know she'll want it."

I almost choked. Adams was a spectacular but terrifying editor, and despite the fact that I'd worked for her, I never stopped being terrified. She was the kind of woman who might be fifty, but also might be seventy-five, and could make references all the way back to when "talkies" were big but you were too afraid to call her out on it even though she was obviously not *that* old. "Um," I managed to eke out. "You did that? Already?"

"Uh-huh. Why is your face that color? Oh no, did I fuck up? Who is it? Is it someone she already hates?"

"Not...not exactly. I mean. I don't know. I don't think." I sagged against the doorjamb of her office and Puzo used his beak to pull himself along the wall of his cage until he was at eye level with me.

We gave each other this long look, me and Puzo, and I halfway hoped he'd say something. Not that Puzo was the kind of macaw who'd speak on command—ever—but two or three times over the years I've worked with Maggie I've actually heard him say "hello" (just that) and it's always kind of cool.

He didn't, though. Just stared at me with his intelligent, totally no-fucks-giving bird eyes.

Maggie pulled me in and pushed me into her own chair, since it was the only one in the room. "What the hell."

"I wrote it." I swallowed, feeling somehow ashamed, as if I should apologize. "I really did write it. You...thought it was lovely?"

She looked at me with an expression oddly similar to Puzo's. "You wrote it."

"Um. Yes?"

A pause. Then she kicked the door shut and sat down on a pile of boxes. "You're for real. You wrote this, like, half-finished love story about a sweet nerd and the bumbling fool who loves him?"

I gasped. "He's not a fool! I mean. Okay. He's not great with feelings—"

"Ya think? He pines for his friend for apparently years! Like, bro, just tell him! But in the book it makes sense because he's written so well, like it's actually believable that he just can't figure out how to do it." She narrowed her eyes. "You're not fucking with me? You wrote this?"

I was beginning to feel slightly insulted that she didn't think it was even possible I wrote something decent. "Hey, I write stuff. I can write! You've read stuff I've written before!"

"I know you can write—short stories, essays, things like that. But this... PK, it's a real book. I mean. I, it's a mess, you backed yourself into a corner with your main character's internal conflict, you changed the names of at least two of the friends, and the pacing flags for the entire middle, which you haven't finished, because you have no black moment and no actual resolution, just a PUT MORE HERE before a happy ending, but all that can be fixed." She shook her head slowly, her eyes never leaving mine, and Puzo, next to her, did the same thing a beat later.

"You really think it's okay?" I asked, my voice small, like a little kid begging for approval.

"I sent it to *Adams*. Oh my god, she's going to kill me when she finds out you wrote it. Shit. I told her it was some random, which to be fair, I thought was true, because I didn't think… not gonna lie, I didn't think you had the emotional depth for something like this." Pause. "Sorry."

I laughed. Not like a genuine, heartfelt laugh, but a high, slightly manic laugh. "Deeply offended, but whatever, you think it's good? Because it sounds like you think it's good."

"I think it's fucking fantastic, you asshole. Okay, so, let's strategize." She started tapping her foot against my chair. Puzo bobbed his head to the beat. "She might not want it. That's possible. In which case, no big deal."

"Um." I raised my hand. "Wouldn't that be bad?"

"It would mean I wouldn't have to have a super awkward conversation with a terrifying woman, so no."

It was honestly reassuring that even Maggie found Adams terrifying. Though at the moment, Mags avoiding awkward conversations wasn't exactly my priority. "But…"

She leveled this very Speaking Look at me. "You didn't even know she was looking at it until thirty seconds ago, so you can't now claim it would break your heart if she didn't want it."

I gave this serious consideration while she rambled on about how she was going to break the news to Adams about, like, me, but in the end I decided her argument was flawed. "I think I really could be heartbroken though? Like you dangled this whole thing in front of me and then—poof—you take it away?"

"I'm not *poof*ing anything. I'm not dangling anything either, I—"

"Carter!"

Both of us jumped at the shout. Puzo moved to the other side of his cage and pretended to be super engrossed in a hanging toy. The door opened.

Adams. Five-foot-two stocky lesbian, mullet included, with encyclopedic knowledge of all things romance. "Carter! This piece of absolute shit you sent me—I want it. It has a lot of potential if the author can be forced to trim down the poetic nonsense and actually stick to a plot thread for longer than a page and a half. I don't care if your anonymous friend runs a factory farm and votes republican, I want this book." She glanced at me for a split second. "Oh. Harrington. I need the room."

I scampered up out of the chair, but Maggie pushed me back into it. "He doesn't vote republican, anyway. PK wrote it." I shrank into the smallest form I could, which was still not that small, but Adams only cough-laughed.

"Is this April Fools? Get me the contact info. Quickly. I want this book on my list. I haven't felt this much clarity about a book since I signed Carlos."

I was torn between flattery and feeling very slightly aggrieved—Carlos was one of our young hotshot authors, and I liked him, or at least, I thought he was genuinely funny *and* a good writer, even if he also had an ego the size of Manhattan.

"I'm serious, Carter," Adams added, as if we weren't convinced. When wasn't she serious?

"I know. And I realize it's hard to believe, but PK is the author." Maggie's voice sounded all sorts of dubious even as she said it.

"Okay, why does everyone think I can't write? I can write! I've been writing since I was a little kid!" To be clear, the early stuff was MCU fanfiction, and the graphic novels didn't have any actual graphics to speak of, but the point stood that I had an established pattern of having written stuff. I wasn't new!

"You." Adams turned all the way toward me. On the other side of her, Puzo peered out from behind his hanging toy, like he didn't want to see the execution but couldn't stop watching. "You. Harrington. How do you explain the fact that your main character utterly fails to take any opening to share his feelings with his love interest?"

"Okay, that's not fair, he *tries*, but see, the way he was raised, it's like not really allowed? So no one ever, uh, role modeled the way you do that. His parents weren't demonstrative, you know? So he has no idea how it's supposed to look when you like…talk to someone about how you feel? And all he knows is he doesn't want to screw anything up and the one time he tries to ask his friend out the friend thinks it's a joke and he basically dies of shame and after that—"

She held up both hands. "I believe you wrote it. Only an author can spout that much bullshit about a book."

I gasped. Maggie laughed. Puzo came out from behind his toy.

"The book isn't finished," Adams said.

"No. I um. I kind of. I mean, I know something has to happen to really get them together, but I couldn't figure out what that was, and everything I thought about doing seemed dumb, so I kind of…stalled out."

"You have an internal conflict issue that starts in the first act."

"That's more or less what Maggie said."

"And your second act is a mess."

"Um. Yeah."

"I also said that," Maggie added (not helpfully).

Adams gave me a long, appraising, super uncomfortable look, that I tried to meet without flinching or fidgeting or running screaming from the room. "This could be the next big thing. It's exactly what I'm looking for. But it needs work."

I nodded. "I know. I wasn't sure where to go and got a little muddled."

"You got *a lot* muddled. But there are moments in it that shine brightly, Harrington. Brighter than you even realize."

Which seemed like a weird thing to say—how did she know what I realized?—but she was still looking at me so I gulped and nodded again, wishing I could hide behind a hanging toy with Puzo. "I want it to be good."

"Oh, we're not going to settle for *good*. By the time you're done with it, it's going to be fucking *extraordinary*. Now I need to have a few conversations and look at the calendar, but do I have your permission to move forward with the project?"

Everything stopped. I stopped breathing. The earth stopped turning. Puzo stared at me with his dark, knowing eyes, like he could tell the world had stopped.

This kind of thing? Wasn't supposed to happen while I was cowering in someone else's desk chair, being loomed over by a short, terrifying lesbian. Was this a book deal? Was I being offered a book deal right now?

"Um. Yes?"

Maggie kicked the chair.

"Yes," I said, more firmly. "Yes. I want it to be extraordinary. Thank you."

Adams nodded. "I'll be in touch when I have more of the particulars ironed out. How fast do you write, Harrington?"

"I don't know. I mean. I guess that took me a month?"

Her eyes glittered. "Good to know." Then she turned and was gone. Not like she'd disappeared—she walked away—it's just the office has thick runners down the hallway to dampen noise so you literally don't hear footsteps, it's actually kind of creepy sometimes.

Wait.

What was happening.

Um.

I looked up at Maggie and whatever she saw in my face made her giggle, this delighted sound, like a kid laughs. She tousled my hair and said, "Let's get coffee."

Puzo sped over to the door and cawed at us, head bobbing all over the place.

"No, you can't come, we're leaving the building." She handed him a treat stick instead, which he immediately dropped, protesting his abandonment. "Sorry, buddy, it's too windy out. Eat your candy."

I watched her grab her coat and hat but I still couldn't move. "Did that just. Did I. Did Adams. Uhhh."

She poked me. "Yes. Yes. And yes. Now get up, I'm buying you a mocha to celebrate. PK, you're selling your first book. At least, if Adams has her way you will be."

"It still has to go to acquisitions," I protested. "They could veto it."

"I bet they don't. Especially after her last two debuts hit the bestseller lists." She grinned. "Hey, I wonder if your book will be a bestseller."

That jolted me back to reality. "Oh my god, shut up, don't even say something like that!" I stood up, my body going from *hide and play dead* to *jitter and freak out* in a heartbeat. "This might not actually happen," I said as I followed her down the hall.

"First things first, you should get an agent. Seriously."

"I don't want an agent. I mean maybe someday but I just—this morning I didn't even have a book!"

She pushed open the door to the stairwell, the one I'd been about to take a distraction walk down before, you know, before my entire life changed in the blink of an eye. Or the flip of a page. Or the bellow of an editor. "You had a book, you sent it to me. Why don't you want an agent?"

"I want everything to be simple!" Even more truthfully, I was afraid anything I did would somehow make this miracle disappear, like if I said "agent" the whole deal would vanish.

And no, that's not really how it should work, but what if, in this one case, it did?

Maggie rolled her eyes. I could tell even though her back was to me. There was an implied eye roll in the stomp of her boots down the stairs. "Whatever you say. I'm just glad Adams took that whole you-being-the-author thing well. Makes my life easier." She glanced over her shoulder. "Ha, PK, you're totally going to have a book."

I gasped like she was jinxing it. "They might not buy it, I might suck at it, Adams might fire me. Seriously, Mags, this might not really happen."

Spoiler alert: it happened. It actually, really, seriously happened. By the end of the week I was signing my name to a book contract. And the one person I really wanted to tell was Art, because he was my best friend, because he was the person I wanted to share everything wonderful with, but I couldn't tell him.

He'd want to read the book and I couldn't let him do that. The second he did, he'd know.

There was this line, this line I was really proud of. *The sight of your profile as you read your book at night fills me with contentment.* And it was true. It was so true it was almost painful.

I thought about it from every angle, but all of them came back to this: Art would know I was writing about myself, that I was writing about my feelings for him, and I couldn't let him see it until I was ready to tell him. They were rushing the release, putting it out in spring, in May, just in time for all those "beach reads" lists.

May. I had seven months to figure out how I was going to tell him that I loved him. Go, team.

Oh god. *What have I done?*

Chapter Eight

Ramping up to the holidays was a wild time at the bookstore where Art worked. It was a small chain, four locations: Manhattan, Philly, DC, and Boston. Small footprint, huge fan base, that type of place. Their Instagram had literal millions of followers, all hearting their dozens of book pictures and squeeing over their #bookasmr Reels. He'd gotten a job there when we were in college and he'd gone through three interviews to get it—that was the kind of competition Art could bulldoze when he wanted something—and he *loved* working at the store.

If you wanted to be precise, my work and his work were at different subway stops, but I didn't mind walking a few blocks out of the way to bring him a sandwich or something if he was working late, which was what I was doing the day I walked in and discovered *Wade* of all bright and shining people already there.

"Preston, darling!" He kissed my cheeks with all the elegance of a freaking prince raised to perfectly cheek-kiss.

I tried to cheek-kiss and ended up basically smearing my face across his like a cat searching for chin scritches. "Wade. What're you doing here?"

"In the neighborhood, thought I'd say hello!" He turned back to Art, and wow, Art had on this slightly shimmering vest that flowed out at the bottom and flattered the shape of his…shape. "Wink wink, sweetness, see you soon!" He actually leaned in to kiss Art's cheek, not like in an airy TV way, but in a saying-goodbye-to-a-close-friend way. Also I thought he might have whispered something in Art's ear.

A suspicion confirmed by Art laughing. "You are so naughty, mister! Get out of my shop, and get home to your—home!"

Wade—and I swear I could not make this up—*flipped the end of his scarf* and let it trail over his shoulder as he walked out the door and into the night.

Who does that. Who.

I wanted to exchange a *who does that* look with Art, but Art was looking fondly after him and I had to control the urge to demand answers. Why had he been here? What had he whispered? Naughty *how*? Instead I held up the bag I was carrying and said, grumpily, "Got you a sandwich."

He snatched it out of my hand. "Oh thank god, I am famished! I've been setting up the alternative Thanksgiving display all day now, but don't you think it's looking good?"

I followed him to the back right corner of the store where there was always a seasonal table of some sort. Right now it was covered in books about the evils of colonization and a fair serving of first-person accounts written by people who'd experienced those evils firsthand. I picked up one and turned it over, scanning the back cover copy. "She's one of ours," I said, pointing to one of the author blurbs.

"Yes, I picked all these books specifically based on whether or not you can play three degrees of insider publishing with the big name authors who gave quotes." He sighed, but I could tell the exasperation was tempered with affection. Or maybe with the sandwich I'd just bought him. "Anyway, the coolest part about the table? No. White. Men." He beamed at me.

"No white men?"

He gestured at the table with the hand not lovingly gripping his sandwich. "Yes! These books were all written by people who aren't white men! Isn't that cool?"

"Yes? I mean, yes. I recognize that not-white-men should definitely be considered experts in the area of colonization, for sure, agreed." That obviously wasn't enough. "It's really cool, Arty."

"Thank you!"

And oh, oh god, the way the angle of his arm changed as he Vanna-White-ed at the table, the graceful, lovely lines and curves of him, the planes of his mind and the things he thought so much about. Me? I'm a white man. I would have made a table with a lot of books, and not *all* of them would have been by white dudes. I don't think I would have thought to make a whole table with *no* white dudes either.

But Art? Thought about things like that. Was undaunted by things like that.

"This sandwich is bliss, by the way. Thanks."

I tried not to bloom under his smile like a flower opening in spring, but it was hard. "Course. Anyway, what was Wade doing here?"

"That, my dear, is a secret!" I could tell he was doing Wade by his voice. I mean "doing" in the sense of "imitating," not "doing" in the sense of, y'know, *doing*. He was definitely not *doing* Wade. Probably. Right? Yes. They hardly knew each other. Not that that mattered. After all, I'd known Art for years and I'd never—

"Are you having sex with Wade?" I blurted out like an absolute jackass at a volume that wouldn't have been appropriate in the bookstore for any question and certainly not for *that* question, which wouldn't have been appropriate in any setting, oh my god, why was I like this? "Um, that's what I said to, to um, that was a line in the play," I continued at that same volume, like I could play it off somehow. "In the play I just saw about this guy, um, Wade, and um—"

"*Shut. Up. PK.*"

I shut up. I shut up so hard I bit the inside of my cheek between my back teeth.

For a really long moment we both just stood there. I stared down at the cover of a book (I wasn't a huge fan, graphically speaking, and I thought our in-house designer would have a serious problem with the fonts being used) and Art stood there not moving. At all.

"The only reason I'm not about to push you in front of a cab right now," he said, voice low, "is that it's kind of adorable you have a crush on Wade, but I have to tell you, because you're my friend and I don't want you to embarrass yourself, that he's completely and totally taken. *Not* by me. Obviously. You doofus. But I can't tell you anything about it because I told him I wouldn't." He shook his head sadly, pretend-sadly, I was pretty sure, but maybe with…with something else in the mix too. "Alas, Wade is not for me or you. But he is very happy, so at least there's that. Anyway, don't ever ask me about sex in the middle of the store again or I will ban you. For *life.*"

I winced. "Fair. Very fair. Also sorry. I should not have said that."

"You really shouldn't. In fact, I think you should go home and clean the bathroom to show your sincere remorse." His eyes stared right into mine.

"You know," I said, taking a step back. "I have this sudden urge to leave. Very sudden. Gotta go. I, uh, didn't catch whatever you just said, but I'm sure it was great. Um, yeah. So enjoy your sandwich, see you later!"

"With the brush! Don't just dump the bleach in and leave it!" he called after me. Because apparently talking about toilet cleaning at high volume in the bookstore was totally fine.

Obviously the thing I should have done is gone home and cleaned the bathroom, but then I was on the train, and I was thinking about Art, and Wade whispering to him, and the two of them laughing, and how if this happened in *Peak Romance* (a title Adams had actually not criticized), what would my main character do? Well. He'd probably clean the bathroom.

But then he'd do something romantic. Bathroom cleaning was *not* romantic. It was maybe not the opposite of romance, but the—what's it—the inverse of romance. Those were different, right? Opposites and inverses? Or did I mean antithetical? I pondered my inability to remember what words meant for the whole walk up to our apartment and then, once there, I pulled out my computer and…wrote a scene in which my main character bought all this cool new bathroom stuff and remade the bathroom (which was already clean because, I dunno, it just seemed like cleaning would be boring to write about).

Of course, it was all sort of a symbol. For how he felt. About his love interest. Except he *also* made this really nice dinner and they cuddled together after and—that's when Art got home from work.

I slammed my laptop shut and hid in my bedroom so I didn't have to see how disappointed he was that the bathroom was still dirty. This was also the prime moment to feel bad about not having cleaned it, which with the benefit of super recent hindsight it would have been nice of me to do, even though I kind of felt like the person more annoyed by the lack of cleanliness should probably be the one cleaning?

When I'd made that argument to Art back in college he looked at me like I was missing something very obvious. "Yes, but what if the other person doesn't find filth annoying until it's so overwhelming he can't bring himself to clean it?"

I didn't have a great answer for that. And, upon mature reflection, it was probably where our bathroom was at right now, except for the shelf where Art kept his stuff (which was always neat) and the towel Art used for his showers (which was always either over the shower door drying or folded on his shelf). But eventually, when my dirty laundry bag started bulging so much I could probably use it as a beanbag chair, and the area around the sink was cluttered enough with socks and the occasional shoe that the door had trouble closing, I really did clean up after myself, as long as by "clean up after myself" you included kicking stuff down the hall so the door could close, and doing enough of the laundry that the bag was no longer bulging like a venomous plant about to pop open and devour the hero in a video game.

It was one of those things I always promised myself I'd start doing soon. Tomorrow, maybe. I needed a system. Should I clean the bathroom once a week? Should I do something small every day? How could I keep it from feeling like such a huge mess? Did I need special equipment, like a certain type of scrubber? Or an antibacterial spray? Should I research that? Maybe someone online had an example schedule for bathroom cleaning?

I hid in an internet guilt spiral until I decided to venture into the rest of the apartment. Art was in his room doing whatever he did in there, probably some mix of video games and reading, semi-simultaneously, because he always kept a book next to his computer to read during loading screens. Since the internet had assured me I could clean my bathroom with things I had around the house (like paper towels and basically any cleaning spray), I decided that now was my moment. Better late than never, right?

I gathered my quest items and braved the new level—only to find that Art had already cleaned.

Not just cleaned. But like, the bathroom was *immaculate*.

He'd washed the floors. I swept sometimes, but why wash a floor when you know it's just going to get dirty again?

In related notes: had this bathroom always had light gray flooring? I would have sworn it was brownish. Oops. Maybe that's why you washed the floor.

I stood there, looking around at the shining fixtures, the stained-but-obviously-clean sink, the scrubbed tiles in the shower, the fresh hand towel hanging on the wall. And the toilet, oh no, he'd cleaned the toilet. Scrubbed it for sure. And cleaned the *outside* of it. Which I had definitely never done. I didn't know anyone did. I just assumed the outside of the toilet was a lost cause of...of dust and...like...pubic hairs...and... ewwwww gross OMG ART HAD CLEANED ALL THAT.

The thought of it made me feel like *I* needed a shower.

The bathroom felt so much bigger when it was clean. Because of the cleanness, and also because of the *textures*; without dirt, the surfaces were all so much more expansive. Oh. Also. Where was my dirty laundry beanbag chair?

Should I knock on his door and ask? But no. I couldn't face Art right now, after he'd cleaned up the whole bathroom, which I'd been using way longer than he had. I could not ask him. Plus, the apartment was not large. Surely if I went on a dirty laundry side quest I'd be able to find it.

And I did.

I found roughly half of it in the washing machine.

(Yes, the apartment had a washer/dryer combo, "in the European style," as my mother put it.)

So not only had he cleaned the horrible bathroom, which was dirty mostly because of me, but he'd also *thrown my laundry into the washer.* Was it angry-laundry? Passive aggressive-laundry? Grow-up-and-do-your-own-laundry-laundry? Maybe I was overthinking it and it was just there's-nowhere-else-to-put-this-laundry.

Whatever flavor of laundry it was, it was now in the wash cycle, and I felt *terrible*. Like really awful. Like throw myself on my toilet brush horrible. Only not literally because that would probably be even less sanitary than throwing myself on my sword. Not that I had a sword. In fact, swords not used for killing people might be clean, or at least cleanable, in a way that toilet brushes really weren't. Too many surfaces. Too much yuck.

Since I didn't totally know what to do, I settled for texting him to ask if he wanted some ice cream. When he didn't immediately get back to me I dithered in the kitchen for half a podcast episode wondering what to do, then made a bowl of ice cream. Then I felt a little weird about it, so I made another bowl, like, you know, super casual, *I was having some cookies'n'cream and thought you might want some.* And knocked on his door with my elbow, hands full of ice cream.

Me, standing in the hallway, holding guilt-stricken apology ice cream, trying to make my face do a thing that communicated how deeply I understood the nature of my poor roommating and how much I regretted it.

The door cracked open. Dark inside. "PK? What're you doing?"

"Oh, um, I texted, just, I thought you might want ice cream?"

He pulled the lace-edged green bathrobe he had on tighter around him and I realized, suddenly, that his eyes had that I've-already-taken-my-contacts-out bleariness to them. "I put my phone on silent. Ice cream in the middle of the night?"

"Um. Is it...really late? I wasn't paying attention. Sorry."

Me, standing in the hallway with my guilt-stricken apology ice cream, apologizing for the wrong thing.

He squinted down at the ice cream. "Cookies'n'cream?"

"Yeah."

"Let me get my glasses."

Relief washed over me in a wave, like deigning to eat ice cream was akin to accepting my apology. "Cool," I said. "Thanks."

He smiled in this sleepy-sweet way. "You're thanking me? You're the one who got the ice cream."

I had no idea what to say to that. The ice cream wasn't the point, obviously, but I didn't think I could...articulate the point. So I just laughed awkwardly and said, "Uh, right, so I guess, you're welcome?"

Thankfully he ignored this and took his ice cream. "Want to listen to scary podcasts in the dark?"

"Definitely."

So that's what we did.

Chapter Nine

Time passed in this weird swirlcone of Book and Life, twining around each other like the chocolate and vanilla you can get from a soft-serve machine, where every bite is made up of the same basic flavors but in slightly different proportions. I'd be a little bit lost in finishing *Peak Romance* and go out to grab fresh donuts from the shop a block away, and it'd be a little transparent, like those two worlds were overlapping, but then I'd get a text from my mother, or Art, or Maggie, or an email from Adams about this or that cover/edits/back cover copy/ whatever, and then my actual life would move to the forefront until I got back to my computer and started writing again.

It's weird how much of life just goes along like normal even when inside your head there are these Huge Things Happening. Like conversations about my pseudonym (H.K. Pierce because I know how to fictionalize my own initials, thank you), and deciding I didn't want my picture on the back cover for reasons of anonymity (you could tell they were all like, aww, the baby author thinks he's going to be famous, that's so cute). In the beginning it was almost impossible not to tell Art about it just because he was the person I told about stuff. But after a while it was almost like I was a secret agent in my own life, like I was undercover as boring old ordinary PK, hiding in plain sight when my much cooler alter ego was the mysterious debut author of *Peak Romance*.

To be clear, literally no one outside work had ever heard of *Peak Romance* or H.K. Pierce. Even after the deal was announced it wasn't a huge wave of fascination or excitement. But in my head it still felt like I was going in all stealth-like, about to burst out of thin air and, like, uh, do something amazing? Or something? There was no really cool visual for having written a book. It's not like authors have a sport. What would it even be? Mouse juggling? Fastest keyboard shortcut wrangler in Microsoft Word?

The point was, my life split into two timelines: the H.K. Pierce timeline in which I was writing a book, a real one, an about-to-be-published one. And the PK Harrington (the third) one, in which I didn't clean the bathroom enough and occasionally tripped over my own shoes.

And then? After Thanksgiving, which Art spent with bookstore friends and I spent with my parents ("Honey, have you spoken to Wade lately?"), there was Christmas. Which Art, even after college, usually spent with my family. Except last year, when he was with what's-his-nut-mononymous-artist-asshole.

The thing about my mom is that she's kind of the worst, but every now and then, she's the greatest? She actually called Art directly to plan Christmas. Like, not through me, and not to *invite* him, but to *include* him. Maybe because she knew that would make him feel good or maybe just because she totally missed their planning session last year, but it didn't matter. What mattered was how much he smiled when they were on the phone talking about, like, ham versus turkey, and which craft they wanted to do to decorate the table, and what the schedule would be—could we go the night before so we'd be there in the morning? Would we spend the night after dinner? Surely we didn't want to brave the streets *on Christmas*, as if the whole world shut down or something.

I felt slightly bad about the fact that Art was on the hook for that whole negotiation, but also? He laughed so much when he was talking to my mother. And his voice would go high and silly with her in this way it didn't usually go unless he was talking to a dog. Not that he treated my mom like a dog, just that she got the benefit of his unguarded voice more than most humans did.

And hey, I didn't want to talk about green bean casserole anyway. Win-win-win. Three-way win. Wait. That sounded…like the kind of thing you didn't want your mother participating in. Me not being part of Christmas planning was good for everyone, was my point.

The other thing that was happening? I had to finish the book. The first draft of it. And make it "an actual book, Harrington, not a collection of lovelorn scenes that popped into your head while you were brushing your teeth with one of those trendy vibrating toothbrushes you kids today think you invented." I didn't get what Adams had against vibrating toothbrushes, but she was inscrutable as usual.

And I loved my Quip so whatever.

I needed to email it on December thirty-first. Which meant…by New Year's I'd have turned in my first draft. Like. Of a novel. For publication.

Unreal. Surreal. One of those. Maybe both.

So I had to work on it a lot. It helped that Art was putting in longer days at the store in the holiday rush (he only had Christmas Day off because of seniority), so he wasn't around to ask what I was doing on my computer all the time. It was a lot like the year I started playing *Skyrim* and then basically did nothing else but play *Skyrim* for three months? That's how finishing the book felt. I'd come out of my room to pee and realize that Art had gotten home from work, eaten, gotten ready for bed, and gone to bed, and I hadn't heard any of it because I'd had my ear buds in blasting static. White noise. Technically brown noise. I didn't know the differences, I just listened to the one that slid under my awareness enough to keep me focused.

Then, boom it was Christmas Eve and we were on a train out of Manhattan.

Christmas with my family is a whole thing. My grandparents from both sides show up, my mom's sister and her husband with their three pugs (you read that right), the couple from next door who never had kids and were basically my second set of…not quite parents, but sort of more hip, slightly-older-than-my-parents role models. I loved it when I was a kid, but as I grew up I was…okay, this is going to sound messed up, but I was kind of jealous of the cynical people who hated family holidays? As if there was some kind of virtue in feeling alienated from this thing that had always made me feel kind of warm and full and happy before then.

At college a lot of people whined about *having* to go home for the holidays, so I did too, and it took me until Art described what his family Christmas was like for me to realize that some people weren't just whining because everyone else was whining. Some people genuinely didn't want to go home.

So I basically forced him to come home with me instead. Not nonconsensually. But that thing you do with people you care about where you kind of wear them down on a thing for their own good? Err. That's a thing, right? I think it is? Anyway, later he said he'd wanted to come all along but just wasn't sure I really meant it and wasn't offering out of pity. Which I definitely wasn't.

Even if a very small part of me *did* feel good that I could offer this actual (what I considered) "real" family holiday experience to someone who'd had a lot of tense dinners, passive-aggressive gift giving, and increasingly drunken arguments in their own family holidays, always punctuated by their older brother either white-knuckling himself through withdrawals or, more often, going on one last drugged-out binge before quitting everything for New Year's (again).

That was the first time Art came home with me, and he's had a standing invitation ever since. When we showed up at like eight p.m. on Christmas Eve, my dad picked us up from the station and gave us both two-handed handshakes, you know the kind, the handshake and additional clasp with the other hand thing. It was as close as he got to hugs, and it made me feel pretty jolly, not gonna lie.

Art, though, used my dad's hand to pull him into a hug, and I could tell by Dad's wide eyes that he was just as shocked and uncertain of what to do as I was. He allowed it and said, slightly gruffly, "It's been too long since you visited, young man. Come on, boys, let's get back to the house." Then he did a *look* at me, like he was demanding to know if Art was secretly dying or something, and stepped back.

"Thanks for having me," Art said softly, his words almost lost in the bustle of holiday travelers and excited greetings.

"Not a problem, not a problem."

We went to the car and made the kind of small talk one always made with my dad—*How's work? The City treating you all right?* (you could always tell when my parents capitalized "city" like Manhattan was the only city on earth that really counted). We gave all the usual answers and showed up at the house in time to see the Andersons from next door leaving. They greeted Art like a long lost friend, hugging him like only genuine huggers could, with those big, engulfing hugs that made you feel like nothing bad could penetrate the safety of their arms.

And Art? Leaned into those hugs like he wanted to bury himself against Mrs. A's wool scarf and Mr. A's fluffy coat.

Both of them sent me the same *Is he dying?* look my dad had sent me. Which didn't seem fair, since I wasn't Art's keeper or something. I didn't know why he was acting this way! Sure, he'd had a rough patch after dumping what's-his-name, but he'd been fine since then. Right?

We dropped our stuff in my bedroom since the guest rooms were taken and then went to say hi to everyone else, but the whole thing was having this weird effect on Art. Like he seemed so genuinely glad to be there, but also there was this undercurrent of me thinking, *No, really, ARE you dying?* at him across the room.

At dinner my mom made a big deal of saying how happy she and my dad were to have Art back for the holidays again and I almost thought he was going to cry, it was awful.

I wasn't sure if I should bring it up or not (wasn't saying, *Hey, you look like you're having terrible feelings* about the worst possible thing I could do?), but I thought if my mom asked me how he was in that intense way she had and I told her I didn't even check in, she'd be annoyed. So I tentatively asked if he was okay, fully expecting him to do what I would do and say, "Sure, yeah, everything's fine."

But he didn't.

"Yeah, just, you know, last year? Last year I was with Roman, and we were so in love, and everything seemed really...wonderful. And I thought that was it. I thought I'd spend all of my Christmases with him, that I was finally all grown up. And I'm so grateful to your parents for being so sweet and lovely, and I feel *so, so* guilty for not being able to stop being sad. But I just...miss that fantasy."

"But... I thought... I thought things were going okay?"

"They are, but I want *more* than okay, I want *marvelous*

and *extraordinary* and *splendid*. I want fireworks, you know? I want…grand gestures and intimate moments and…and… more than I can even imagine now. Surprise and joy and stuff. Which is what I thought I was getting with Roman. But it wasn't. Anyway." He gathered up his pj's. "I'm going to take a shower while everyone's still downstairs."

I would have said something—*sure* or *okay* or *can't things be marvelous and extraordinary and splendid with me?*—but he left for the bathroom too quickly. Which was probably for the best.

He'd broken up with a guy and moved in with me and then, well, I thought everything was fine. After all, it had been four months ago already, it's not like he'd dropped what's-his-nut the other day.

Plus, he was *happier* now. Shouldn't that sort of…make it better? Than being with that prick Roman? And how could anyone think about a future of *Christmases* with a guy like that? Did Roman have a family who already loved Art? I didn't freaking think so. How was *anything* about that better than this? It made no sense.

I couldn't bring it up again. And there was no polite way to say, *Your boyfriend was a loser and there was never a future with him and how can you possibly compare him and that to me and this and still feel sad???* He'd already said he felt guilty about it so I wasn't going to bring it up, even though I could not under-stand it, like, at all.

We'd shared my room at holidays before, so it wasn't tech-nically a big deal, but something in me had shifted since he'd showed up at my apartment in the rain. Or maybe since I started writing *Peak Romance*. Almost like I couldn't go back to acting like I didn't think about him the way people think about, you know, their…others. Their special, uh, friends.

I guess how Art had been thinking about fricking Roman. That was super depressing.

I had no idea how I'd be able to sleep listening to him breathe from the chaise lounge. He was so close! He was so far away! He was right there next to me! He was obsessing over his ex! Basically I was lying there on my back practically thrumming with all the muddled thoughts in my head.

His voice came out of the darkness when I'd pretty much given up on ever falling asleep. "Sometimes I put on a classical playlist and wander around the oldest parts of the city, pretending I'm a character in one of those artsy films you act like you don't hate, like I have my own turbulent soundtrack."

I wanted to argue that I didn't hate those movies, but I did. And Art knew it. I stayed quiet instead, trying to hear the sound of his breaths. Or maybe trying to hear all the things in his head, wondering if any of them were like the ones in mine.

When he spoke again his voice was so soft it was almost drowned out by my own heartbeat. "I imagine I'm back in time somewhere in Europe, that I have no hope I'll ever be happy, but the audience knows it's a romance and that by the end of the story I won't be alone anymore. So even though the me in the scene is sad, the meta-me keeps it from being crushing."

I turned toward him, the sound of my body moving so much louder and more intrusive than I wanted it to be, not like the way Art moved, as if he made no ripples. "But you're not alone. You have me. You always have me." For a moment I thought I'd said too much.

His face moved just slightly, eyes meeting mine, and they seemed to glitter as if full of tears. But that was probably just how the light had hit them. "Do I?"

"Oh my god, yes, of course, you always have me, you've always had me, since that day they were talking about Willa Cather and you were like 'I find the idea of a lesbian writing an aching book about longing for a woman who didn't want her really depressing' and the professor tried to be all like 'Your feelings have no place here' and then you destroyed him by saying that without feelings no one would read literature at all." I paused for a breath, realized I'd probably said way too much, and shut up.

Art's eyes shimmered for another moment and then he looked away. "We should sleep."

No! We should talk! You should let me make you feel better! But I couldn't say any of that. So I just kind of lay there, with all these unspoken thoughts clogging up my brain until I felt like a backed-up toilet of emotions—wait—that was gross—until I felt like a backed-up drain of emotions I couldn't flush. And oh my god, why was I so obsessed with toilets? *A backed-up drain of emotions, overflowing all over me, unable to get clean.*

You know, probably I should leave the wordsmithing to actual waking hours, when I had coffee. When Art wasn't lying next to me in the dark, so close and so totally unreachable.

Chapter Ten

And then… I turned in the book. *Delivered* it in publishing lingo, like it was a baby or something, like I'd labored and gestated—uh, not in that order—and here it was, here was this thing I'd put so much of my energy into creating out of almost nothing, sent off as a file attachment to an email, which seemed anticlimactic somehow. I almost missed the days of getting a book printed, shipping it off in a manuscript box, to be received on the other side by someone who would lift the top off and *behold* it. Like it was a real thing. A tangible thing. Like all of those words, when put together, had *weight*.

But this is the modern era. So I attached it and hit send and that was that.

I wanted to feel, I don't know, elated or something. *Achievement unlocked: book written.* Except I work in publishing, so I know that the moment of finishing a first draft is like maybe the halfway point for a book being really finished. (Minimum four rounds of edits, hours of reshaping and adjusting and polishing, all the promotional stuff, all the endless back-and-forth over covers and copy and "Do you want to write a blog post about Your Process for SomethingBooks-dot-com?" and then writing it and then tweeting about it and ahhhhhh. One of the authors I worked with said the first draft was the easiest part of writing a book because she just got to sit at a keyboard and reckon with the empty page.)

I didn't feel elated. I didn't feel happy. I didn't even feel satisfied.

Maggie, though, was thrilled. If *Peak Romance* was a baby I'd delivered, Maggie was the midwife. "We should celebrate! I'll bring some bubbly over later. Will Art be there?"

I choked. "Oh my god. No. We can't. He can't. I can't. No!"

Her face did a thing I recognized as flashing from hurt (that she'd been excited and I'd been horrified) to irritated (that I'd made her feel hurt) to suspicious (that I was having an unexpected response to her proposal). "Excuse me?"

When people say "Excuse me?" as if it's a specific question to which you're then obligated to reply I never know what to say. On one hand it seems like they've really left themself open to not get whatever information they're looking for since it's not actually a question, but on the other it's almost always said when I *do* know what they want from me, so am I a liar if I pretend I don't?

In this case I just wanted to talk about something else, so I said, "Art's working late," and hoped she'd drop it.

Yeah, of course she didn't.

"Don't tell me you haven't actually mentioned you have a book coming out."

"Whoa. I have *a book coming out.*" I hadn't actually figured that out myself. But I did. It was on the editorial calendar and had a publication date. "Oh my god, Mags, *I have a book coming out.* Did you know that? I mean obviously you knew that but I hadn't thought about it like that and now I am and—"

She laughed, not like she was letting me off the hook, but maybe like she was delighted by my sudden insight into my situation. "Yeah, genius, you have a book coming out. Adams has been working on it all day, which I know because occasionally she makes this almost-laugh noise"—she did? I made her laugh???—"and then at other times she says, 'Harrington, you dumbass,' and furiously types for a few seconds. Her edits are going to be amazing, you have to let me see them, and also I recommend a stiff drink."

My initial excitement about making Adams laugh was immediately consumed with *oh no, why am I a dumbass.* "Wait, has she said anything? Does she hate it? Am I the worst?"

Maggie ruffled my hair. "Aww, look at you, with all your new author angst! And no, of course she hasn't said anything, she wouldn't talk shit about you to your coworkers, that'd be wrong. You know full well that when Adams wants to talk shit, she'll do it right to your face. Anyway, why can't we celebrate with Art? We need to celebrate, PK. This is a big thing. You finished the first draft of a novel!"

I hunched forward. "I haven't told anyone, I guess? I don't know." I totally knew. I hadn't told my parents for the same reason I hadn't told Art: I was pretty sure the second they saw the book it would be starkly clear to them that it was about him, that *I* was about him, and I couldn't have them knowing that. Not like this. Not when it was just this…this unrequited *thing* that had no real place in my world, almost like boring old PK Harrington didn't get to have the kind of real love that his alter ego H.K. Pierce wrote about.

Which was a mildly troubling thought. Since technically I was both of those people.

Maggie sat back on the edge of my desk, which was tucked into a corner under a sort of eave, or at least I pretended it was an eave. It was probably just a weirdly angled area of ductwork under the roof, but in the right light I told myself I was a Dickensian character toiling in my cramped little corner where I couldn't fully stand up without banging my head. "Art's your best friend."

"Yeah." Sort of. Ish. Best friend with a side of longing.

Hey, that was a good line, I should find a place for it in the book. *Best friend with a side of longing.* Or maybe it was a terrible line? Now I couldn't tell.

"Why didn't you tell him? It's kind of bizarre."

"The whole thing is kind of bizarre. Like. I don't know." My toes fidgeted in my shoes, wiggling with emotional discomfort. "It doesn't feel real yet."

"Having champagne with me will make it feel more real. And anyway, you have to tell him eventually, right? His store's on our usual ARC list."

"I'm not using my name, though," I countered, suddenly desperate to justify keeping it a secret, to make it less about me maybe doing something shady, and more—uh—more something that was definitely *not* about me doing something shady. "Even then it's not like he'll know."

Maggie straightened up, the better to survey me disapprovingly from above. "Okay, this has gone from bizarre to actively unhinged. Are you trying to *hide* the fact that you wrote a book? And why? It's not like it's a tell-all gossip rag about"—her voice took on a deep intonation—"*politicians in high places and the depraved acts carried out on their behalf, as told by a Washington insider.*"

"I think that should be 'a longtime Washington insider,'" I suggested.

"Oh good, that's better. And he's probably 'afraid for his safety' or something."

"Totally. All the reviews will talk about his 'slow descent into a situation no one could imagine' and how it 'upended his promising career.'"

"Unless it's a woman, in which case they'll talk about which of the married politicians she was having sex with."

"True. And she definitely seduced most of them."

Maggie nodded. "Because she's a home-wrecking slut who should have stayed in the kitchen."

I wrinkled my nose. "I hate this book now."

"But it would sell a billion copies and stay on the *Times* bestseller list for years."

"Gross."

"Seriously." Pause.

"We should get lunch soon," I said quickly.

She did not jump up and start walking. "Are you...embarrassed? About this book?"

Argh, why wouldn't she drop it already? "No. I mean. I don't know. It's not the book I ever thought I'd like...write. I thought I'd come home and tell my parents I'd penned a literary novel exploring deep themes of like...culture and identity and with a backdrop of the Great Plains or something to symbolize isolation with small clusters of communities dotted around so I could talk about inclusion and exclusion through the main character's concrete experience."

This time she wrinkled her nose. "Oh. You wanted to write white guy jerkoff litfic. I'm glad I didn't know that when we met because I would not have become your friend."

"Ouch." I was genuinely hurt. "That's kind of mean."

She shrugged. "It just sounds like you want to write a book about some middle-class white dude discovering his life is not the template from which all other lives derive, and that book has been done before. And glorified. It's really not my bag. And PK? *Peak Romance* hits a lot of those themes without being jerkoff litfic that also makes normal people feel dumb and pretentious people feel smart." She glanced up at the clock on the wall—an actual wall clock, with a clock face that had, no joke, Roman numerals on it. "Lunch sounds good. But the coffee shop so we don't have to actually leave the building. Let me get Puzo."

What did it say about me that I still sorta wanted to write that book? The one with the desolate setting and vibrant interactions between people? I knew the kind of book she meant, but I thought I could write it *better*. Then again, that's what privileged people always think, right? That they're the exception to the rule?

In any case, it didn't matter what I wanted to write. *Peak Romance* had taken me over and it hadn't even felt like a choice; it felt like a *need*, like I had to get those words out of me or they'd back up and…no, not toilets, not even drains, what else backed up in a really catastrophic way? Um. Well, anyway, I had to get those words out, so I did, and I felt better, and I must not have done the worst job because Adams and Maggie had both liked what they saw.

And yes, maybe sometimes I was a dumbass, but I'd also apparently made Adams laugh. What a wild thing that was, to make someone laugh from your keystrokes, from the arrangement of words, from the feelings those words evoke. I made someone *laugh*.

"You ready?" Maggie asked.

Puzo offered a squawk.

"I'm ready."

Was I being weird about this whole thing? Maybe I should just tell Art and figure he wouldn't understand what the book meant?

Except no way. He would. He'd seen too much of my writing.

Then again, he was the one who said I didn't understand romance. So maybe he'd think what Maggie thought and just assume I couldn't write romance any better than I lived it?

Honestly, it was a subject that still felt like this deep bruise inside me, but whatever. It's not like there was much you could say to someone to convince them you were romantic, right?

Actions speak louder than words. I'd have to demonstrate it. And I could! I totally could. I just needed him to give me the chance, and I kind of...used to think he would? But now? I had no idea.

What would he think, if he read *Peak Romance*? Would he even like it? I was kind of...excited about the idea that his store was on the ARC list—that's the thing where a publisher sends out early copies of books to stir up some excitement about them before they're out, and specifically so booksellers like Arty will hand sell copies to customers after a book is actually released. I'd seen him do it. He'd go all sparkly and bouncy and tell someone just how much he'd *loved* the book, how much it had *changed* him, that it brought him joy, excitement, even *adventure*. Art was the kind of person who could read print on paper and have it be an adventure, genuinely, and then communicate that to other people. It was a thing I really admired about him, and a thing I tried to learn from so I could do it better at work too.

At some point, in the not-too-distant future, *Peak Romance* would land in the break room at the store, and people would hold it, turn it over in their hands, decide in seven seconds if it looked interesting enough to read.

Art loved romances. I'd never read an actual romance novel until Art introduced them to me in college, and then? I loved them. Not that I wanted to write them, but I couldn't stop reading his whole bookshelf because it opened this world of people having all these feelings, like I could get this contact high from reading about other people's intensity. It made me feel good. It made me feel...maybe a little voyeuristic, but also a little like I understood Art better. He had so many thoughts and feelings about stuff, and these books were my way of getting what that felt like in his head.

In my head? Feelings were this loud, clanging, confused

mass of noise. But for Art, feelings were colors and textures, things he could make sense of, could sort and organize. What would he see, if he read my book? Would he see chaos or order? Would he see me, or himself, or both of us, or neither of us?

I had no idea. And until I had to think about it, I wasn't going to dwell on the whole thing. I was going to go to lunch with my work BFF and her macaw, and definitely not obsess over the badass, take-no-prisoners editor now working on *Peak Romance*.

You always think having someone read your book is going to be amazing, and sometimes it is. But also? It felt like I had emptied my insides onto the page and then sent it to another person and now she was picking me apart, bit by bit. Poking and prodding and laughing and cursing at all of my pieces until nothing was left that hadn't been examined. Ahhhh.

Chapter Eleven

Normally the first round of edits comes back after a month, but because Adams wanted *Peak Romance* to come out in spring, we'd pushed it. Hard. And she'd gotten me a very, um, *thorough* response in ten days. Which was good? Except maybe it would have been nice to have that full month to come away from the book a little before basically being ordered to tear it apart.

God, I so wished I could talk to Art. I just had this feeling that if I could show him the edit letter he'd make me feel better about it. He'd point out that there were only really two major things I needed to fix, and yes, they'd take time, and energy, but also the book would be stronger after I did them, and didn't I want the book to be stronger?

And I did. I really did. Not just for me, but also because Adams and Maggie and the rest of the team believed in it so much they were doing a big push to get it out there. When a publisher decides you're Kind of A Big Deal, it's hard not to feel responsible for holding up your end of things. My end of things was the book. I needed it to kick ass.

But ugh, I had so much work to do. I couldn't help moping just a little about it. Adams had sent the email on Friday, so I gave myself the entire weekend to not think about it. A job I was doing so badly that Art asked me if I was okay because I seemed depressed.

When your bestie-slash-roomie, who's still mourning the loss of some imaginary future with a total jerkwad, says you seem depressed...things are low. But then he brightened. In this beautiful but also *alarm bells* way.

"I just had the best idea I've ever had!" He pulled out his phone and sent a text but didn't put it away, like he was fully expecting an immediate response. His phone buzzed. He rolled his eyes and sent another message. His phone buzzed again.

Who the heck was he even texting like that, all alert and excited and *oh my god, stop being jealous of someone on the other side of Art's phone, that's creepy.*

"I am, like, a candidate for MENSA right now. Except I think maybe MENSA is a joke." He slid the phone into his back pocket and said, "You're coming with me tonight, cancel your plans to sit around feeling sad."

"I wasn't going to do that! But where are we going?"

"To Wade's," he said, with this...effervescent smile on his face. Effervescent in the sense that looking at it made my insides bubbly. "Well," he added, "Wade and Ray's."

I just blinked. And blinked. And blinked. "You're spending Saturday night at Wade's?"

"Not the night, you goof, but he invited me over. And now you're coming too!"

"Am I, though? Why would I go to Wade's? I don't even *like* Wade." My conscience prickled and I said, grudgingly, "I don't *dislike* Wade. I feel neutrally about Wade." I'd probably like him more if Art didn't like him quite so much, but that definitely seemed like an inside thought.

"Tough. You're moping and I can fix it, so you're coming with me."

"I'm not moping, ohmygod." Sure, I'd thought of it as moping myself, but other people shouldn't be able to see the mope.

"Don't be a butthead," Art said affectionately. I think it was affectionately. He didn't sound annoyed or anything. "We're leaving in an hour."

I bit back the urge to groan like a little kid being forced to go to my grandmother's house instead of play outside with my friends. "Fine."

He grinned. "This is going to be so much fun!"

I sincerely doubted it.

"You *what?*" I goggled at the woman standing next to Wade as if she had a leg sticking out of her head. "You have a *girlfriend?*"

"Well, *I* don't," she said, smiling, and held out her hand. "I'm Ray."

Wade laughed. "This is exactly how I hoped he'd react. I take back everything I said, Art, this was worth it."

"You're making it worse." But Art, too, was laughing. He patted my arm gently (making me forgive the laughing). "Wade needs your help."

I managed, despite the acutely distracting sensation of Art's hand on my arm, to glare at Wade.

"Oh, don't be mad!" He reached for my hands like we were sisters running through a field of wildflowers in a Jane Austen movie. "I have a girlfriend! But I can't tell my parents, you know how much they love having a trendy gay son. Will you please be my beard to the birthday party they're throwing me? It would mean *the world* if you'd do it. Please, Preston?"

"I…you…what?"

"Refreshments," Ray said distinctly. "Get poor Preston a glass of wine, Wade." She patted my shoulder. "Ignore him. Come in, sit down. I can't believe you've known each other since you were children."

"We hated each other, for the record." I followed her, feeling dazed, and also weird that in the span of like two minutes all of them had touched me, like my body, not in a weird way, in a casual way. Like we were just people who could do that. Was I a person who could casually touch other people? I literally did not know.

Ray led me to a sofa in a very cute, very thrift-store-chic living room area, with a galley kitchen area tucked away in one corner, like the afterthought it most definitely was in a building this old. "Tell me how dreadful Wade was as a kid. Let me guess: he was the kid who got a tiny scrape on his arm and then cried inconsolably for an hour."

"Rude!" he called from the kitchen. "Plus, crying wasn't allowed for boys. Right, Preston?"

"We were supposed to play, like, field hockey. Or...some other game with a stick. Or something."

Wade and Art returned carrying trays of appetizers and I wondered how many times Art had come over before, since he seemed too comfortable for this to be his first time in the apartment. "Games with sticks, but I'd always pretend the sticks were my canes—for some reason I thought all fancy men had canes—and I'd walk around like an actor in an old movie."

"And do horrible British accents," I added, reluctantly drawn in. "Your British accent is criminal. Or was when we were kids."

"It hasn't improved," Ray said, grinning at him, an expression that just slightly stabbed me directly in the heart, like it was this reminder I'd never have what they had.

Art sat in a comfy-looking velvet-lined chair with ornate scrollwork on the arms. "That sounds completely adorable. Did you do a British accent too?" he asked me.

"No—"

Wade gasped dramatically. "Lies! You absolutely did!"

"Only once! Because they made us watch some old movie that was supposed to be 'enriching' or something."

He raised his eyebrows at me. "You don't remember *The Singer Not the Song*? Preston, that movie was like the queerest queer thing to ever queer. How can you not remember it?"

"It was?" I wracked my brain. "I thought it was a western."

"A western with British accents?" Art asked.

"I'm googling," Ray said.

"It takes place in Mexico, and it's about this super sexy war for a small town between a bandit played by the ever so fab Dirk Bogarde and a well-intentioned priest played by John Mills—"

Art waved a hand. "Wait, *Swiss Family Robinson* John Mills?"

"Exactly! Or, I should say," and he paused, so I winced in anticipation of the terrible accent to come, "cheerio-chap, got it in one!"

All three of us groaned and Ray threw a decorative pillow at him, nailing him directly in the head. I was starting to like this girl. Lady. Woman. Whatever.

"I am going to *break up with you* if you ever subject me to that again. But get back to the movie, it sounds fascinating."

"Oh *it is*." Wade leaned in. "So the rumor I read was that Dirk Bogarde refused to work with John Mills but they hired him anyway—one of those production company power plays—and I think *that's* why he camped it up so hard in the movie. I can't believe you don't remember, Preston. I swear that film basically formed my sexuality. Here." He pulled a laptop over and loaded YouTube.

I did not want to sit in Wade's lovely, adult apartment, with his lovely, adult relationship on display, and crowd around a small screen to watch a seriously Very Old, as in all of the main actors were now totally dead, movie. But then Art sort of pressed against me in order to see and Wade hit play on a clip that was rife with all this incredible sexual tension—like whoa, how did they cram that much *pure sexual tension* into a movie made before people were allowed to be queer, like weren't the sodomy laws still totally on the books in ye olde ancient whenever-they-made-this-movie? But there was Dirk Bogarde in leather pants vamping at John Mills and ahhhh.

And we just kept loading more clips, and Art kept leaning against my arm, his weight and warmth so, like…precious almost? We'd sit next to each other on the couch at home, but it wasn't like this, I didn't get to feel the form of him, I didn't get to feel his breaths when he laughed, or hear this little murmur he made when the tension on the screen got even more *extra*.

"This movie…" Art said, softly, not really in my ear but I could pretend.

"I know." Ray's arms twined around one of Wade's. "This is like…hot and tragic and absurd and amazing. All at once."

"Thus its magic." Wade sighed happily. "But this is why I did accents when we were kids."

"I just thought you were being ridiculous," I said, but it didn't come out cutting or critical. The thing about Wade— the thing I'd always hated about Wade—was that he did what he wanted and didn't seem to care who saw him doing it. Like carrying a hockey stick around and pretending it was a cane and saying things like "cheerio."

"It was fun! And anyway, look at them."

The two men on screen, one of whom was genuinely closeted, the other of whom was the straight man in basically every sense of the term, were embroiled in a deeply intense conversation about God or religion or women or responsibility.

And despite the fact that it was just a movie, despite the fact that a lot of the awesomeness of it was rooted in this horrible context of homophobia and relying on audiences not to fully understand what they were seeing, I was kind of jealous. Because Dirk Bogarde was playing his character like he was a man who DGAF about what anyone said, who had this very meaningful connection to another person, and who knew it, even though he never verbalized it.

My face heated up, scrunched in between Art and Wade. How could I be jealous of this? It was so dumb. And yet when Wade shut the computer I was like…sorta emotional, as if I couldn't let go of those thoughts.

I definitely wasn't ready for Wade to say, "And that's why I need you to be my beard, Preston."

"Umm." I grasped for clues. "Because…you don't know how to tell your parents that despite their best efforts you didn't grow up to be Dirk Bogarde?"

"Oh my god, right? Do you think they just didn't know that movie is like *rife* with homosexuality? Or do you think that even when we were five they were planning on us getting married?"

"No way. They didn't know. And that wasn't the only movie they made us watch. There was the one about the journalist or whatever."

"*His Girl Friday*?" Art asked.

"No, the other one, the one with the journalist."

"That *is* the one with the journalist!"

"No, the one with the journalist and the girl he's supposed to marry. Or did marry. Or didn't marry, I forget."

"That *is* the one with the journalist and the—"

"*The Philadelphia Story*!" Wade announced. "Which *also* has a journalist and a—"

Ray clapped her hands. "Thank you, all of you, for coming to our group TED Talk on 'old-ass movies about journalists and girls they have married, might marry, are marrying.' Please remember to tip your servers."

"TED Talks don't have servers," I objected. "Wait, do they?"

"Who knows, have you ever been to one?"

"No, but—"

Wade reached for his computer again. "Dear Google, do TED Talks have servers?" Pause. "Oops, yeah, that did not work. Waiters? Food? What am I looking for here?"

Art shifted away from me (sadly, so sadly) and said, "Maybe we should focus. And also eat."

"Good point." Ray picked up what appeared to be some kind of stuffed pepper thing. "It's just that Wade's parents like to get over-involved and if we told them we were—what are we again?"

"Partners in crime," Wade supplied.

She kissed him lightly. "Yes, of course. I meant what did we decide to call ourselves for other people?"

"None of your business? Or no, we decided on 'partners' as the public version of our relationship, which I still resent us needing to have." Wade made a face at us. "People are so *nosy* about things. You can't just be two consenting adults who happen to have a penis and a vagina without people getting all in your face about when you're getting married and when you're having babies and blah blah blah *none of your freaking business.*"

"To be fair, I got that when I was with Suzanne too," Ray said. "Is this like…a triumph for equality? Now we're all equally badgered by relatives and strangers demanding private details about our lives?"

Art sighed. "I know it's terrible, and I agree with everything you're saying, but also… I wish someone was badgering me for the details of my private life. I wish there *were* details of my private life to badger me about."

"Chin up, sugarplum." Wade reached around me to pat his shoulder. "Your time for badgering will come. But yes, Ray's right, it's not like I'm offended by my parents and their borderline creepy desire to marry me off to the nearest acceptable queer man because they've been planning my wedding announcements in their head for a decade now, but I just don't *care* about their narrative, and I can't be bothered to confront them about it." He beamed at me. "That's where you come in, Preston, my oldest friend."

I slumped. I could probably say no, but Art would hold it against me and I liked Ray, and Wade was really way too *Wade* a hundred percent of the time, but also, I knew his parents, and the problem wasn't that they were fixated on him being gay. It would take maybe a week for them to transfer all of that energy into him marrying Ray, which, yuck. "I'm going to hate this, right? What do I have to do?"

He leaned forward to kiss my cheek. "You are the very bestest oldest, most loyal—"

"I hate you, remember?"

The wide, somehow guileless and simultaneously too-knowing smile didn't leave his face. "I know! Tell me you're free Saturday in two weeks."

Art clapped his hands. "Yes! He's totally free"—I shot him a look—"and so am I! Ray, girlfriends night?"

"Best idea ever!"

Oh god. So Wade's partner was going to be hanging out with my—with my—with Art, while I was stuck at Wade's side pretending to be his boyfriend at some horrific thing his parents were throwing. I closed my eyes. "This is the worst idea ever."

"It'll be fun! Plus, your parents are not that different. This will get them off your back too!"

Except I didn't want to pretend I had a different person. I wanted to tell my parents I had the right person. Who was, in this very moment, excitedly planning a "girlfriends night" with someone else's girlfriend. Super annoying. "You owe me," I said to Wade. "You owe me *so much*."

He hooked his pinky around mine. "Promise I'll pay you back. Now tell me what you're going to wear."

I groaned and surrendered to the cause. Which was noble and pure and basically just making Art happy. And he was. He was maybe even proud of me for saying yes.

And that would have to be enough to get me through the nightmare that was to come: Art, leaning against me again as he spoke to Ray, lips shiny with oil from the olives he was eating, so close I could kiss him, except I could not kiss him.

Which was a good point. "I don't have to kiss you, do I?" I said to Wade.

He laughed. "Perish the thought, darling!" he said in his terrible British accent.

Ray tackled him to the couch and I just sat there, still jealous, and also, *I already regret this so much.* Except Art was still maybe-proud of me, so I would do it. Nobly. Without complaining.

Okay, with just a *little* complaining.

Chapter Twelve

"This is the literal worst," I informed Puzo as I reworked the same sentence for at least the tenth time. Maggie had lent me her office while she was out at a meeting so I could better concentrate on my line edits. It had been an hour and a half. I was on the second paragraph.

But the first paragraph was pretty much the best thing anyone had ever written in the history of the English language.

Maybe.

Actually.

Maybe there should be a comma in the third sentence? For flow, not grammar. I said it aloud, then frowned. Was "fluid" the word I wanted, or would "liquid" be better? Was there a meaningful difference between the two? I'd picked "fluid" because I liked the way it sounded more, but "liquid" was nicer looking on the page…

It was possible I had not just spent an hour and a half working on the best paragraph that anyone had ever written in the history of the English language. In fact, now that I was re-reading it, the vocabulary was too basic, the cadence unexciting, and the point of it was beginning to seem unclear to me.

Puzo one-eyed me from his perch where he'd been sleeping before I'd started verbally processing the worstness of line edits.

"You don't understand how awful this is because you're a

bird," I told him. "But believe me, it's awful." Then I imme-diately felt bad. I was *so* lucky. I knew I was lucky. I waded through loads of emails from prospective authors trying to get a shot at publishing. And I'd just kind of stumbled into a publishing contract. Well. After a few years working in the industry and also I did actually have a book and stuff. And Adams wasn't into nepotism. But still, getting a contract is easier when you're like in the same room with a bunch of people who have the power to give you that than it is when you're on the other end of an email from people who have the power to give you that.

Blah blah privilege blah editing was still the worst omg.

Maggie came in while I was lecturing Puzo on how he should be more sensitive about my tribulations. "Are you still on the same page you were on when I left? PK. Come on. Your deadline is in like...five days?"

"Shhh, don't tell my brain that, it'll freeze. It's okay, brain, don't listen to Maggie, she doesn't understand, uh, time, or something."

She sighed heavily. "Close the laptop."

"Didn't you just point out that I'm running out of time?" I demanded. "How can I edit if my laptop is closed?"

She closed my laptop. It was the kind of move I wouldn't have dared do (and even Puzo made a sound I chose to take as disapproval), but honestly? I was relieved. I was beginning to hear my own book in this high mocking tone, like the whole thing was just waiting for me to fall flat on my face.

Puzo said something that sounded suspiciously like, "Poopy."

"Be nice," Maggie said to him before turning back to me. "PK, you're having a minor imposter syndrome breakdown, which, as you know, is totally normal. Now listen up."

I slumped forward with my head in my hands. "What?"

"Take the rest of the day off."

I eyed her through my fingers. "That's the dumbest idea ever. Weren't you just saying I had to finish this?"

"Yeah, but you're done for the day. Take the rest of today off, go home, have some food, hang out with Art, watch some bad YouTube, get some sleep, and start again tomorrow. And tomorrow you gotta start doing it like when you were trying dating apps but you just kept reading every single profile and thinking deeply about it without swiping."

"But I thought it was important to actually pay attention to the profiles! How can I make an educated decision about whether I want to date someone if I don't read their profile?"

She shook her head. "Every single profile is not worth reading. Remember? Some are, so you should, but most aren't. It's the same with edits. Sure, some lines are vital, for voice or character development or plot. If you're in the middle of a super important scene, spend some time on that, get it right. But that's not every single comma, PK. And it's not every single paragraph. Think about the you in five years: will you remember this comma? If not, just swipe. Or in this case, accept or reject. That's it. Just swipe."

"Just swipe," I repeated, more in desperation than anything else. "Okay."

"But not today."

"Right."

"Hey, I know what you should do instead of obsessing over commas. Why don't you go home and tell Art you wrote a book? That'd be good."

This was like the fourth or fifth time she'd mentioned it. "Oh my god. I told you, I'll do it when I'm ready, okay? It's obviously not today. Today is already The Worst."

"You're running out of time here, pal. They're not gonna

hold the presses so you can last minute be like 'oh bee-tee-dubs, I wrote a book.'"

"I'm not going to!"

"I just think he's going to be super weirded out when he realizes you kept this whole thing a secret for absolutely no apparent reason. But hey, it's your life, buddy. You do you."

Which was Maggie's way of saying, *Hey, it's your life, buddy. You screw it up as much as you want.* "I'll tell him at some point. Just not today. I'm already stressed out enough by these stupid edits."

She patted my shoulder again. "You're such a baby author right now, it's kind of adorable. Right, Puzo?"

Puzo squawked.

I shot both of them glares. "You two are so insensitive."

"Uh-huh. Noted. Now get out of my office." As she said it she smiled. Sweetly.

"Fine."

"Don't work on that any more until tomorrow."

"*Fine.*" But I couldn't quite keep up the petulant teenager thing. "Did you bring me back leftovers?"

She reached into her pocket and pulled out one of those red and white mint candies, dropping it in my outstretched palm. "Body of Christ," she intoned.

I made a face. "Ew, what?"

"You're supposed to say 'amen.' That's how communion works."

"Okay, gross. And I'm not—uh—whatever Christian thing it is that does that, so."

Maggie sighed. "I need more former Catholic friends to understand the depths of my attempted blasphemy."

I stared down at the peppermint. "I think you've ruined this for me now."

"Ha, sorry. You can give it to Puzo if you really don't want it, he hasn't had candy in like two months."

Puzo, hearing his name, climbed over to the corner closest to us and pressed himself against the bars.

"Um, no, I'll eat it."

Puzo made a very clear protest noise as I left the office. I could hear Maggie opening his treat container to give him something more parrot-treat, less human-treat. *Just swipe*, I told myself as I walked back to my desk. *I can do that.*

But first, I wasn't allowed to work on the book the rest of the night, per Maggie's orders. And Art had the day off. Maybe we could play video games or something. A distraction. A way to pass the time. A way to distract myself. Yeah. Good idea. Go, me.

The first thing I noticed was that the apartment...smelled like smoke. The second thing I noticed was that all of the windows were open.

"Um. Art? Is something on fire?"

"Only my ego! I'm trying to make dinner."

I poked my head into the kitchen, where the smoke was still hanging heavily in the air. "And...how's that going?"

"Here." He handed me a magazine from my stack of never-read magazines. "Will you just stand there and try to wave some of the fresh air this way? I really wish we had a window in here."

"Sure. Can I take off my jacket first though?"

"God, sorry, just, I walked away for a second and things were somehow boiling over even though there was nothing there to boil and I think I mostly salvaged it but also I was worried I was literally burning the apartment down." He spun away and crossed the kitchen—so took three whole steps— which is when I noticed that he was wearing this very cute peacock blue skirt with some sort of vine pattern on it, and an apron over the front, and the whole thing kind of flowed around his legs as he moved.

"Is that a new skirt?"

"Oh. Um. Not really. I just don't wear it that much." Was he blushing? Or just flushed from the whole near-fire experience?

"It looks nice on you," I said, and then immediately wanted to take it back. That was not the kind of thing you said to your roommate who you totally in no way might be in love with oh my god what was I doing ahhhhhhh.

Art smiled, only glancing at me for a second before directing the rest of his smile at the frying pan. "Thanks, PK."

I gulped. *Smile at meeeeeee.* No. Down, PK. Bad PK. "So, um." Why did this silence feel so awkward? I dropped my messenger bag and jacket so I could begin flapping around the magazine, as requested. "What're you making?"

"Curry. Or trying to." Another glance over. "Just, you've seemed kind of stressed out? So I had this whole plan that I'd make you dinner. Well, both of us dinner. Obviously I'd also be eating dinner. Anyway. *Are* you stressed out? Did I make that up?"

"Oh. Um. No. I mean. Yes. Kind of." *Tell him, tell him right now, tell him everything, this is the perfect moment to tell him EVERYTHING.* "I, um…" Sweat broke out all down my back, all over my face. I could not tell him. I couldn't tell him about the book unless I was also going to tell him about the other thing. I mean. The book basically *was* the other thing. At least, he'd know I had non-best friend feelings for him the second he read it. No, not *non*-best friend feelings. I had those *plus* other feelings. *Best-friend-plus* feelings.

He looked over and smiled again, and he'd pulled his hair back to cook, so it was this little sunburst of wavy tendrils coming out the top of his head and oh god, I couldn't tell him, I couldn't tell him like this, when he seemed so happy. What if I ruined dinner? What if I ruined *everything*? Maybe he'd see through the book, maybe he wouldn't, but I could not tolerate waiting to find out.

If I told him about *Peak Romance*, I had to tell him about my feelings, and I couldn't do that. I didn't know how.

"Are you so stressed you can't talk about your stress?"

I forced a laugh, shying away from how close he'd gotten to the truth. "Nailed it. That's exactly what I am. So stressed I can't talk about how stressed I am. It's just a lot going on. At work." Which wasn't a lie. Technically the book *was* work now. "But dinner smells—um—well, it *looks* really good."

"Now that the smoke's clearing away, right?" His laughter was this sort of terrible self-mocking thing, which I wanted to erase out of the world because he deserved so much better than that, he deserved to be proud and never, ever self-deprecating.

"No! I mean. Not at all, it's not even that smoky." I flapped the magazine faster. "And anyway, I'm super hungry so I'll be happy with anything." Oh god. That did not come out right at all.

"Thanks, PK."

"I didn't mean it like that! I meant—I just meant—I really appreciate the thought! It's the thought that—wait—no, that's not what I meant either. It really does look good, I swear!"

"Thou dost protest too much," he said, but his tone was a little lighter at least. "I think maybe I just accidentally dropped a snap pea on the burner coil and panicked when it started burning. You can probably lower your magazine now. I may have overreacted."

I wanted to protest, but if I protested his overreaction, I'd be supporting his panic, and what was my goal?

Before I had to untangle my possible responses, Art was pulling two bowls of rice out of the oven where he'd apparently been keeping them warm (and also, genius, I always just left my rice out where it got cold and gummy while I was cooking other stuff), then carefully ladled two beautiful bowls of curry. Was it "bowls of curry" or "curries" in noun form? I couldn't remember. Should I google it? No, I should help with dinner.

"I also got us fancy drinks from the Asian market, though they're probably not Thai. This is like fusion Asian cuisine for white people who can't tell the difference, basically."

"I'm still super excited for it. Thanks, Arty."

Did he blush again? No. Probably not. I couldn't tell.

"I mean, I feel like I should be thanking you. I did just show up and move in without asking, like, at all. And you let me have my D&D group over. And you've never put pressure on me to like...leave." He dropped a sprig of, uh, green thing on top of each bowl-slash-curry. Herb! It was an herb. A green sprig of herb. And yes, I knew they all had names, but who can be bothered to tell the difference when you could buy them in handy little bottles with the name printed on the side?

"Dude, no, you can move in with me anytime! Or sorry, maybe you're not in a 'dude' mood, I just mean, you can always move in with me, um, I can't think of a less dude-ly version of 'dude.' Like, 'madame'? Or maybe...does 'lady' work? I feel like that's not really the thing. Or 'sis'? Sis! You can move in with me anytime, sis. You definitely shouldn't feel like you have to leave, oh my god, I don't want you to leave! That's not a thing." I swallowed more rambling. "Plus you force me to accept rent money when I totally don't need it, so it's not like you're just, um, tenanting unofficially."

He wasn't looking at me. "Yeah, but still." He picked up both bowls/curries and used one to gesture to the fridge. "You can get our beverages if you want."

"Yes! Yes, I do want. I want to help. Get our beverages.

Whatever you need." But before I could do that we had to pass each other in the tiny space of the kitchen and I guess I should have backed up into the hallway, but I was still kind of flustered from the whole conversation, and I didn't do it automatically, so by the time I realized I should have we were already two ships very awkwardly attempting to steam past one another in a very small—was it a lock? maybe a canal?— in a very small space, the clearance no more than an inch… half an inch…a centimeter… "Sorry," I murmured as his skirt brushed against my pants.

"For what?" His voice also seemed…soft somehow? Soft like the flowy fabric now swirling away from me and out the door before I could reply.

It was still hot in the kitchen, hot and kind of humid. I could tell because I had to blot my face with a paper towel before I brought our drinks out to the living room.

"Speaking of me living here," Art said, like we were just continuing a conversation, "I'm thinking about having my book club over. Not this coming week, the one after. I didn't want to volunteer unless that was okay with you."

Ugh, this again. The D&D club, the book club. "You can have over whoever you want because you freaking *live here*, this is your freaking *apartment*, and you're a grown-up! If you want to cosplay as a dragon and"—I searched the bottom of my brain for some idea what people did at D&D meetings— "roll dice for hours, you can do that, because this is *literally where you live*. I'm not Roman, okay? I'm not going to, like, lay down the law and shit on the things you care about!"

He stared at me for a long moment in the wake of my, okay, call it what it is, *outburst*. His eyes were wide and his mouth was just slightly open, a picture of *what just happened*.

"Um, control-z all that. Sure, book club, sounds good." I very seriously began eating my food.

"I just meant… I was making sure that you don't have anything big going Thursday in two weeks. I don't want to disturb you."

Umm. I swallowed the bite of food I was mashing around in my mouth and said, "Oh. No, that's solid. Cool. Yeah." Then, because that seemed super inadequate, "Sorry."

"It's okay. And I think…you're right. At least a little." Now he was the one staring down at his food. "I did do that. I did sort of…edit myself to fit in with what Roman thought was important." One of his hands stole to the side, smoothing the skirt over his leg. He'd taken off the apron at some point and now he was all peacock blue and pale fingers and glittery nails that were chipped at the tips.

I wanted so badly to reach out. What would I even do? Touch his hand? Trace the bird bones of his fingers? Draw a line from the knobby bone of his wrist all the way to the glitter of his pinky? The impulses from my brain—*reach out, touch him, do SOMETHING*—were so strong that my own fingers twitched. God, he was… I was…we were… Was this The Moment? Maybe this was The Moment where I reached for his hand and told him everything. About how much I'd wanted to kiss him since That Night, about how much I admired him and cared about him.

Would that even be romantic? We were talking about his ex, after all. This was probably not The Moment. Or maybe it was? But how was a guy supposed to know? Was he vulnerable right now? Would I be taking advantage somehow? I didn't want to do that. I wanted to… I wanted to do something so special that he'd never forget it, not sort of mumble my feelings over the dregs of his last relationship like when you take your last sip of coffee and it's all grounds.

But I also wanted to touch his hand where it lay against his skirt.

The two factions of my mind were possibly going to war, all clanging logic and feelings, when suddenly the silence was split by—

A "Who Let the Dogs Out" ringtone.

Art perked up. "It's Ches," he said, and jumped to get his phone. "Hey!"

Ches was Art's older brother. I really liked Ches, like, as a human. He was fun and funny and sort of absurd in a way I didn't think I was brave enough to be? But also over the years I'd realized it wasn't so much bravery with ol' Chester. It was...not to be judgey about it? But he just didn't pay attention to what other people needed. Sometimes it seemed like he didn't even realize other people *had* needs.

Watching Art's face fall, I suspected this was one of those times. "But I thought you had another week on your program? No, but Ches... I know it does, but...that's what you said last time, though..."

I picked through my curry, spearing chickpeas with my fork. If he'd left rehab (y'know, again), he'd be hiding from their parents. He'd done it a couple of times when we were in the dorms, and I knew he'd shown up at Art's when he lived with Roman, which was just another thing for Roman to look down on. But now?

"You can't randomly call because you have no place to go—" Now Art just sounded resigned. "Of course I do, but..." He looked up at me when I happened to be looking up at him.

I offered a shrug and an attempt at a supportive smile. *Whatever you want to do, I'm here for.*

"I have to ask PK, I can't let you crash on the couch without at least talking to him... That's *not* what I said, Ches! Just hold on." He lowered the phone.

I tried the smile again. "So Ches is on his way?" I asked.

He sighed, this heavy, like, age-old sigh. "Is it okay? I mean I know you'll say yes. I just. It's always the same with him."

"Where is he now?"

"Couch surfing in the company of some woman he left rehab with, but she's going to stay with a girlfriend and he's not invited, so."

"So he'll come here. It's cool."

"Okay." It didn't seem like the response he really wanted, but obviously I wasn't going to pull a Roman and tell him his brother could get lost. Actually, Roman was a lot like Ches in that way: charismatic and totally insensitive. Art lifted the phone and said, "I'll text you our address, just call when you're downstairs and I'll let you in… Yeah, okay." A slight smile. "Yeah, I'm excited to see you too."

"When's he getting here?" I asked when he put down the phone.

"Three hours. I can't deal with him, I swear. Anyway, thanks, PK."

"I didn't do anything."

He sat back down, close enough for our knees to touch. "You never make me feel bad about who I am."

"Um." Now I was super confused. Did Ches do that? Were we still talking about Roman? "I mean, yeah. Because that would make me a serious shithead."

"Still. I appreciate it. Do you like your curry?"

"Love it." I scooped up a whole forkful of curried rice. "It's freaking delicious."

"Thanks."

We kept eating, talked about the blankets we could gather together for Ches to use, the possible location of an extra pillow. He told me about the various Black History Month tables he was putting together at the store. I filled him in on some drama with one of the authors at work and their possible fabrication of a story in their memoir. Normal roommate stuff.

Now that the moment was past I was relieved I hadn't spurted out all my feelings like a fountain without a pressure control. It would have been The Wrong Time. For sure. Because now Ches was coming over and also because I wanted it to be special.

In *Peak Romance* there's this moment where all the feelings come out, and it's super special, like there's a midnight picnic and battery-powered tea lights and it's the most romantic thing I could think of. *That's* what I wanted for Art. Something perfect.

A perfect, life-changing moment. I just needed to, y'know, find one.

Chapter Thirteen

Having Ches around was honestly fun. For a while. And maybe more fun for me than for Art, who was happy to host him right up until he turned on some music at almost-midnight and started banging around in the kitchen "making late dinner, you know, linner," cue big smile.

To be fair, he did turn the music down, at least that first night, and mostly cleaned up when he was done. The thing I'd learned about Ches over the years was that he required a lot of energy. Even just talking to him for a minute on the way out the door to work took *a lot* out of you. You'd be standing there, boots on, coat on, hat on, bag on, keys in hand, and he'd randomly be awake (or he'd jump off the couch in a tangle of blankets when he heard you leaving) and he'd stand there right at the door talking for like…whole minutes. While you were slowly beginning to steam and sweat and wilt inside your appropriate-for-February-weather coat, which was definitely not appropriate for the wildly tropical temperature the building always seemed to be in winter.

But aside from his general, uh, attention seeking, he was an okay house guest. Art wasn't super keen on giving him keys to the apartment, but I pointed out that if he needed us every time he wanted to go anywhere that would mean we'd basically be imprisoning him all day long and then attached to him the rest of the time. And nobody wanted that.

Throughout the day we'd get texts—and I say "we" because Ches was a big fan of the group text, though the group
in this case was just Art and me—mostly selfies: Ches outside
the Museum of Natural History, Ches in Times Square, Ches
at the arch in Washington Square Park, Ches at the Central
Park Zoo. It turned out Ches was a consummate tourist, something that had somehow escaped me before. Or maybe this
was some new phase of his, though I definitely remembered
him mooning the Statue of Liberty at some point. Later at
home he'd tell us stories about all the people he talked to, the
French couple he took a picture of so they'd have one with
both of them in front of the New York Public Library (also,
best nerd tourists, now I kinda wanted to get a picture of myself in front of libraries wherever I happened to go). Or the
German family he helped with directions to Kmart.

"They were looking for shoes, you know, because one of
the younger kids had lost a shoe playing in a fountain, and the
dad looked really tired of carrying the kid, you know, but it
was okay, they only had another couple of blocks to go," he'd
say, beaming as he told us about it.

"That's so cool," I'd say, every time, because it *was*. It was
cool that Ches rocked up and went all over the city having
these cool encounters with random strangers. I had no idea
how anyone could do that, but I thought it was slightly amazing, and it was easy to get caught up in it, in this wild post-
rehab adventure Ches was living in the city.

Until one night Art knocked really quietly on my door and
when I opened it, he slipped inside. But not for any of the reasons I'd ever imagined him slipping inside my room at night.

"Look." He fidgeted as he stood there, rocking from side
to side. "I know you like Ches, and that's awesome, it really
is, but also. Also, PK, um, remember that he doesn't always
tell the truth."

Which, now that he mentioned it, I did know. At least, I knew he sometimes embellished stuff, because Art had pointed it out before, but I'd sorta forgotten. He'd been staying with us for maybe a week by then, long enough for me to have heard handfuls of stories about what he did while we were at work, and they'd all *seemed* believable. "Yeah, okay, but… why would he lie?"

"I don't really think of it as *lying* exactly. He just makes stuff up." Art's voice was low, though Ches was in the kitchen making food again, so it probably didn't need to be. Still, there was something compelling about the way he was talking, the way he wasn't really looking at me. Almost like he was…what? Embarrassed? Ashamed?

"But…why?"

He shrugged, shoulders shifting under the satiny bathrobe he called his dressing gown. "Not to be mean or anything. I think he always just wants to seem interesting. He wants to have something to talk about, you know?"

"But…" I still couldn't really wrap my head around it, like I couldn't wrap my head around it the other times he'd told me, which was why it was so easy to get caught up in Ches's stuff again. "But…they're so specific. Like. The thing about Kmart? Who would think that up?"

"I don't know, PK. And maybe it's not *all* a lie. Maybe it was one lady and one kid. Or maybe it was one German person. Or maybe it was a person buying shoes. But I'd be super shocked to find out there was actually a little German kid who lost a shoe in a fountain. Plus aren't the fountains all shut down for winter? And definitely people aren't *playing* in them, it snowed literally last week. You know what I mean?"

I did. But also I didn't. "I just…but…why?"

He glanced back out at the kitchen, like Ches might hear. "It's just a thing that he does. Try not to let it bother you too

much. Anyway, I'm gonna go play some *No Man's Sky*." And
then he was gone. Leaving me sorta confused about the whole
thing, up to and including Art's apparent nonchalance about
it. Maybe not *nonchalance*. I guess it was acceptance? But it was
hard for me to imagine just accepting that someone you cared
about might open his mouth every day and tell you stories
that weren't true. Like, now that he said it, the thing about
the kid playing in a fountain made *zero* sense, but had seemed
reasonable when Ches was telling the story, mostly because
who would make something like that up?

After the first few days, having Ches around seemed pretty
normal. I had no idea what he did during the day, but he
couldn't seem to sit still long and his Instagram was full of him
in front of allllll the tourist destinations. Since I'd never randomly shown up at someone's apartment and kind of vaguely
asked if I could crash on their couch, I didn't know what
typical behavior for that was. I did get the impression there
was some tension between him and Art about when he was,
y'know, going to be leaving the couch.

Still, I had *Peak Romance* to think about. ARCs were going
out, which meant advanced readers everywhere would soon
be getting their copies and, um, reading it.

Obviously when you work with a publisher to publish
something you know that someday it will be...published. It
therefore followed that, like, also someday people would...read
it. But the reality of that? *Seriously freaking weird*. Also the fact
that I'd done almost all of my rounds of edits, the cover was
designed, the back cover copy was finalized, the blurbs were
gathered or mostly gathered (I'd told Maggie I didn't want to
know what Real Authors were saying about the book, it was
too terrifying), so now I was just kind of floating in this weird,

still calm where my work was done, but the book hadn't been formally introduced to anyone yet.

Which led to, not gonna lie, a lot of obsessing over how everyone would hate it.

The other plans that had now been semi-finalized were about the release. Specifically, we were going with a reading, which I agreed to before I really thought about it and then didn't know how to get out of. Also I wasn't sure I wanted to get out of it because, well, it was a reading. A real one. With me. As the author. Doing the reading. The night of the day when the book, like, came out. Which I thought might be a problem, but I was assured that with enough buzz, it wouldn't be. "Plus," Maggie added, "you know romance readers glom stuff in a sitting. We could hold it at nine a.m. and everyone with a preorder would have it read already."

Which was meant to be supportive, but also: GULP.

Obviously people would also be able to *buy* the book at the reading, so we were trying to capitalize on intrigue, which was all well and good, except what if there wasn't any? I'd been worried about no one showing up, but Maggie said they were having Carlos, of young-gay-author fame, introduce me (and therefore bring his legion of fans). Which was kind of reassuring—at least, I knew Carlos, and liked him, and he'd read the book and apparently liked it—but also intimidating. Like the main act was opening for me and everyone would be super disappointed when he stepped back and I was all alone. With my book. Which maybe no one would even read. Ahhhhh. What was worse: people reading the book and hating it, or no one reading it at all?

I definitely wasn't against having a distraction around, and Ches was a great distraction. When he told me he had this friend who made a few thousand dollars a month—"a few thou" as he put it—taking online surveys, I was for it. It was something he could do from his phone anywhere he wanted and hey, even if it was only half that much money, it was a start, right? A couple days later, I heard him telling Art that some friend of his from high school had moved to the city and he was thinking about hitting him up for a job. (Art didn't say much about that, or at least not that I could hear from the hallway where I was on my way to the bathroom and definitely not intentionally eavesdropping.)

In retrospect, obviously Art knew Ches was full of shit. But despite being warned, I still didn't.

He'd been at the apartment for a week and a half when they had their first real fight about when he was leaving. I was trapped in the kitchen, where I'd gone to eat a late dinner of Lucky Charms, and it had started as another one of Ches's stories, this one about a girl he met at a coffee shop who said she worked at a department store in midtown that was currently hiring.

"Hiring for what?" Art's voice was flat. "You're not qualified to work at a department store."

"I can work at a department store! Anyone can work at a department store, little brother, it doesn't take a degree."

"You think they're going to hire a completely inexperienced applicant when they probably have five others who have relevant work experience? What store would do that?"

"Why are you shitting on me? I've had *jobs* before! It's not like I've never worked."

"I'm not *shitting on you*, I'm pointing out a logical flaw in your plan. Did you go to the store and fill out an application?"

"I was going to, but—"

"I bet you can fill one out online, did you check the website?"

"I didn't think of that—"

"You do know the name of the store and its location, right?

Because a lot of stores have multiple locations and obviously you want to find the exact one that she was talking about since the job market is so crummy. Which store does your new coffee shop friend work at?"

"Listen, Arty, you want to be a dick, fine, but I'm really trying to get my life together here, and I could use a little *support* from you for once!"

"Excuse me? You're sleeping on my couch and eating my food, exactly how much more support do you expect from me when you've done literally nothing lately except leave rehab before you were supposed to?"

"Seriously? I think you mean *PK's couch*, since this is his apartment, last I checked."

"I pay rent!"

"You want me to pay rent for sleeping on *PK's couch*, is that the problem? You want twenty bucks or something, Arty? Fine, here."

I winced so hard that my head hurt. Also I really did not want to be part of some dumb fight they were having.

"I'm not taking your money. Maybe you should use that to catch a train back to Mom and Dad's, since we both know that's where you're going to end up." A few footsteps later, I heard the sound of Art's door closing. He didn't even slam it, which felt almost more cold, like fighting with Ches wasn't worth a door slam.

"Screw you, little brother," Ches called, though not super loud. I also couldn't decide if repeating "little brother" was some sort of microaggression or just a normal brotherly attempt to put Art in his place.

I was trying to decide how I'd escape from the kitchen without Ches noticing when he showed up in the doorway, which was also the entryway, and started pulling on his boots. Maybe, if I stayed very still, he wouldn't see me.

Yeah, of course he saw me, I was standing three feet away from him, frozen, with a cereal bowl in one hand and a spoon in the other.

"Uh. I'm going out. Also, your asshole roommate is a piece of work. He acts like I'm not even *trying,* when I am this time! That's why I'm here! Fresh start, new perspective, whatever." He burrowed into his coat, which was actually an old one of mine, and fumbled with the zipper.

"Oh, you have to kind of twist it a little—here." I stepped forward and, um, then I was zipping up Ches's coat, which used to be my coat, and it was this super weird moment because he was pissed at Art, and I was trying to be the most neutral of neutral countries, and also we were definitely standing closer than we'd ever stood before, but that zipper was super tricky, and I didn't think I could describe how to do it.

"Are you hitting on me, Mr. Robinson?" he teased as I went back to my cereal, and he must not be that pissed, because he was right back to laughing. "Sorry, bro, you're definitely off-limits, even if you don't know it." He laughed again. "See ya, PK."

"Bye, Ches." In the quiet aftermath of the fight I did what any rational person would do: I poured another bowl of Lucky Charms. Also, ugh, fighting siblings, worst. Addendum to the last also: what did he mean by me being off-limits? Not that I was at all interested in Ches (eek, no), or had any reason to believe he wasn't totally straight, but "off-limits" implied something. Didn't it? Imply something?

But, like, *what?*

Chapter Fourteen

Book club was on a Thursday. Art told Ches about it the day before. And by "told Ches about it" I mean he messaged our group thread to say, broadly to both of us, that he'd need the living room all evening, so if we could stay out of it, that'd be great. (I chose to believe that was more for Ches than me.) He added that the kitchen was okay, he just didn't want any big interruptions during the meeting.

Basically the message was, if you squinted very slightly, *I'm not telling my friends that my older brother has been sleeping on my couch for two weeks so please stay out of the apartment until they leave at ten.*

At least that's how I interpreted it. Ches probably did too. His reply was, *Ha ha ha ha book club, that's adorable! I'll try not to DISRUPT it or anything!* With a smiley face that looked extra mischievous-slash-maybe-kinda-shitty in the context of the text.

Alarm bells went off in my head. A lot of alarm bells. Big firehouse alarm bells you could hear for miles. Or no, maybe those booming air-raid alarms, like at any moment the two of them might go to literal war with each other and I'd have to hide in a bunker. Actually, that was probably a seriously insensitive metaphor? And yet still felt accurate.

I did not want them to go to war. So I did what only a desperate man would ever do: I called in a favor. To Wade. Who answered his phone, "Preston, darling, we were just talking about you! When are you and your lovely boyf—*oof*—room-mate coming over again?"

I was way too preoccupied to play stupid games with him. "You know how you totally owe me for being your beard at your parents' birthday party? I mean the birthday party your parents are throwing you like you're six years old? Remember how you definitely *owe me* for that?"

"Do I *owe* you, though? I thought old friends just did small favors for each other out of pure altruism?" His tone was light, amused, as if nothing he was saying mattered in the least.

"This is important, can you please be serious for like five seconds? And also, it's not a small favor, it's a massive one, and you know it!"

He laughed in my ear, that same tinkling laugh he'd per-fected sometime after puberty. Wade had always specialized in performative ridiculousness, but I knew if I could cut through that, he'd help me. "It's not the *smallest* favor, maybe. What do you need, sweetheart?"

"First, never call me 'sweetheart' again. Second: I need you to babysit Art's brother tomorrow night."

Silence for maybe three whole seconds, which was a lot for Wade.

"Is Art's brother a toddler? In what way does he need to be babysat?"

"He's—he—actually most of the time I like him, but in this case Art's hosting book club and I'm worried that Ches is going to be a jerk and walk in and—"

"Make a scene?" Wade suggested.

I paused to picture it. "Either he'd be outwardly a jerk about it, or he'd be charming and everyone would love him and… that would be worse."

"How could people *liking* Art's brother be worse than him being unlikable?"

"Because everyone's always *liked* Ches. Art's the one who works hard, and tries to be a good person, and tries to be there for other people, and Ches is just this self-absorbed overgrown kid who's always been the one their parents and basically everyone else paid attention to, and I don't want that to happen again, so if you could just do me this one favor then we'll be even."

"I don't mean to insult you, Preston, but it honestly never occurred to me that you were perceptive enough to notice complex interpersonal dynamics. Of course I'll babysit Art's brother. But if you like him, why aren't you doing it?"

Which was a good question. And I didn't think I could explain my instinctive desire to stay at the apartment, specifically in the kitchen for as long as I could, to be Art's first line of defense just in case Ches managed to shake his nanny and find a way to come home before the end of book club. It didn't reflect all that great on me that I saw myself as Art's knight in shining armor, standing guard over his, uh, book club, which...all right, that sounded absurd, but the good relations were fraying between them and I didn't want any of that to come out when Art was having friends over the way he couldn't do when he lived with stupid Roman.

"I have to work tonight," I lied. "I mean, I'll be in the apartment, but I have...deadlines. And stuff."

Wade laughed. "I hear you loud and clear, honey. Tell me when I'll be dropping by to abduct this gentleman."

I felt better after getting off the phone with Wade. He was—well—*Wade*, but he seemed to understand that I needed him to do me a favor for Art, and he and Art, okay, obviously not going to run off to a fake music festival on an island in

South America with each other, but they did seem to really like each other.

He probably would have babysat Ches even without me calling in that favor he owed me. Best not to chance it, though.

I'm not sure what I *expected* from book club night? But this… wasn't it.

First: there was a lot more wine than I realized would be needed to sit around and discuss books. I swear they had a bottle apiece and maybe an extra. Aside from seeming relieved that Ches was gone, Art was super focused. On book club. He'd never hosted it before and he wanted it to be completely perfect. Maybe that's why all the wine.

Second: piles of cheese and crackers and fruit. Not just one cheese, *multiple* cheeses. A variety of crackers, all on their own plates. Pretty much every dish we had was now being used to entertain Art's friends, which was fine, just strange. The last time Maggie came over I'd offered her a beer and dusted off an old box of Girl Scout cookies I'd bought because someone at the office cornered me into it.

Third: they were *loud*. Not that I had a problem with it, but I guess when I thought *book club*, it conjured pictures of like… tea and polite murmurings about the thematic resonance of blah blah blah. Not raucous laughter and raised voices.

I'd tried to stay in my bedroom after I'd met Art's friends, but curiosity got the better of me. The plan had been to wait until an hour had passed—I figured Wade could at least keep Ches occupied that long—then go to the kitchen and make a full meal, AKA guard the door just in case I needed to divert Ches to anywhere that wasn't the living room. I'd pictured herding him past the low-voiced discussion about literary motifs and into my room where I could force him to play video games until book club ended.

I would gladly make that sacrifice. If Wade making that sacrifice wasn't enough.

As I passed by, sort of hunching over to make myself smaller, I heard Art say, "Okay, okay, we have to get to the book now because I am *in love*."

Um. Art was *in love*? Since when? How? With who? I forced myself into the kitchen and stood there, completely still, forgetting to keep up even a pretense of not eavesdropping, which didn't matter, because book club did not care about me in the least.

Not that I wanted to disrupt them, obviously, but it was a tiny bit unsettling how little notice they took of my existence.

"I know!" one of the book club friends said. "How much do we love this main character? He's *so hopeless*, but you just want to hug him!"

"*I* want to shake him," someone else said.

"*I* want to kiss him," Art chimed in. "He's my book boyfriend, it's official, no one else can have him. He is the *perfect* boyfriend."

They all laughed. Someone clapped.

I stood in my kitchen with a heavy feeling of *ugh* in my guts. Not that I was against Art kissing, obviously, but because I considered Art kissing like…sacred. His lips. His skin so close. His eyes…

More laughter and talking. How did they understand each other when all of them were talking at once? Whatever it was, they seemed to be having fun. I stopped myself in the act of reaching for the cereal, which wouldn't take long enough for me to eavesdrop more—er—stand guard over the front door. Definitely that. Definitely being noble, not, like, sneaky. Yeah.

I hadn't even been interested in book club except as a thing that showed off how much better I was than Roman, because I *wanted* Art to have his friends over. But now? Now I wanted to be a fly on the wall and hear *everything*. Which was challenging because after the initial outburst about how *perfect* the book was, they started doing some overlapping talking, and also discussing deeper things I couldn't track because I hadn't read this book or the three? seven? fifteen? other books they seemed to be comparing it to.

I paced the kitchen restlessly, waiting for water to boil. What was I doing? I didn't feel like pasta, and I didn't even have sauce, so it'd be butter and salt pasta, out of a box that looked like it might have been there when I moved in, and it was angel hair, which I didn't like because it was so slippery, you can never get a good bite of the stuff without it sliding back into your bowl. And I'd *tried* the spoon trick, but I wasn't very good at it and—

God, I wanted to be a fly on the wall in the living room. What were they talking about now? They weren't as loud and I strained to hear but it was hard to make out whole sentences and arrrrrgh. Maybe someone wanted pasta? I could go in and offer pasta. To book club.

Before I could think too hard about it (surely it was a normal thing? To make food and offer it to people?), I stuck my head out of the kitchen to call a totally normal, casual, *Hey, does anyone else want pasta?*

Except I hadn't timed it right. So then I was just…a head in a doorway, facing the group of people, but not part of the group of people, but also awkwardly floating there in space, mouth slightly open, prepared to speak, but not able to, because someone was currently talking about, y'know, the book.

"…way the arc plays out, with all the pining and then the transition to a relationship? I didn't think it was working for me completely, but by the end I really…" They trailed off and glanced up at me.

Or at my floating head.

The others turned to look at my floating head too.

"PK?" Art asked, looking flushed with wine and laughter, his hair a little mussed like he'd been pushing it back too much. "Do you need something?"

To kiss you, I need to kiss you, please let me kiss you. Oh god, I'd almost said that out loud. I choked for a second, then said, "Pasta." Right, not a sentence. "Does anyone want any? I'm making some, but it's too much for me."

One of them kind of laughed. One of them looked at me with that slightly condescending kindness, like I was a big oaf who just didn't know any better than to interrupt book club to offer pasta. One of them said, "Hey, have you read this book? It's really great. You can join us, you know, you don't have to hide in the kitchen."

"Yeah, join us," said the one who'd laughed. "We'll catch you up!"

"But no spoilers," said the condescending one.

I really needed to get better at names. "Um."

"PK doesn't read romance," Art told them, in this tone that like...was sort of offensive? He said it like we'd talked about romance and I'd *shat* on it. Like I'd rolled my eyes at the whole genre, which I very much had never done.

"I've read romance!" I immediately defended myself.

He gave me *a look.* "Kirk/Spock fanfiction doesn't count."

The one who'd asked me to join them (Pigtails) turned to Art. "Um, of course it counts. It's romantic, isn't it?"

"It's thinly veiled porn."

"So? If it's porn with romance, it's still romance." Pigtails stuck their tongue out at Art. "Don't be judgey."

"Okay, you make a fair point, I just mean PK wouldn't read *this.*"

Which could not be stood for. "I could read that! I don't not-read romance! I read all your books in college!"

"Yes, you read romance for *a month* this one time years ago." Something in his face almost stopped me, like maybe it wasn't just Art annoyed, there was something almost too exposed in his face just then.

But all his book club people were looking at me, and the gauntlet had been thrown down. I made my way into the living room to better defend myself. "I'm not a snob about romance!"

The one who hadn't spoken (Locs) held out his copy of the book. "It's genuinely good. I don't think you have to be a romance reader to enjoy reading a book about people who care about each other."

"I don't think PK is tuned in enough to his feelings to really like this kind of book," Art was saying as I took it. "No offense, obviously, it's not like anyone *has* to be tuned into their feelings, I just think…"

But whatever he thought was lost in the sudden waves-rushing-past-my-ears sound of my heart kicking up to high gear.

Peak Romance.

Peak.

Romance.

Peak Romance by H.K. Pierce. Which was me. Change the initials around, make up a last name. Have yourself a pseudonym.

I was holding *my own book.*

"Um." I stood there, mouth dry, staring down at my own freaking book.

"Even the word 'romance' is too much for you," Art teased.

"It's not!" *Heart, stop pounding, I can't think.* "Um." What do you do when someone hands you a book? Um. Right. I flipped it open and scanned a random page.

The way he looked at me in that moment, like I was all the colors in the dawn sky, like he could see everything about me and loved me anyway... I couldn't breathe. Then he pressed his lips—

I shut the book fast and handed it back to Locs. "Looks good," I said weakly, my legs feeling wobbly beneath me. "I'll, um, borrow Art's copy."

"Let me guess," said the slightly condescending one (Buzz Cut). "You read hard SF, right? Or no, only nonfiction, because you 'can't get into fiction.'" She said it like she was quoting someone.

"He's not one of those," Art said. "He just doesn't read romance."

"Except Kirk/Spock, which counts," Pigtails added.

"I don't... I mean, I went through a Kirk/Spock phase, but it's not like I..." Words were hard. Sentences were hard. How had I managed to write an entire book? I stared at the ARC in Art's hand, where he was holding it with his thumb in the middle, like he'd picked out a part he especially liked. In the middle, ish, but toward the back...what scene was that? I tried to memorize the exact place so I could look for it later.

"I think your water's boiling, hun," Locs told me, kinda gently, like he was giving me an out.

"Oh. Right. Thanks." I could not stop staring at the words *Peak Romance* on the book Art was holding. He was in love with *my* book? My book? The book I'd written? The book I'd written *about him*?

Not really, not totally, but a little? A little about him. And me. And us. And romance. And...

And he thought I thought I was too good to read a book like that. A book like the one I had literally *written*?

For this one wild second I thought about saying it. Coming out with it. Right there in the middle of book club. "Actually, I've read this book. A few times now. Because I *wrote it*." Just to see what would happen.

But I couldn't. I could not. I should not. They would laugh. Or they wouldn't believe me. Or they'd think it was a joke. And then I'd just be one more person who took something that was important to Art and hijacked it for my own. I refused to be that guy.

Oh, also, it was terrifying to even think *I wrote it*, so there was no freaking way I'd be able to say it, not in front of all these people. Not when only one of them was the person I needed to tell, and definitely not like this.

"PK." Art's voice.

I dragged my gaze from the book to his face.

"I can hear the lid of the pot, like, flipping out because the water's boiling."

"Oh. Right. Yeah. Got it." And I did. I backed out of the living room and went to the kitchen and turned the burner off.

And stood there.

Very still.

In front of boiled water and a box of pasta I no longer wanted to eat.

Art was *in love* with my book.

My character.

Me.

The character I'd come up with to prove that I could be romantic, that I understood how to do that. He was *in love*. With the thing that I wrote to prove I could do love. The thing I wrote to prove I could do love with *him*. And he loved it.

Me.

Me in every sense but the obvious, like, it-was-fiction sense.

I was still standing there when my phone rang and jolted me out of myself.

"Mayday, mayday, mayday," Wade said. "The pigeon has flown the coop, repeat, the pigeon has flown the coop."

It took me a second to remember what was happening in

the real world. In the world that was not me, my book, and Art. Who was in love.

"Preston?"

"I'm here. Okay, thanks. I'll make sure... I'll take care of it."

A pause while I listened to cars driving past Wade, and conversations being had by strangers near him, before he said, "Are you okay? You sound strange."

"I'm fine. Sorry. Thanks for doing this."

A longer pause. "Of course, darling. No problem at all. He's a charming, if ridiculous, person."

"Yeah. He is."

"Wellllll, that's that, I guess. Speak soon?"

"Sure. Yeah. Okay."

"And you're *sure* nothing's wrong?"

Wrong? What even was wrong anymore? What was right? Was it right that I loved my best friend and he loved a character who was basically just me, but acted on the things I only thought about? Was it wrong that part of me desperately wanted to run back in there and pull him into the hallway and say, "It's me, it's me, the book is me, *I'm* the one you're in love with!"

I could not do that. I was not the person who could do things like that. "Nothing's wrong," I told Wade.

"If you say so. Talk soon!"

"Talk soon," I agreed mechanically and hung up.

Twenty-five minutes later I was herding Ches into my room and forcing an Xbox controller into his hand, but my brain was still reeling. Art was in love. He loved my book. He loved the main character. The *me* character. His perfect book boyfriend.

His perfect boyfriend was *me*.

Chapter Fifteen

The last thing I wanted to do on earth was go play Wade's boyfriend in front of his parents, but I didn't have much choice now that I'd already called in my favor.

"You're making too big a deal out of this," he said, standing in my living room in a flamboyant pink dinner jacket with a rainbow scarf trailing down his back. It's not like it was that different from what he'd usually wear, but knowing he was basically in costume made it way more annoying. "It's not that hard to pretend you're dating me, Preston. Plus, we're having dinner at [clearly fancy restaurant the name of which I immediately forgot]." He paused, waiting for a response.

Which he got. "Oh my god, *you are?*" Art clapped his hands together. "Bring me back something! I know doggie bags are gauche but I don't care, you have to bring me back something."

"Darling, I'm the birthday boy, I'll be as gauche as I like." He did a ridiculous scarf toss over his shoulder as if to prove it.

Meanwhile I accidentally caught Ray's eye while I was failing to get excited about the restaurant and she grinned. "Your face right now is exactly how I feel. Who has the energy to think about some place I A) couldn't afford, and B) wouldn't spend my money on even if I could?"

"Right?"

Wade sighed theatrically. "What are we going to do with

them? And where's your lovely brother? I thought he'd be taking part in girls' night with you and Ray?"

Shit, I should have briefed him, or at least texted him, since Ches was a sore subject, but Art waved it off. "Gone back to our parents with his tail between his legs like he always does. I'm over it."

"Oh, I *see*." That tone in Wade's voice seemed like it was about to be mocking and I braced to tell him off (maybe if he was rude enough I could refuse to go to this stupid birthday party), but instead of saying something mean, he kissed the side of Art's head, as if *he* were Art's older brother. "There's at least one in every family, try not to worry about it. Hate to abduct your roommate and run, but Preston and I are quickly losing our 'fashionably late' window."

"We could just not show up at all?" I suggested hopefully.

"For that to work we'd have to elope, and I don't think either of us is ready to take *that* plunge."

I wrinkled my nose. "Ew, no."

Ray laughed out loud and covered her mouth as if maybe she was keeping in the rest of the outburst.

"Um, PK?" Art was biting his lip. "I think you have to at least pretend not to find the idea of eloping with Wade, like, viscerally disgusting."

Wade grabbed my arm and tugged me toward the door. "Hard as it may be, my love, my sweetness, my *lover*..."

"Oh god, I can't do this, please don't make me do this." I didn't even know who I was begging, but Ray was the one who came up to me and kissed my cheek (as Wade was still pulling me away).

"We really appreciate it. No matter what happens tonight they'll be happier with you there than they would me."

On that note, I allowed myself to be dragged out of my apartment and down to the street, where, no shit, there was a car waiting for us. It had probably been double-parked for the entire ten minutes we were upstairs clowning around.

Which was a ripe opportunity to mock Wade, but I was still hearing Ray's words in my head. "You will eventually tell them, won't you? It's crappy that you're making Ray your dirty little secret, man."

Wade, like, *bubbled over* with mirth. "My dirty little secret? What, because I won't tell my parents? Darling, please, the less my parents are involved in my life, the better. Everyone who matters not just knows about Ray but adores her. And everyone who didn't adore her, well, they can fuck right off."

The thing about Wade—probably the thing about the Wades of the world in general—was that he could be so good at displaying a personality he let you forget that there was a man beneath it, a man with edges and moods and sadness and anger. Just like everyone else, but he was so good at pretending to be an unthreatening gay dude that even I could forget, and he'd once shot me directly in the eye with a Super Soaker.

Into the slightly awkward silence I did not say, "So some people were assholes when you hooked up with a lady?" because the answer to that was obvious. Instead I went with, "Ray is great, and also, Art loves her, so she must be completely amazing."

He turned to face me in the plush backseat of this hired sedan (it wasn't an actual limo—presumably Wade's family reserved those for like weddings, not just birthdays—but it was a super luxury black vehicle with dark tinted windows and a little basket with complimentary refreshments). "Yes, isn't it interesting how much stock we put into the opinions of those to whom we're closest, darling?"

"Uhh. I guess? Are you going to call me 'darling' all night? Because you've already done it like fourteen times."

His eyes lit up. I'd clearly made a serious mistake. Nothing that made Wade that happy would be good for me. "You're so right! We should have pet names. What do you want to be? Snookums? Sweet pea? My little goldendoodle?"

I was brought up short. "Wait, why would you call me a dog?"

He reached out and I dodged before he could ruffle my hair. "Because you're so sweet and adorable, of course!"

"I am not!" I couldn't completely understand how that was offensive, but I could *feel* the insult in my bones. "I am *not* sweet. Or adorable."

"You really are. I bet Art would agree, and then you'd have to admit it, because, as you said, Art is your north star."

My mouth opened. Nothing came out.

"Your pet name for me will be Pennyweather. You can call me Penny for short."

I recovered valiantly. "Hard no. And also why does that ring a bell?"

"You remember!" He clasped his hands to his chest. "Because, my little goldendoodle, when we used to play drag race, Portia Pennyweather was my drag name!" He sighed happily and snuggled up against me. "We really were meant to be, Preston."

"Were *not*, gross, stop it." I shoved at him but he remained pressed against me, the pink jacket bright against the darkness of the car. "Oh god, tonight is going to be *horrible*."

"All you have to do is look pretty and be my arm candy," he said soothingly. After a moment he added, "And we appreciate it. It's just so much easier letting them believe what they want to believe."

"Yeah but…don't you care? About what your parents think? About lying to them?"

"In order: no, no, and they're lying to themselves. Preston, you've met my parents. Don't you think they'd rather keep lying to themselves than be faced with the truth?"

He kind of had a point. "I don't think I could do that with my parents." The car felt confessional, somehow. A little pocket of space where my words didn't have to matter anywhere else. "I want them to know..." *how much I love Art.* Couldn't say that out loud, not even to Wade. Especially not to Wade. "...what's important to me."

Wade patted my leg. "You'll get there, apple blossom. Never fear."

"What do you—"

"We're here!" He jumped out of the car before I could finish my sentence, calling back, "Thanks for the ride, darling!" To the driver.

I paused for a long moment and closed my eyes, hoping I'd open them and be literally anywhere but outside a fancy restaurant about to masquerade as Wade's boyfriend.

"Good luck," the driver said, in accented English. He said it with feeling, too.

"Thanks." Wade had done me a solid with Ches, and now I was going to do him one in return. This was how things worked. I took a deep breath and stepped out.

"Come along, my little goldendoodle!"

Seriously, I might have to stab Wade with a steak knife. Technically it would probably just add, what's it, authenticity to our charade. But Ray might be annoyed.

"Coming, my little wiener dog," I muttered, and surrendered to my fate.

Wade's birthday party was exactly the nightmare I'd imagined. "Just an intimate gathering of his closest, darling," his mom assured me, and while I'd thought he was a little cold to say he didn't care what his parents thought, I had to concede his parents both didn't know him very well and possibly weren't that interested in getting to know him better. This "intimate gathering" was an *entire restaurant* they'd rented for the occasion, and it was only Wade's "closest" if the median age of people he liked hanging out with was sixty.

Watching him with his folks really...bummed me out. Like. You can know someone doesn't have a lot of regard for his parents but seeing it in action was another thing, and it wasn't just one way. I'd thought it was harsh because it seemed like Wade's parents adored him, but the more I stood around awkwardly pretending Wade and I were cute gay boyfriends (technically both of us were obviously, like, pansexual, but I didn't think the nuances would make a difference to his great-aunt Maryanne), the more I realized that he was right. This whole night might as well have been a staged performance, with us as the unpaid actors.

After the seventh or eighth or possibly fiftieth coy joke about when we were going to "make things official" I said, "Actually, I think marriage has gone out of fashion for our friend group, don't you, Wade? These days it's all about making our own commitment rituals."

Wade, eyes glittering, picked right up on the thread. "True. We *have* considered that thing where couples hold hands and jump into a volcano together to proclaim their undying—well, I suppose quite literally *dying*—love for each other. But we're still on the fence about it. It's so hard to find a good accessible volcano these days, you know? But doesn't it seem *sooooo* romantic?" He batted his eyelashes at me in a way that would have been insufferable before.

But now? I got it. "We have time to find a good one," I assured him, and led him away.

The last time I took Wade's hand we were like seven and our parents were trying to get photos to put in their scrapbooks. This time was way more satisfying: we walked out of frame, leaving a group of slightly stunned but covering it up quickly adults behind us.

"If Ray and I ever jump into a volcano," he whispered, "you'll know we've staged our own deaths and are living a beach-bum life in Hawaii."

"Noted," I whispered back.

Mostly, though, it was not that exciting. Small talk and ignoring political asides and *was that a microaggression or am I crazy?* Wade's mom took me aside after dinner to let me know that if we were trying to be modern and not accept their financial help for the wedding we were being very silly and there was nothing she and Robert would like more than to help us with our dreams.

Before tonight? I'd have thought, *Wow, that's so nice!* But now? I thought, *So you can show off to your society friends?* It wasn't a feel-good thought. But that was probably because none of this felt good.

I thanked her and couldn't think of anything else to say to this woman I'd always sort of liked in a vague my-parents'-friends way.

"We're so glad you two kids finally managed to take the hints we've been dropping for years," she said, smiling, and was she being smug or was I imagining it? "We all just *knew* you'd be perfect for each other! Your mother was *delighted* when I told her!"

I went very cold. So this was what the ice bucket challenge felt like. And I didn't even have to change my clothes. *Oh god, oh no, my parents, frick! I didn't think of that! Oh god!* I tried to mumble something, but couldn't form the words.

Only to be saved by Wade, grabbing me around the shoulders and resolutely tugging me against him. "Sorry to eat and run, Mummy darling, but we have to be off! Kiss kiss, thanks for a lovely evening!"

I wouldn't have had the balls, or the ovaries, or the guts to do it, but Wade extracted both of us from his birthday party with ruthless efficiency. Five minutes later, having said goodbye to no one else except the owner of the restaurant (who received the most genuine thanks of the night), we were getting back into the same car as before, and he'd even remembered to get a doggy bag for Art.

"How was it?" the driver asked after a moment.

"Dreadful. The usual." Wade leaned his head back against the seat and didn't say anything else the whole way to my apartment.

I expected him to stay in the car, but he walked back up with me and allowed himself to be engulfed in Ray's arms. You wouldn't think someone that short could hug so all-encompassingly, but she did. I wished I could hug Art like that, but instead we just awkwardly stood beside each other.

"Preston told them we were going to jump into a volcano," he said against her neck.

"I did not! You told them that! I just said we were too fashionable to get married."

A huffed laugh. "True. The volcano was starting to sound good right then, though. More of a fantasy than anything."

Ray rubbed his back and met my eyes. "That bad?"

"It was..." What word did you use to describe someone's family being at once well-intentioned and also totally self-absorbed? I looked at his head, where it rested against Ray like she was the only thing holding him up. "Brutal," I settled on.

"And yet we march on." He straightened, but kept Ray tightly at his side. "Thank you, Preston, for a terrible evening."

I shook my head. "I feel like I should apologize for how

awful it was. Or punch you in the nose for making me do that."

That got me a tired smile. "Good man, Preston Kingsley Harrington, the third."

Ray cackled. "You're a *third*?"

"Wade's a junior!" I protested. "That's not much better!"

She turned to Wade. "We should get a pet and name it The Third."

"Not tonight, sweet one. Tonight we should go home and drink sleepy tea and go to bed."

It was such a calming, domestic thought. I was immediately jealous. "Do we have sleepy tea?" I asked Art.

"I think we have a dusty box of chamomile somewhere?"

"Maybe we should make some?"

He wrinkled his nose. "I hate chamomile."

"And on that note," Wade said, watching us, "we're off." He broke away from Ray long enough to kiss my cheeks, then Art's. "Thank you both. And Art, darling, your makeup is gorgeous."

Art preened. "Thank you! We did a few tutorials, but I'm not very good at it."

"You're *so good* at it." Ray turned to Wade. "We have to have Art come over early the next time we do a costume thing, they have unparalleled makeup skills."

"Aww, thanks," Art said, still preening.

"It's a future date." Wade sagged against her again. "Now take me home and pour me into bed."

"My pleasure."

They went and Art locked up and I stood there, hesitating, before saying, "Um. So, like. Ray used 'they' for you?" I paused, but Art said nothing to fill the silence. "Should I... do that? Use they/them? Because I can! I can totally do that. With you. If you want me to."

"I… I've been thinking about it. For a while. And then she asked and it seemed right? But like. You don't have to." He wasn't looking at me. Or no, *they* weren't looking at me.

"If it seems right, then I'm doing it." I gulped. "If that's okay? I want to do what seems right. To you. Or, like." Ugh, how could I be so bad with words when it mattered? "If it seems right to you, it seems right to me."

He glanced up, then away. "Okay. Then yeah. That would be good." After a second he—no, *they*—added, "Thank you."

"I mean, sure, but I've literally never thanked anyone for using my pronouns before, so you don't owe me thanks, Arty. Okay? Like, it's just a service I offer for free."

That time I got a smile. "It feels bigger than that? But yeah, okay, I take back my thanks."

"Good, because I won't accept them."

"Fine then. Anyway, was tonight that bad? It seems like it was bad."

"So bad. So, so bad. I could eat an entire gallon of ice cream levels of bad."

"That's pretty bad. We don't have a gallon of ice cream but we do have the mined-of-all-add-ins end of a pint of Chunky Monkey."

"I'll take it."

I told Art about the party while we sat in our living room amidst the remains of an epic makeup party. I didn't realize he—Art—they—had that much makeup, but the shimmer on their cheekbones and careful cat's eye on their lids did accentuate their features in a beautiful way. A way that made me want to kiss them, honestly, but not more than usual. Just that with makeup on their features drew my attention differently.

I did not kiss Art. I practiced their new pronouns in my head while we talked (*their mirror, their eye shadow, their lipstick, their lips…*) and they did actually make me a cup of chamomile, which felt sweet and sort of precious and also like a salve after all the affectations of Wade's parents.

Maybe this wasn't all-encompassing-hug-and-pour-me-into-bed levels of coupledom. But it was a really nice level of roommateness. And tonight that was enough.

Chapter Sixteen

I was in this weird haze of sending off the final-final proof-read edits for *Peak Romance*. The last-chance-to-fix-anything-you-fucked-up edits. And it felt good. But also strange. Like I was giving it away now, officially, to other people. To readers and reviewers and everyone else. Art told me that he'd—*they*'d read it now three times, that even after three times they still considered the main character their book boyfriend. And for this split second I thought—hoped?—they'd be like, "Okay, fess up, I know your writing better than anyone, did you really think I wouldn't know you'd written this?" We'd laugh, and they'd tease me, and I'd blush and admit it, and then they'd get a little more serious but still playful, and ask if the book was really kind of about a real situation, and I'd blush more and say maybe, and we'd kiss, and it would be perfect.

Except that's not what happened. They just, y'know, were really passionate about books they loved...probably. Though they didn't usually bring up the same book over and over again. I didn't think. Not like this...not in this intense way.

Art wasn't the only one who had strong feelings about *Peak Romance*. A lot of other people were reading it too, and when I was still in edits, that was one thing, but now it felt...permanent. Carved in stone. My words etched forever on the page. On the file. In people's ears, because there was an audiobook, and the sample they'd picked was this...this moment of yearning and sweetness and *awww* that people were super into even though they couldn't hear the rest of the book yet.

It felt impossible on some level. Unreal. Like it must be happening to someone else. And it sort of *was* happening to someone else. My superhero alter ego, The Mystery Man Who'd Written *Peak Romance*. Maggie said there was a subreddit dedicated to figuring out who was really H.K. Pierce. Since the book was getting a splash, people thought it might be an actor or a musician, someone in the public eye who was taking a spin at writing.

Which: *gulp*.

No pressure.

He said.

As he was flattened.

Under all that pressure.

I'm not a depressive type of person. Not that I never felt sad, just that I wasn't deep enough to be depressed, not really. I had simple emotions. Basic emotions. If you were going to compare my, like, emotional geography to an organism, it would have more than one cell? But not by much. It'd be early on in the evolution of organisms.

My ability to feel stuff was a creature that hadn't dragged itself out of the primordial ooze yet.

Even so, I started to feel very slightly panicky as the days crept by. Four months until release, three months until release, two and a half months until release, all the ARCs out, all the buzz starting, my name on the cover, in the promo copy ("debut author H.K. Pierce"), tagged on Twitter even though it wasn't my account and had no tweets, just my silhouetted author photo. Maybe Maggie had grabbed it? I had no idea. I just knew Things Were Happening.

I needed a distraction. So I said, in a perfectly calm way,

on a perfectly ordinary evening, to my supportive (though in this case clueless) roommate, "I need a distraction."

He snorted. No, no, they snorted. Like a great big meanie from mean town.

"Hey!"

"Sorry, PK, but like…ya think? You've been jittering all over the place for twenty minutes."

"I have not!" I protested, deeply offended by this gross mischaracterization of my behavior. "I have not at all. I have been…mindfully pacing. Which is totally a thing. That mindful people do. When they pace."

"Mindfully pacing. Uh-huh. And in your research on mindful pacing did that practice also include chewing on your cuticles and occasionally mumbling to yourself?"

I frowned, ready to argue my case more diligently, but then also, was Art, like, *paying attention* to me? Because maybe that wasn't such a bad thing. Maybe it kinda…was a good thing? In a big picture way. That wasn't about my pacing. "I don't think I was mumbling to myself," I said. With dignity.

"I'm pretty sure you were." They seemed so amused, though, that it made all of my jittering worthwhile. "And I'd hate to see the damage you were doing to your poor nails." In a direct contradiction to what they'd just said, they held out their hands. For mine. Err. My nails, but same difference.

What else could I do? I surrendered my (perfectly acceptable) fingernails for Art's assessment.

They *tsked*. Out loud. "Tsk tsk, what are you so stressed out about? Is this about work?"

It wasn't *not* about work. "Kinda."

They pulled my fingers higher, like they needed to see more closely. "Some big book you've been working on?"

Suddenly it seemed like… I dunno. A weird question? Maybe? Or maybe it wasn't. "Uhhh, yeah. You could say that." Which was the sort of thing you only say when you're leaving the door open to other interpretations of a thing.

They raised their eyebrows, this time at me, not my hands. "Is it at least coming out soon so you can stop eating your fingers to nubs?"

"I'm not! They aren't nubs!" Was he—they—fishing for information? I mean. Would you. If, for instance, Art had a *suspicion* about *Peak Romance* and was trying to confirm that suspicion…maybe this was the kind of question they'd ask?

Before I could say anything more, they sighed. "Your poor cuticles."

"I—um—" Wait, I thought we were going to have A Moment, was that over? Were we back to my nails again? My nails were in no way that interesting.

"I have an idea for a distraction." They practically jumped up from the couch. "Oh my god, this is going to be so fun. I'll give you a manicure!"

I'd thought Art had long forgotten about my manicure set. My impulsive, confused, "I read it in a magazine and thought I'd try but was too scared to really do it" manicure set. The symbol of my attempt and failure at taking myself seriously manicure set.

Art, though, wasn't super into forgetting things. Which you'd think I would, like, expect from them (from them! I congratulated myself on getting their pronoun right) this many years into our friendship, but I was still surprised sometimes.

Art still surprised me sometimes.

I perched there awkwardly, uncertain if my hands were still my own or if even now I was supposed to be Doing Something Manicure-y with them. When you thought about it, hands were strange. Like, basically they're multi-tools just sitting there at the ends of your arms, right? Sure, it seems normal. But look at your fingers. They're *weird*. Why are they all different lengths? The opposable thumb makes sense, but why four fingers instead of three? Or five? Why isn't your pinky also opposable? Would it be called something else if it was?

What is even the *deal* with fingernails? If the tips of your fingers need protecting, shouldn't they be thicker, like a dog's nail? When you think about it, they're really not doing much to provide shielding, are they? And why don't they go all the way back to that first knuckle?

Thankfully Art returned before I fully redesigned the human hand, but make a note: if I ever get a hand amputated, which could probably happen, I want a new blueprint for my prosthetic. I'm just not convinced that the old one is as effective as it could be.

Anyway.

Art sat down with my manicure set (still in its little case), a shoebox full of nail polish, and a bowl of warm, soapy water. "Here, soak your hands while we talk color. Oops, I forgot a towel. I'll be right back."

So then I was awkwardly perched on my couch with my hands trying to soak in a bowl that was not quite large enough, and also, the human hand is not really laid out in such a way that soaking all your nails at once is easy unless you're dunking most of your hand in, and Art had left me with, like, a small bowl that only had an inch of water in it. Trying to cover my thumbs and pinkies at the same time was proving something of a challenge. I felt like I was in some kind of game show and there was a clock ticking down as I tried to curl my pinkies and flatten my thumbs.

"I don't think there's enough water," I observed neutrally to Art when they returned.

"If I put in more the displacement would make it overflow, but anyway, it's working. It doesn't have to be perfect. So what color do you want? You can pick more than one, obviously, but I'm not great at fancy designs, FYI."

"Um."

He fished out—no, they fished out an array of bottles. Red and pink and blue and purple. Glittery gray and sparkly yellow. "You can do one for each hand, or a different color for each nail. Or you can layer one of these holo toppers over one of the other colors."

"Um."

They laughed. "Do you want me to pick? Are you having choice paralysis?"

"Um."

"What about..." They selected a darkish blue and a darkish purple. After a moment of deliberation they added a clear polish with silvery glitter stuff in it. "Similar enough so they won't be shouting at people from your fingers, different enough so they'll keep your interest, and the holo flakes will look *amazing* in sunlight, just wait till you see them."

"Um."

They looked up at me with this excited, anticipatory expression, like they were offering me a gift. "What do you think?"

"Sounds good. Sounds fantastic." *Please keep looking at me like that.*

"Yay! Okay, let's try to neaten things up here. You should stop chewing on yourself, PK."

I bit back another *um*.

And then.

And *then*.

And then they took my hand. Lifting it out of the water, patting it dryish, setting it down on top of the towel, which was *in their lap*, or at least on their leg. Their thigh. They were next to me, and their legs were there, and the towel was over them, and they set my hand down over it, and then they were—oh—doing things—clipping and pushing and touching and oh god, Art was touching my hands, their own fingers so confident on mine.

I was light-headed. With the closeness. The Artness. Of it all.

Right up until they pulled out this piece of sand paper on a stick thing and started *sanding down my nail ahhhhhhh—*

I pulled my hand away and hid it under my armpit. "Oh my god, what was that, don't ever do that again, ahhhh, that was horrible, why did you do that to me?"

"It's…a nail file? PK, have you never filed your nails before?"

"I mean, I've heard of nail files, but if that's what they are, I opt out. Completely. Forever. How can you stand that feeling?"

They blinked at me. "It doesn't bother me?"

"How. How can it *possibly* not bother you?"

They glanced down and applied the thing to *their own nail*, where it scratched across with this horrific *sound*, this scraping, agonizing *sound*.

It drew across their fingernail like the most discordant bow striking the most discordant note across the most discordant violin string. I shuddered. "Stop! Oh god, that is…there are no words for how awful that is. Nail filing should be a torture technique. I would sell out my mother if someone started doing that to me and I couldn't escape. Ahhhhh."

"Shh, it's okay. Look, we won't do that." They put the *sandpaper of torment* down and gently tugged my hand back to the towel. "I can shape with the clippers, it'll just be a little less finished. That's okay. Here." They held my hand comfortingly in both of theirs. "I've never seen anyone react that strongly to a nail file."

"Torture device," I corrected.

Art smiled. "Sorry, I meant, *torture device*."

"Thank you."

"We won't use the torture device again. Are you all right?"

The reassuring warmth of their skin against mine was grounding. "Yeah. That was just. Unexpected. Unexpected and *horrible*."

"I can see that. But it's over. The clippers don't bother you?"

"No. It's fine. Sorry."

"Completely okay, don't worry about it." They bent over my hand again, shaping each nail with tiny little applications of the clippers, and I didn't really think it made a huge difference but it seemed to satisfy Art. Once the first hand was done, out came the second, and the same process repeated (without the sandpaper of torment).

And then the color went on. And I saw why they'd spent so much time perfecting the shape of each nail, because once the dark polish was on, you could see each shape. Also, I'd never really put on nail polish except every now and then I'd wear black as a teenager to show how counterculture and independent I was. (I got the idea from TV, which is where all the best markers of counterculture independence are born.)

But this? Was totally different. This was *legit*. I could watch Art paint my nails forever. Each stroke of the brush seemed more deliberate, more real, when it was in their hands. They told me about how good this brand of polish was, how they could leave it at one coat, even for dark colors, but two would last longer. They instructed me to hold my hands in front of the space heater to dry them faster—but not close enough to mess up the smooth finish of the polish.

And I just followed along. I did what they said, and otherwise just allowed them to do whatever they wanted. They turned my fingers this way or that to get to the edges, pulled my hand forward or rested it farther back. And I let them. Obviously.

It did take half of forever before they finally sat back and declared both of my hands fully manicured. But man, it was worth it.

"Here, let me show you." They turned on their phone's flashlight and pulled my hand to it, letting it hit all the specks of reflective stuff and bounce back, like the way light hits water on a lake, where it's just all these shards of bright white constantly moving.

"Oh wow. That's so beautiful." I didn't want to pull my hand away, but I did move my fingers just to catch the light at other angles. "That's so... I could just keep staring at it."

"I know, right?" Sadly, tragically, they let go of my hand and began packing up all the things. "I really like this manicure kit, you picked well. I'll keep the file, though, so you don't have to see it again."

"Oh. Yeah. Thanks." Did that mean they would never give me another manicure? Because that would be such a bummer. Still, I gender-bendingly manned up, you know, with my sparkly fingernails, and squared my shoulders to face the world. "This is so awesome, thanks, Arty."

"Course. It was fun. And now you know how to use your manicure kit."

"Um, I might need a like refresher class or something. I don't think I know how to use it quite yet."

They gave me this playful coy look. "You're just trying to get me to do your nails again!"

Yes. Omg YES. "Um, maybe?"

"You should try it on your own, mister. It's good for you to know how to do your own nails." But the way they said it didn't seem like a *No way* so much as a *For your own good I should make you do it yourself.*

I pulled a puppydog face. Or attempted to, anyway.

They laughed and gathered up their shoebox and the bowl of water. "Maybe sometime. But it's late, I need to actually sleep tonight. I always forget how long a really *good* manicure takes. Night, PK."

"Goodnight. Thanks again!" I watched them go. With my sad puppydog face still in effect because it just...fit. My feelings. My sad puppydog feelings.

But at least my sad puppydog face and feelings were attached to some truly freaking fabulous nails. I turned on my flashlight so I could watch them twinkle again.

Chapter Seventeen

I got used to my nails being amazing, but I didn't stop staring at them when they caught the light. Or when I was bored. Or when I was supposed to be typing an email but didn't really know how to phrase the thing I was saying and oh, hey, look at my sparkly nails. And when my gaze happened to be captured by my sparkly nails, I wondered, again, if Art knew. About me. About the book. About…everything.

My nails became an ongoing reminder. Other people noticed my manicure, too. People complimented me when I was reaching for my coffee at the shop in the bottom of my office building, and once someone broke The Sacred Oath Of Pretending No One Else Exists in the subway and said, "I just have to tell you how much I *love* your nails." She said it as she was getting off the train, like she'd timed it so her transgression would be brief.

Which was kind of unfortunate. I wanted to tell people about my nails. I wanted to brag about them a little. "Oh, my best friend did them. I know, they look great, right?" It's not weird or conceited or whatever to agree about how badass your nails look if you're giving someone else credit for them. And if a random complimenter wanted to hear more, well, that wasn't a problem. I could glow about Art forever.

I brought them lunch at the bookstore one day when I was in the neighborhood. (Also, I was really on it with the pronouns after almost a month of practice.) I was waiting for them to finish up what seemed to be a really long conversation about nature photography with a little old man who had a very battered camera on a strap around his neck when a woman accidentally bumped into me.

"Sorry, dear, wasn't looking—oh, you must be Art's young man." She grinned with this stunning deduction and gestured at my fingers. "I recognize the color. He's really something else, isn't he, our Art?"

"Um…yes?" Did I correct their pronouns? Did I correct the "Art's young man" thing? Did I just go along with it because it didn't matter?

"I've been coming in here for years," she continued, like she just started talking to random strangers all the time. "I remember when he was just a baby and now he's all grown up."

I blinked. A baby? "He's only been working here since college."

"That's what I mean! But you're still so young, both of you. I'm sure that seems quite adult, but someday you'll look back at yourselves in pictures and think, 'Oh, we were babies back then!'" She put her hand on my arm. "That's how it happens, you know. Time goes so slowly until you look back and poof! It's flashed right past you."

"Uh-huh." Okay, I can be as nice to a little old lady as the next guy, but I sent Art serious mental signals to wrap it up with Nature Photog and come rescue me.

"But he always showed such potential. I do keep an eye on things and a lot of young people come through this store, but not all of them are as bright and shining as our Art, are they?"

"Um. No?" *Save me, save me, give the guy the book he wants and come save me ahhhh.*

"No. That's right." She patted my arm with one crocheted half-gloved hand.

Art finally, *finally* said goodbye to the old dude.

"That's right. But I'm so pleased that Art has such a lovely boyfriend, dear. He deserves the very best. He deserves a young man who will bring him lunch."

I could tell by the color on Art's cheeks that they'd heard that. "We're not boyfriends," I said quickly.

"Well, partners, whatever it is you want to call it, dear, you have so many choices!" She turned to Art. "I was just saying hello to your partner, but I really do have to go. Have a good night, boys."

And then. At long last. She left.

She left us standing there in the awkward wake of her misunderstanding. My cheeks were hot. Art's were still pink.

"Um so." Despite having brought them takeaway many times before, I felt newly strange about it. "Lunch?"

They took the bag. "Thanks, PK. Sorry about Rose, I think she's considers herself everyone's doting grandma."

"That seems nice though?"

"It can be. Um. When she's not..." They faltered.

I opened my mouth.

No one said a word.

Art coughed. "Well anyway. Thanks." They lifted the bag in explanation. "For lunch, I mean."

"Sure. I mean. I was in the area. So. Yeah."

"Yeah."

A terrible voice in the back of my head suddenly poofed into existence: *Tell them you want to be their boyfriend. Ask them if they already know. Ask them if they* want *you to be their boyfriend.*

I couldn't do that. I couldn't. Could I? I swallowed. Opened my mouth.

"She just thinks that every time two queer people are in the same room they must be dating, that's all," Art said.

"Oh. Right." I closed my mouth.

"It's no big deal."

"Sure." *It is, though. It could be a big deal. I want it to be a big deal, don't you?*

They shifted from one foot to the other. "So I'll see you at home?"

"Yeah. Definitely. It's a date." I grimaced. "I mean. Not—not it's a *date*—like—obviously yes, you will see me at home because both of us live there. So it's where we'll see each other. Later. When both of us are…there. At home. Where we live."

They cracked a smile, but still weren't quite looking at me. "Yeah. I'll see you at home, where both of us live, later, when both of us are there. Bye, PK."

I might literally die standing in the bookstore blushing. "Um. Yeah. Bye, Arty."

Thankfully, they walked away. Which seemed to free my legs up so I could also walk away.

It was only a twenty-minute walk to my office from the store but the day was cold and I had to hunch into my coat against the wind.

Art.

Was not.

My partner.

They'd blushed, too, though. Both of us had blushed. At the idea of it. Was that normal? I mean. I knew why *I'd* blushed. Because, y'know, the whole…well, the whole maybe being in love with them thing? And also just feeling like it was so *close*, like maybe if I could just say the right thing—like my character in *Peak Romance*—I could be the perfect actual boyfriend instead of just being the perfect book boyfriend.

I couldn't help but wonder if it was…possible Art had some idea? That I felt that way? Maybe that's why they were blushing. Or maybe they…maybe they also felt that way?

I'd already wondered if they knew about the book. Did

they also know about my feelings for them? They'd have to, if they'd figured out that I'd written *Peak Romance*. Was that nuts?

Except by the time I got back to my desk my brain was on fire with the idea. With the sudden near-certainty of it. After all, they knew me better than anyone. *Wouldn't* they know my book when they were reading it? Wouldn't they recognize me through the words, even in fiction?

I was staring dreamily at my nails, which I was holding underneath the little string of white Christmas lights I'd pinned to the under-eave to make it less dark and shadowy, when Maggie and Puzo showed up.

"They really are great," she said, like we'd been in the middle of a conversation.

"I know, I love them so much." I sighed. Other things I loved: Art holding my hand in theirs, Art bent over to concentrate on clipping my nails, Art pulling my fingers to a lamp to make sure the little holo flakes were equally distributed.

Puzo squawked something that didn't sound like a word to me at all.

"He says you're distracted," Maggie translated.

I looked up. "He did not. Puzo, you did not say that."

"Fine, *I'm* saying you're distracted."

"I'm not distracted."

"I sent you an email before lunch."

"I didn't see it." I went back to turning my nails under the lights and thinking about whether Art would manicure me again. Could you use "manicure" like that? You could, right? As a verb?

"I know, I have return receipts turned on," Maggie continued. "PK, it's been two hours since lunch and you're sitting here with your monitor dark, staring at your hands."

Two hours? I pulled my attention away from the dancing light reflections and checked the time. "Whoa. Um. It's later than I realized." I straightened up and hit the space bar. I was locked out of my computer, which meant it had been *over an hour* since I'd used it. (I got so annoyed that it would time out while I was thinking that I set it to not go dark for sixty minutes. Which usually was not something that happened during the workday. When I was, y'know, *working*.) I punched in my password and cleared my throat. "Sorry, uh, what was the email?"

Maggie pulled over a chair from the corner where we collected chairs (there was also a music stand, don't ask me why) and settled Puzo on her shoulder. "Are you freaking out right now?"

"Ummm." I mean, *freaking out* seemed a little strong, but I wasn't *not* in a state of…something freak-out-adjacent. "I don't…not too badly. I don't think."

"I know this is a big thing, like maybe even life changing, but I think it's important that you not think of it like that, okay?"

How could being with Art not be life changing? "It's not 'maybe' life changing. It's pretty seriously life changing."

"Right, but remember this happens all the time. I know it's getting closer and probably feels like increasing pressure, but realistically it will all work out and it won't seem like that big a deal in a year. You know?"

"Seriously, no." I looked at her. A year from now. Me. Art. Together. "Still gonna be a big deal."

"Well…true. Granted. But it won't be as scary. The scary part will be over. Until the next time, anyway."

I gasped. "Oh my god, *next time*? I don't want there to be a next time! I want this to be The Time!"

"You don't want to write more books? I mean, I just assumed, I guess."

I gaped at her. "Wait, what? Of course I want to write more books!"

"But you just said you didn't want a next time."

"With *Art*. I don't want to fall in love with anyone else."

Which was when both of us realized we were having totally different conversations.

Maggie recovered first, because of course she did; she wasn't wishing the earth would open up and grind her to dust between its tectonic plates. "You're...in love with Art. That actually...makes perfect sense. Huh."

Puzo nodded enthusiastically. I didn't know if he was being supportive or mocking me.

"I." I swallowed. "Um. I. I." Maybe if my face stopped burning so hot I'd be able to think.

"So...what were *you* talking about? I mean, why are you freaking out about Art? Is he not...attracted to you?"

"They," I said, relieved to be able to focus on *something*. "Art goes by they/them now."

"That's cool. But doesn't answer my question. Are they not attracted to you, or...?"

"I think. I mean." Oh my god, I had to form a sentence. "I don't know. Sometimes I think maybe? But then... I think they might have figured out that I wrote *Peak Romance*."

"Oh. Wait. PK. Is *this* why you didn't tell Art about the book?" Her eyes widened. "Did you write *an entire book* about Art? Oh my god. PK. Please, please tell me that is not what you did. Please tell me that's not what I *helped* you do."

Puzo pecked gently at her hair as if to comfort her. Which I thought was kind of rude since she was making a huge deal out of nothing.

"What? No. I mean. Kind of? I didn't mean to! Well. I mean. I didn't mean. I only sort of meant to do that. And then it was happening. And it's not like I asked you to bring Adams into it!"

"It's not like you told me it was literally about your roommate!" She shook her head slightly. "PK, you could have just said, 'Hey, Art, I have a crush on you, maybe we should date.' Like you wrote a whole novel about emotional bravery and you couldn't use your damn words?"

"Obviously not or I would have done it! And anyway, it's not like it's completely about Art."

Okay, yeah, it was completely about Art, but also characters are a thing, and fiction is…fiction is a thing. *Peak Romance* was fiction, after all.

"If it's not completely about Art, why do you suspect he's—sorry—they've figured out it's you who wrote it? Isn't that the number one biggest tip-off?"

"No! I don't think so. They've read a lot of my stuff. Like. All the stories I wrote in college. This time I tried to make a blog but failed at it. Essays. Half-finished novels. Art's a really good first reader. Always so supportive, and encouraging, and…" I trailed off when I realized she was staring at me. "Anyway, I just think they'd know my voice. In my book."

"Your voice."

"Yes."

"Uh-huh. And having deduced from the *your-voiceness* of it all that you wrote this book Art, by your account, loves, why haven't they asked you about it?"

"Well, because." Actually. Huh. But no, I didn't think they would. Not right away. "I mean, I'm sure they're not totally convinced yet. It'd be a weird thing to be wrong about, wouldn't it? They probably just want to wait for corroborating evidence."

Maggie chewed on that. "Which would be what?"

"Well, they did ask if I was working on a really big book because I seemed so distracted."

"That is literally your job, so I feel like that's just a normal question."

"No, but there was something more to it," I insisted. "You had to be there. Like. They were more, like, earnest than usual." That clearly wasn't all that compelling either. "I mean, maybe they're waiting for an author photo when the real copies come in, or something."

"And when they see that there's no author photo? Which you stipulated, remember."

"Oh. Right."

Puzo squawked and even though it clearly wasn't words, Maggie nodded and said, "I know, he's a mess."

"Hey! I'm not a mess. And anyway, I guess we'll find out the answers to all these questions eventually, and right now I have work to do so. So you can leave now."

"I can't believe you're kicking me out of your office," she said wryly, and put the chair back in the corner of the hallway. "Maybe Art *does* know. Maybe the two of you are playing some weird game of emotional chicken. But PK, don't you have to ask yourself why you're wasting all this time when you could be enjoying it together? You only get a first book once, you know."

She really didn't know what she was talking about. I couldn't say anything to Art. That was just batty. My armpits were sweaty just imagining it. And anyway, there was no hurry. I'd only have a first book once, so probably, for the next one, I'd be less of a manic weirdo about it, bouncing from *this book I wrote is brilliant* to *who even lets me write books, I'm the worst* like five times a day.

No one needed to see that. Least of all Art. I wanted them

to think of me as sweet and strong and romantic, like my character. Not like a hot mess, which was what I actually was.

Anyway, who cared what Maggie (and Puzo) said. A little old lady had thought I was Art's boyfriend. And Art? Had blushed. So there.

Chapter Eighteen

I should have guessed my mother would eventually bring up the whole thing where I'd gone to Wade's birthday as his date, but I...did not guess. I was so wrapped up in my own, y'know, *life* and stuff that when I saw she was calling I actually answered. Like a fool.

Well, answered in the sense that I immediately put it on speaker and muted *Call of Duty* so I could keep playing.

"Darlinggggg!" she exclaimed, as if surprised I'd answered my own phone. "How *are* you?"

"Good." It was a noncommittal "good." It was a "I know you didn't call to ask how I am so what are we *really* talking about" good.

"That's what I hear! I hear you're *so* good that you're dating a certain someone we both know. Preston, how could you not tell me? Do you know how *delighted* Pamela was to think she knew something I didn't about my own son?"

The thing I'd found profoundly confusing when I was a kid about my mom and Wade's mom was how much they loved each other, but also how deeply they were in competition with each other. Not that I'd actually figured that out as an adult, I guess I'd just stopped thinking about it. "Um."

She laughed. "Of course you don't have to tell me *everything*, you're a grown man now"—why did my mother calling me a grown man always make me feel like a five-year-old in his first suit?—"but I do think it's strange you didn't let me know about you and Wade. Tell the truth: it started when we threw that get-together, didn't it?"

"You mean when Wade's grandma threw that get-together?"

More laughter, broken up by the sound of the locks turning on the front door and Art's steps in the entryway. "Cheeky boy, I can tell you're trying to dodge the question! I won't have it, tell me about Wade!"

"Ooooh, what about Wade?" he called. "Hi, Cristine!"

"I assume *you* know about Preston and Wade, don't you, dearest?"

Their grin was all sparklers. Mom was really missing out by being on the other side of a non-video call. "I know a lot of things! But what do *you* know about Preston and Wade?" They disappeared into the kitchen to wash their hands before settling down beside me with a pastry bag and two plates, all that time filled by my mother recounting the call with her bestie/mompetition opponent, and how I'd let her down by not telling her about Wade.

"I didn't tell you about Wade," I began firmly, "because…" then fizzled out. He lied so easily to his folks. Did he want me to lie to mine? Was my mom even capable of keeping a secret? "Um. Well."

Art settled a bear claw on the plate in front of me and a maple old fashioned on their own plate. "It's complicated," they said.

I put my controller down so I could better bear claw. "It's none of your business?" I suggested around a mouthful of food.

"Excuse me, but you are my son, so I consider who you're dating plenty my business, mister."

"I'm not *dating* Wade, Mother, oh my god. And you know, just because I'm your son doesn't automatically make my life your business!" Which sounded like just the sort of thing Wade might say, but actually, it didn't feel that good when I was saying it.

Silence on the phone. Art looked at me as if I'd farted in church.

"Um. Right? I mean." I shoved another bite of bear claw into my mouth.

They sighed and leaned toward the phone. "Wade is dating a very nice girl called Ray, we like her a lot, and we totally support their relationship."

"A very nice…girl?" my mother asked faintly.

"Yes. A very nice girl. Woman, obviously, though I don't think she'd mind use of 'girl' in this conversation for cultural import reasons."

Cultural import? I mouthed.

They ignored me. "She's great, they're great together, and PK was only trying to help by going to the party."

I recovered myself. "And you *can't* tell Pamela, Mother, promise me you will not do that."

"Well, but I… *Wade* is dating a *woman?*" The idea of it seemed to have shocked her beyond what made sense.

"He is very much dating, and living with, a woman." *Sorry, Wade.* "And actually, if you think of it in a certain light, this is just a sign that I trust you more than Wade trusts his folks."

Art nodded vigorously, which *I* took as a sign I was on the right track.

"Because he doesn't trust his parents to respect his relationship, but I know that, no matter how surprised you are, you wouldn't *dream* of disrespecting Wade, would you?"

"No, of course I wouldn't, I'm just…surprised. That's all."

"Just remember, the next time you talk to Pamela, you have to go along with whatever she says, even though you secretly know different. Okay, Mom? Just nod and smile and pretend that I'm dating Wade even though you know for a fact that I'm not. She *can't* find out before Wade tells her, that wouldn't be right."

"No, I see that." She still sounded iffy. "It's just that I've always felt that honesty was the best policy..."

"I agree *completely*," Art said, with a sudden burst of energy. "Honesty in relationships, whatever the relationship is, is absolutely vital. It's really sad that Wade doesn't feel like he can be authentic with his parents, and I sympathize with that so much, you know."

My mom, on more solid ground, made noises of commiseration. "Well, you know you can always count on *us*, dear." She took an audible breath. "This has all been quite interesting, boys, but I should run."

"It's not like *I* called y—"

Art punched my arm.

"Please give Wade and his..."

"Partner," Art supplied.

"Yes, please give Wade and his partner my best and let him know that I wouldn't dream of spoiling anything for him." Pause, which I expected to end with a flourished goodbye. "And for whatever it's worth, you can also tell him that I know Pam can seem a bit shallow, but I do believe she actually wants to support him. She's always wanted that, you know. *Always*." With that slightly emphatic send-off, she hung up.

I looked at Art.

Art looked at me.

"Um." I took a bite of bear claw.

They pulled out their phone. "I'll let Wade know—"

"Wha—no—" I tried to swallow quickly and a chunk of pastry got stuck in my throat. "No! Don't do that!"

"I'm not letting him talk to your mom without knowing she knows," they said, fingers already moving on the screen.

"What? He won't! It's not like they're Facebook friends! Err, I take that back, they might be Facebook friends, but it's not like they *chat*."

Art huffed a laugh. "If you think your mom's not going to find an excuse to casually call him as soon as possible just so that she can express her explicit support for his lifestyle choices…"

Which, okay, fair. "Shoot. I didn't think of that."

"It's fine." No sooner had they'd set their phone down than the screen lit up. "See? He sent back a laughing-so-hard-he-cried emoji. Or five of them. On separate lines."

My phone vibrated the table, making my controller rattle. I winced and picked it up. *Don't worry, poppins, you don't have to sink to my level of parental dysfunction. Plus, your mom will LOVE having something to hold over my mom's head.* And then only one of those emojis.

I took a deep breath. "Okay. Um. I guess. I guess that's okay then?"

"Definitely. Now eat your sugar, I'm ahead of you but I don't want to crash first, so you have to catch up."

And abruptly I realized we were sitting beside each other, on the couch, with pastries, our legs almost touching. And they were looking at me expectantly. Because of pastries. Not, y'know, anything else. Though some mental voice distantly assured me that if I kissed them now, they'd kiss me back.

I couldn't do that. I couldn't. Could I? Would my character in *Peak Romance*? He would, definitely. Maybe if I did kiss Art they'd sort of swoon against me and whisper, *I knew you were my book boyfriend all along…*

I was so busy imagining kissing them that I missed it when they picked up my bear claw—and crammed it in my face. "Eat!" Then they grabbed the controller and loaded a new game.

Whew, close call. I chewed and cheered their game and

gave thanks I hadn't done anything stupid. Like kiss them, thus ruining any possibility of finding The Right Moment to tell them. I couldn't *believe* I'd come so close to doing that! Like. They'd brought me a bear claw, my favorite. They'd talked about rose petals and horse-drawn carriages. I had to do something special for Art, something to show them how well I understood them. Something *better* than a dumb horse-drawn carriage.

Now I just had to figure out what that something was and, y'know, do it.

Chapter Nineteen

Here's the thing nobody tells you, and it's a kind of big thing. It's a "seriously, how has no one ever mentioned this before?" thing. When you write a book and people start reading it? It's like you kinda become two people.

The person who wrote a book that other people can hold in their hands.

And the person who lives out the rest of your life.

That second person is like…you, but not the whole you. It's you, recognizably, but also that person hasn't written a book, or if he has, it's not a book that strangers on the internet can talk about. He's never imagined characters who are real to other people. He's just a regular guy, "soaking" his dishes instead of washing them, occasionally tripping on literally nothing as he walks down the street and then pretending to tie his shoelace so no one knows it happened.

But the first person? The Legitimate Author? It's kinda like being a superhero. You carry that with you all the time but it's this like…latent part of you until it's activated by something. Like Twitter deciding you don't have a penis when last you checked you do, in fact, have a penis. (Actual thing that actually happened.) Then you walk into a phone booth, spin around, walk out and you are The Legitimate Author, ready to do battle.

Okay, less like being a *super*hero and more like being an

*insecure*hero. I'd wake up at three in the morning with this one line from the book bouncing around my head and I'd spend ages trying to remember if I'd used "appraise" when I meant "apprise" and if I had, wouldn't someone have noticed? That's the kind of thing editors, did, right? Or having this blinding white bolt of lightning about some moment between your main characters that would have been *perfect* and catching yourself thinking about where you'll add it in before realizing you missed your chance. That moment, which would have been amazing, is now lost forever.

At least lost to this book. And that's weird. Because at once the book is more alive than ever (alive for other people!) but also not dead, but inert, frozen in time and space. Can no longer be changed. Like it popped out of your head and took on a whole life of its own but now it's a statue, no longer malleable.

It's freaking weird is what I'm saying. And I definitely wasn't used to it yet. Why is it that the second you send off the final version of the file you suddenly think of all the things you screwed up? Does this happen to everyone? Was it just me?

I had no idea. I whined to Maggie, who put up with it for about fifteen minutes before saying, "Okay, champ, that's all the time I have for this right now. I've got to put in a good hour later to hold another author's hand at three, and that's my daily max."

"But I… I…"

She patted my arm. "Go google 'imposter syndrome' and do some work. What's the next pitch? I want to see what you're working on by the end of the day."

"But…how could I… I mean…the first book's not even done yet…"

"It really is, PK. It's totally done. All you have to do now is enjoy the ride."

I made a protesting sound as she ushered me out of her office. Behind her, Puzo squawked in a way I decided was more supportive than exasperated, which actually helped a little, gave me just enough courage to face the rest of my day.

Or so I thought.

"I did not consent to this dinner," I said grumpily as I dumped two bags of groceries onto the coffee table.

"I like that for a welcome," Ray said, only not sarcastically, the way I would have said it. "At least I know if you ever say something nice to me you mean it."

Wade blinked. "I've never considered Preston to be a particularly honest person, now that you're saying that, but I suppose he's not all that *dishonest*. Not the way I am. At least unless you mean—"

She smoothly shoved an apple in his mouth. "No one's asking for your expert analysis, partner. Art, we have to dish about this penis thing. What is wrong with literally everyone?"

"I know!" Art sailed past me to grab her arm. I mean sure, I was the one who'd stopped at the store on my way home, and sure, I was the one being inconvenienced, but they completely ignored me and sat together on the couch, legs all pressed against each other.

It was so wrong. It was super wrong. *I* should be the one sitting beside Art, our bodies touching, the heat growing between us...

"Buck up, sweetums," Wade said, hand clamping down on my shoulder.

I twisted away from him, trying to hear what Art and Ray were talking about. "I did not consent—"

"—to this dinner, I know, but here we are anyway!"

"Do you have to be so loud?" I demanded, y'know, not-loudly.

"Why? Surely someone your age should know how to effectively eavesdrop." Wade sighed. "Some book thing. I didn't follow all of it because it didn't seem worth eavesdropping on. To me, anyway."

He was obviously just trying to be a jerk. I couldn't help being annoyed by that, though I tried really hard. "I guess you're above such things."

"Not so much above as embroiled in my own sorts of dramas, which only sometimes have to do with penises."

I *knew* that's what she'd said. And okay, maybe it was a sign that not a lot was really happening in my life that the only penis-related thing I could think of was the one having to do with H.K. Pierce aka *me*.

Penis-having me, not that it mattered, or should matter, to anyone. Like unless obviously they were interacting with my bits, in which case it would only matter in so much as it would be descriptive information about aforementioned bits.

Wade was staring at me expectantly. While I thought about my bits.

"What?"

"I asked how work was going," he said, slowly, in that emphatic way that made it clear he was repeating something he'd already said.

"Work?" Had also memorably been about my bits recently, until Maggie asked IT to block my access to Twitter. Where people were discussing whether or not H.K. Pierce had a penis, a question I happened to know the answer to. Intimately. Which I wasn't about to share with Wade for any reason. "It's fine. I mean. It's work."

He waved a hand. "Any interesting books coming out? Is that the correct question? I'm not used to small talk with people I actually know."

I made a face at him. "Then why are you pretending to care about my work?"

"God, I'm not pretending at all! I thought that was the good thing about small talk. You don't really have to pretend you care. Small talk is the…garlic powder of conversation. You sprinkle it in everywhere because it can't hurt, but no one expects it to provide more than a pleasant backdrop for the things that matter."

I was still contemplating whether or not I thought that was a fair analogy when I caught the end of Art's impassioned speech about body parts.

"—possibly matter less when it's the *story* that's important! Who cares if a woman wrote it? Or a trans person? Or a cis guy? Or whoever!"

"Amen, sister," Ray said, holding up her fist to be bumped.

Art, realizing we were all looking at them, flushed and kind of hunched over. "Sorry. It just bothers me when people act like genitals have some kind of…inherent meaning. Or value. They just *don't*."

"Agree completely, darling," Wade flourished. "Can't be bothered with that kind of bullshit. Now, what are we eating?"

I withstood an ongoing critique of my snack choices for all of five minutes before I had to escape to my bedroom. Where I sat. On the edge of my bed.

My penis. I mean. My fictional penis. I mean. My very real penis, which was capable of writing fiction. Not like I put it up to the keyboard! Just that—you know—I wrote it and my penis—oh god, when did I start thinking this much about it, I swear I don't have a fixation—it's just that Art, my Art—not *my* Art, but you know what I mean—had been defending me, or not defending me, but defending my right to have a penis—or not—without anyone relating it to my book.

My mouth was dry. I swigged a few sips of warm Diet Coke from my night table and half wished I hadn't.

We ate. Food. I mean. Presumably. I was still totally fixated on the whole thing where penises existed and also books and also books that I, penis-haver, wrote. And Art read. And loved. And...shared with Ray. And now both of them were discussing the controversy about the book, a controversy that still felt complicit in transphobia without even really acknowledging the existence of trans people, a theory that seemed pretty well backed up by Art being upset about it, not that one person who was probably trans (I mean, we hadn't explicitly discussed it but they'd always been very overtly gender-bending) being upset meant they were being upset *on behalf of transness* or something, just that—

Wade patted my knee. "Don't mind him, he's clearly in a contemplative mood. Preston, did you have anything you wanted to add to our conversation?"

"I don't think penises have any inherent value," I stated with total conviction. "I mean, *my* penis has value to *me*, but in general."

The stunned look on Art's face, bewildered look on Ray's, and utterly, suspiciously delighted look on Wade's all made it clear that I had not been tracking the discussion very well.

"I'm so pleased we have covered the topic of your penis," Wade said silkily, "but I believe Ray was offering a cracker, not enquiring about your anatomy."

I gulped. And shoved my hand into the box of crackers Ray was holding out to me. In fact, I stuffed my hand in so hard and fast that it was more like punching the box? Which made it fall—I guess Ray hadn't been ready for that kind of force—dropping to the floor with a little spin that scattered crackers across the floor.

"Sorry," I mumbled, and went to my knees to gather up escaped crackers.

"No problem! And kudos on the penis thing. It's always good to be fond of your own organs."

Art giggled. Wade laughed out loud. I maintained a dignified silence as I picked up crackers from where I'd punched them.

I redeemed myself sometime later by having seen the same show Ray had during our very different childhoods, and thus being able to low-key bond with her over a particularly creepy half-animated dystopia.

"It was the snake things in the sewers that really haunted me," she was explaining to Wade and Art. "They had, like, tentacles somehow?"

"With teeth," I added, shuddering.

"With teeth!" She made a kind of tentacly finger motion as if things were sprouting from her mouth.

"And this was a children's show?" Wade asked. "I'm sure I wouldn't have been allowed to watch something like that even if I had heard of it."

Ray and I glanced at each other, but she didn't look any more certain than I was. "I think it might have been one of those shows that tried to straddle kids and preteens?" I suggested.

"Older than kids, not old enough to be teens." She paused, considering. "Or maybe it was for adults but it looked enough like something kids could watch that no one noticed?"

Neither Wade nor Art looked illuminated, but at least I felt more normal as we kept talking. Normal enough to have lapsed into unsuspicious comfort by the time they were finalizing plans for "the big day."

"I'll just pretend I'm not totally left out right now," I joked, not even feeling particularly left out. It had turned into a nice evening. Ray was smart and funny, Wade was Wade, Art was happy to entertain.

"Art said you refused to read what may honestly be one of

the best books I've read this year," Ray said. "Anyway, we're going to a reading."

Here's where you can tell I got *too* comfortable: it didn't click. Not immediately. I latched on to the first part and didn't process the second. "I never refuse to read books! We don't always like the same books, but that's not the same."

"Excuse me, when you picked it up at book club you looked *revolted*, so it was fair to assume you didn't want to read it!"

"Revolted," Wade said, shaking his head. "So closed-minded, Preston."

"Book club. Wait. You mean." Which was when my brain caught up.

"*Peak Romance*," Art said with relish. And did they look RIGHT AT ME while saying it? You know. As they would if they sort of...knew?

"We're all going to the reading," Wade explained. "But you will presumably be at work."

"Oh. Um. Yes? I mean yeah."

"I'll meet the creator of my book boyfriend at last!" Art pretended to swoon against Ray, who laughed and caught them. "I can hardly wait. Maybe this is it! Maybe my prince has come!"

Wade, eyeing me more obviously than Art had, said, "Maybe he'll be a gargoyle. Or a republican."

"Oh my god, republicans don't have feelings! Do they? I mean, they must. But..."

A half-funny debate about the Venn diagram of conservative politics and ability to emote followed, but I wasn't paying attention.

Their eyes had glimmered at me when they'd said the thing about their book boyfriend. I was sure of it. They had to know. Which meant I had to up my game.

This would be The Moment. The all-important moment

when we both acknowledged what we'd always secretly known: we were meant for each other.

So good. Great. Now I just had to plan The Moment. The Grand Gesture. The thing I'd do to prove to Art that of every other person in the world, I was the one for them. No big deal. No pressure.

Chapter Twenty

I couldn't sleep. At all. I tossed. I turned. I stared at the ceiling. I stared at the various LEDs where things were charging. (I didn't want my phone battery to die during the day so I was charging not one, but *two* power bricks just in case, even though would I even have time to use my phone?)

I took deep breaths and tried to clear my mind. Couldn't. I went from my toes to my head, trying to relax myself. Could not relax. I actually, literally, counted sheep. Not literally in the sense that I had sheep in my bedroom and counted them, but I did the thing where I imagined sheep jumping over a fence, though I'm not sure if sheep do a lot of jumping, but whatever, that was the picture in my head, so I counted them. I don't know how long I counted sheep but it didn't help, just raised an awful lot of questions about sheep anatomy and did they have knees and were their joints really that great at like shock absorption that they'd be jumping all the time?

Despite swearing to myself I wouldn't, I picked up my phone. And googled "do sheep jump." (Yes, but not over whole freaking fences.)

It seemed innocent enough at first. Maybe researching sheep would even *help* me sleep. Right? That was possible. Lying in bed wishing I was asleep wasn't getting me any closer to being asleep, I told myself. Researching sheep couldn't *hurt*.

Except then, I don't know how it happened, I was on Twitter.

And my hashtag alerts were informing me that people had been tweeting about #PeakRomance. And I clicked.

I should not have clicked.

Note to self: *there is never a time when clicking is the wiser choice. NEVER. Just. Don't. Click.*

But I did. I clicked. And then, there were people talking about the book. What I hadn't realized was that people would already be *reading* the book. It wasn't just people talking about the reading or how excited they were to read, it was humans live-tweeting as they read, or calling out inconsistencies (those ones always seemed a little gleeful, to be honest), or picking on one thing they hated and doing, like, a whole thread about that one thing.

Sure, if you wanted to tally them up, there were probably way more people who'd liked it than hated it. But somehow my eyes skimmed over most of those and zeroed in on the ones that wanted to talk about my racist use of "peanut gallery." Which, it turned out, *was* racist, but I hadn't known that! Everyone used "peanut gallery"! I'd never seen it on one of those "Ten Things You Didn't Know Were Super Racist" lists! I couldn't google everything!

I took a few deep breaths, realized my hands were numb from reading my phone in bed, sat up and got my computer.

Note to self: *there is never a time when firing up your laptop at three a.m. because of something someone said on Twitter is a good idea.*

But I did. And felt bad for ever using "peanut gallery." Obviously "Oops, didn't know I was a racist" is not a good look. I was trying to think of something to reply when a new tweet popped up: Maggie. Or rather @puzosmarterthanyou, which was her non-official account.

@puzosmarterthanyou: *This is total news to me! Thanks for pointing it out!* Which was nice and all but wasn't she just feeding the trolls?

Except then the presumed troll replied to say, *I'm sure the author had no idea either! But if we don't talk about it, no one learns, you know?*

And like, fair point. I reread the initial tweet and this time it felt less...mean. And more just "I hate seeing stuff like this because it's racist, so let's all stop using this phrase, okay?" Which I support.

My emotions had gone from chest-tightening horror to rage to embarrassment to horror again, then confusion and finally exhaustion. Though my chest still hurt.

Oh god. People were going to read my book. And find so many things wrong with it. You think you can prevent that with edits and stuff, but it had gone through edits and not one person had been like HEY ALSO RACIST MUCH. Ahhhh. This was terrible. Why had I thought this was a good idea? I should get a time machine and go back to last fall and say *no thanks, I'd rather take on a boss fight against a guy twenty levels higher than me than publish a book.* But I didn't know anyone with a time machine. And I'd done all the work. And all I had to do was get through the day, right?

The day.

The day.

The day when Arty and I could finally talk to each other. About feelings. And stuff. Because the second I walked out they would know that I knew that they knew that I'd written the book. About them. Which would make everything so much easier. No awkward trying-to-bring-it-up moments. None of that fumbling about what to say because I'd already said it. I'd said everything I needed to say in the book, right? And Art loved the book. Desperately.

I was ready for this. Completely ready for it. I put my laptop away and lay back down to think about that second when our eyes would meet and we'd know that the whole world

had opened up for us, that we could walk into the future together, maybe even holding hands, maybe even kissing again,
almost certainly kissing again.

My toes curled at the thought of kissing. Surely there would
be that. Because today was *the* day. The day when it all came
out.

I'd even bought a bottle of champagne for us, stashed at
the back of the fridge. I was going to clear off the coffee table
before leaving and put a few candles there so we could celebrate when we got home. Would we kiss sooner than that?
Maybe they wouldn't be able to control themself and they'd
pick their way through the crowd, come up to the podium,
and kiss me passionately.

Yeah, okay, that wasn't really Art's style, though it *was*
pretty fitting. Still, much more likely that they'd wait. Until
the reading was over. Until the books were signed. The people
dispersed. Wait for me like I'd waited for them all these years.
Maybe it would happen in the bookstore. Or on a street corner. Maybe we'd be in the elevator coming up to the apartment. Or maybe it would be by candlelight, with champagne,
hands touching lightly, lips brushing against each other at first,
then the pressure getting firmer as we grew more confident,
and then...and then...

The blaring of my alarm woke me just in time to hear Art
call, "Have a lazy day while I go out to meet maybe the greatest author ever! Bye!"

Right, they were going to lunch with Wade and Ray before the early evening reading. I called a belated "Bye!" back
before taking a deep breath.

I was not well-rested. I was not feeling fresh as a daisy. What
I was, was *ready*. I could do this. I could be everything today:
mysterious author, smooth reader, pleasant book-signer, and
when all of that was done, I'd be the thing I'd wanted to be

for years: Art's perfect boyfriend. I'd trained for this and now it was finally happening.

Today was it. Today was *the day*.

Also I might puke. Except I wouldn't. Because Art just called me *maybe the greatest author ever.* Obviously they were teasing, but still, it was the kind of tease that felt just a little bit true. And I could coast on that tiny kernel of truth until I could tease them back.

I only had to wait a little longer now. Until we'd look at each other and just *know.* All the truths for all the years. At last.

For about an hour I thought everything might be…kind of perfect? I got dressed. My sharp black shirt looked more or less ironed (it took three YouTube videos and two hours of paranoia that Art would walk in from work and see me doing it the day before, but it was fine, everything was *fine*). My rainbow tie, which was their graduation gift to me, looked great, mostly because I'd let them tie it once and never loosened the knot too much after that. I'd even remembered to shine my shoes, as long as by "shine" you meant "quicky run over it with a sock and some polish I knew Art wouldn't mind me borrowing (again)."

I managed to tell my brain to take a break when it suggested I casually walk half the length of Manhattan to get to the bookstore. No, brain. Don't make more work for us. *But we'd get there so refreshed!* my brain argued. *But we'd be sweating through our nice dress shirt!* I argued back.

I won. I mean, technically I'd have won either way since I and my brain are the same entity, but whatever, I took the train, like a normal person.

I was early. Well, later than Maggie told me to arrive, but well before the actual reading. And yet…there were people there. In fact there were lots of people there, in a literal line outside the store, like I was the freaking new iPhone or something.

What was happening. Maybe there was something else going on. This couldn't be for me, could it? Probably not. Only an egomaniac would see a crowd and think, *Oh, they've come to see me.* Ridiculous. Foolish. Absurd. Probably they were all there for Carlos and the second he finished introducing me, they'd run out of the store because obviously no one cared about some mysterious debut author with a book that just came out.

Until I realized they were all holding it. The book. My book. *Peak Romance* by H.K. Pierce. Me. By me.

Oh god, they were all there *for me*, or at least for my book.

I was so flustered by this realization, and so fixated on all the copies of *Peak Romance* in the wild suddenly, that I literally tripped over my own feet and fell right into a woman with *Peak Romance* tucked under her arm.

It slipped to the sidewalk and I reached for it automatically, trying to think of the inevitable tweet about how an author had banged into her at his own reading. "Sorry! Oh god, sorry!"

"Dude, give me back my book."

I guiltily handed it over, wondering if I should sign it right there for her or something. "Sorry, I wasn't looking where I was going, it's such a crazy day—"

"I know. Are you here to see H.K. Pierce too?" She glanced at the line. "Because you'll have to go back there if you are."

For a really long moment I just stood there. Then I got it.

She had no idea who I was. I was just a clumsy stranger to this woman. This, uh, fan.

"Oh. Right. Yeah. Actually no, I was just…um, I was just going to look for…for a book about…um…"

She rolled her eyes. "Yeah sure. The line's back there, dude."

I sheepishly stepped away. "Um, thanks. But I really…" I began walking again, this time keeping my head down so as to monitor where my treacherous feet were at all times.

Behind me she called, "They're not going to let you in, you know!"

Other people grumbled as I passed, but I just kept my head down. And wished I'd decided to wear some sort of disguise so I could change into H.K. Pierce in the store, like Superman.

The owner of the shop—AKA Art's boss—was standing at the door playing bouncer. "Hi, PK. Art's not here yet but I expect them any moment now, I'm sure you know how excited they've been—"

She was interrupted by Maggie, grabbing my arm and dragging me inside. "Sorry, I need him! *Fifteen minutes ago.*" The second part was growled at me, not Art's boss.

"Sorry, I—"

"Mouth closed, ears open, mister," she ordered, like I was a disobedient kindergartner.

I almost looked around to find Puzo, who usually punctuated Maggie's orders, but he didn't like large crowds in small spaces, so he wasn't there. Which actually made me kind of sad. Like Puzo had been there at the beginning, so he should be here now, not that this was the end, just that—

"PK!"

I snapped to attention. "What? Sorry. I'm here." I was pretty sure fully seventy-five percent of my spoken words today were "sorry" but whatever. "Yes? What? Um, also, I sort of just stumbled into a woman out there, do you think—"

Maggie closed her eyes and took a long, frazzled breath. "PK," she said without opening her eyes.

"Um. Yeah?"

"You are late."

"Yeah, sorry, I mean, I figured as long as I showed up—"

I could hear Art's boss murmur, "Oh dear."

"Come with me." Frazzled breath. "Right now."

"Yeah, sure, I'm with you."

Frazzled breath. "I'm going to kill you." Frazzled breath. "But later."

I laughed uneasily. "Right, kill me later, good call. Because we've got this whole"—I waved an arm—"reading thing now."

Her eyes opened and locked on mine like a targeted missile. "Good tie. Let's go." And then turned on her heel to, uh, go.

I glanced over. "Art got it for me," I added, to Art's boss.

She nodded quickly. "Very nice, dear. You should probably…"

"Right." So I did. I followed Maggie to the back of the store, which was alternately cleared away for storytime or author readings as necessary. (And omg this one time I watched Art do storytime and it was like the cutest thing I'd ever seen, they put on this wig to look like Goldilocks and skipped around the little cluster of kids and ahhhhh it was adorable, like I probably wasn't allowed to get that ovaries-bursting feeling? But whatever it is where you look at someone and want to have their babies? That was me.)

"You will sit here." Maggie jabbed her finger at a chair behind a table. "The books are there." Jab at a couple of modest piles of books on one side. "Pens to sign with there." Jab at, y'know, pens. "Extras, there." Jab under the table, where a couple of boxes lived.

"Hey, Mags," I said, keeping my voice low.

"*What*." No question mark.

"Do you think…today will be okay? I mean." I swallowed around what was beginning to feel like a really big lump in my throat. I reached up to test the outside, making sure it wasn't, like, bulging from my neck, goiter-style.

"You're a jackass, I could seriously punch you in the nose

right now, and of course today will be okay, you jerk." She gave me a brief, tighter-than-necessary hug. "Now pay attention, this is the biggest event I've ever run on my own, and you're already screwing it up."

In all of my anxiety about release day, and the reading, and the Peak Romantic Grand Gesture of proclaiming my love for Art, I'd sorta forgotten that it was a whole thing. For Maggie, for Adams, for the sales team, for the folks who'd acquired the book mostly because Adams told them to (but who were still on the hook for it succeeding).

"There are a lot of people out there," I said. "And FYI, one of them definitely thinks I tried to steal her book. Or trip her. Or trip her so I could steal her book."

Maggie's forehead smoothed out. "Seriously, all you had to do was get here without drama."

"I mean, *and then* I have to do a whole lot of other stuff."

"I guess so. Speaking of which, you should probably get in place. You know what you're reading?"

"Yeah."

"And you talked to Carlos?"

"Yeah, but why aren't you pissed at him for not being here yet?" I didn't love Carlos, but in this moment, with those people outside, I didn't mind having him stand in between me and like…my destiny. Or whatever.

"Carlos is late to everything he does. And he always shows up acting like—"

As if on cue, the bell on the door chimed again. "Sorry, sorry, the train was delayed, and there was this death trap of a pedestrian construction walkway that I had to detour a block to get around—"

Maggie sighed. I dodged a variety of dudebro shoulder shoves. Carlos beamed. "Today's the day, little man. You ready?"

"How would I know if I was ready?" I asked.

"You aren't. No one's ready for their big break." He clapped loudly. "Let's get going! Can't wait to throw PK to the wolves. I mean introduce him to his adoring fans. Hey, do you have a good answer for 'How do you get your ideas?' There's always one of them who asks."

I opened my mouth to speak but at that moment Art's voice came from the back. "PK? You didn't tell me you were going to be here! Hey, Maggie."

"Art! Good to see you. Carlos, you and PK talk shop." Maggie gave Art a side-squeeze and began to walk away. I frowned after them, but only happened to catch the eye of Wade, who was holding Ray's hand and staring at me.

Really hard.

Staring like he wanted to bore a hole through my skull.

I turned fast but thought I could almost feel Wade's gaze drilling into my brain from across the room.

Chapter Twenty-One

Then it was time. Really time. Time in the sense of "either you run screaming out the back door, or at least the door that leads to a warren of narrow hallways down which was probably an exit but who even knew which direction to go, OR you get your shit together and become the mysterious author of *Peak Romance*."

So I did it. The second thing, not the running away thing.

I stood off to the side with Maggie, slightly hiding behind her, to be honest, and watched Carlos give a super theatrical intro. He even managed to passive-aggressively suggest that if I worked hard I might someday write as well as he did, a thing I only caught because Maggie elbowed me so my brain went for a review of the last few seconds to see why.

Because, me? I wasn't really hearing anything. Or seeing anything. My mind was a fog, but an electrified fog, making sweat stand out on my skin like my blood was boiling.

Art was here. Art was in this room. They'd let in all the people who'd been waiting outside, and as much as some of them were probably Carlos's usual entourage, some of them, most of them, were there because of me. My book. How many would we have gotten without the "mystery author" gimmick? I didn't know. And while I thought it would matter to me, in this moment, it didn't.

In this moment the only thing that mattered was Art.

I knew where they were standing, knew exactly where I'd look when Carlos stepped aside and I stepped forward. I knew exactly what I was going to say. I could feel the domino of moments that would follow: meeting Art's eyes, theirs going big, confirming the thing they already knew but hadn't quite allowed themself to believe, which was that I'd written this book entirely for them. The way their lips would curve. The way they'd probably bring their fingers to their lips like they were flustered (and their nails were iridescent rainbows today, I'd even imagined the way the light would hit, all those dancing colors setting off this moment of pure, true recognition).

They might cry. *I* might cry. But I didn't want to think about crying. I only wanted to think about Art. This time tomorrow would we be cuddled together on a couch (or in a bed???), laughing and talking together, making up for all the time we'd wasted? In a few hours we'd be drinking champagne, and we'd probably have to ask Wade and Ray back to the apartment with us, but that was okay, eventually they would leave and it would just be me, and Art, and this precious, fragile little seed we'd been invisibly balancing between us for all this time…

Maggie elbowed me sharply.

I looked up to see Carlos clapping at me, aggressively, his hands moving in my direction like they'd rather be smacking me upside the head.

"And here he is! Again! For real this time!"

Laughter, more clapping, and my legs, numb, starting to move. My face, smiling, but I was pretty sure it looked terrifying, because Carlos grabbed me in a hug and whispered, "You look like you're shitting out a feral squirrel."

Which made me laugh somehow, even in this moment, and that broke, or at least fractured, the surface of my terror.

Then I went to stand there, where he'd been standing, in

this little semicircle in front of the table where I'd be signing books later. And I kind of waved, like a doofus. "Um, hi."

Giggles, shoes shifting, chairs squeaking.

This was it. This was the moment. The Moment.

I looked up to where Art was standing. They looked super confused. They opened their mouth, lips forming my name, even though I couldn't hear them.

Okay, I hadn't expected them to look quite that confused, but I could roll with it.

Seriously though, I thought by now they'd be grinning at me like we shared a joke, like we were in on a secret. The secret of, y'know, *us*. The secret we'd kept even from ourselves.

"So, um, I'm"—I caught myself at the last moment and remembered my pseudonym—"H.K. Pierce." My eyes scanned through the other people before returning to Art.

Now they just looked stunned.

Stunned in a good way? I cleared my throat and said the thing I'd been rehearsing for weeks. Lots of weeks. Maybe, in a sense, for years. The thing I'd been rehearsing since that morning after we'd kissed when Art laughed it off and I...didn't.

"I, uh, wrote *Peak Romance*, as I guess everyone knows. But before we get to the reading I just wanted to say that this book was inspired by my real-life bestie, my closest friend, the person I'd do anything in the world for. I didn't know how to say all that so I...wrote a book."

There were assorted "awww" sounds and more giggles and a few "that's so sweet" and "oh my god adorable"s sprinkled around, but everything faded for me except for Art. "Anyway, this is for you, Arty," I said, as I'd been planning to say, and smiled at them, the kind of smile that splits you open in the best of ways, the kind of smile that you pour everything in your heart into, like you're channeling your entire being into that moment.

Art's expression went from stunned to shocked to very, very still. Frozen. Statue-like. Then, after the longest moment, people turning in their seats to see who I was talking to, coworkers patting their arm like they'd won something, Art finally, finally spoke. And I didn't think it was my imagination that no one in the room was breathing. I sure wasn't.

"You didn't."

That's what they said. Not in a vaguely impressed way. Not like *I can't believe you wrote me a book.* More like *I can't believe you put the leftover pasta in the fridge while still in the pot and then left it there until it went smelly and moldy so now we have a molding pot of pasta in the back of the fridge making everything taste like death.*

Actually the tone in their voice when I left the pot of pasta in the fridge? Wasn't as awful as the tone in their voice after I, you know, said what I said. About them. And me. And us.

And then they lowered their head and pushed through the people standing at the back of the room until they got to the door. Which chimed. As they left.

This one time when I was about six I fell off a play structure and landed flat on my back in sand. I don't remember it hurting. But there was this long moment when I couldn't breathe, and I lay there, looking up into the sky, thinking the words, *I can't breathe.*

I stood there in front of all those people thinking, *I can't breathe.* And then I could. I didn't want to, particularly, but my body remembered how to suck in air and oxygenate blood and a woman toward the back of the room said, "Didn't you almost fall on me outside? I thought you were trying to steal my book!"

Scattered laughter.

In the corner of my eye I could see Maggie take a step. Maybe she was going to help me. Or hit me. Or hit reload so I could play this scene all over again, but better.

I looked once more at the door, but there was no Art there.

Art was gone. I coughed a few times, my eyes watering, and said to the woman I'd seen outside, "Sorry, I'm just clumsy, is the thing. Okay, so let's…"

…finish up so I can go after Art.

…get super drunk so I can stop replaying that look on their face in my head.

….cry. Let's all just cry.

"Let's get started," I forced myself to say, and coughed a few more times until I was pretty sure I wasn't going to start really crying. I didn't exactly feel like crying. I felt…like I wasn't in control of how I felt. But I could hear myself reading the thing I'd marked to read, and the part of me that had picked it for Art, picked it so that they'd know how much I cared about them, the part of me that had desperately looked forward to looking up at the end of this line or that line to meet their gaze, that part of myself began to pull away.

Maggie told me later that I'd done really well. And she meant it. She didn't say I'd done well for someone whose life had just crushed them. She thought I hadn't seen Art leave, so I hadn't totally realized what happened.

In reality it felt like the opposite. It felt like part of me had simply gone with Art. And the rest of me stayed there, in my body, reading from my book, smiling and laughing and talking to people. My hand cramped signing books. It was supposed to be this big Moment in all the ways, but I was barely even there.

What had I done? It had been so perfect. How…how had it all gone so horribly wrong?

Hours later, an eternity later, after Adams had patted me on the shoulder and told me I should be proud, after Maggie and Carlos took me out for drinks to celebrate, after Ray texted to tell me I'd done a great reading, and Wade texted me an ellipsis with nothing else, after all that I finally went home.

Art was gone.

Chapter Twenty-Two

It had been eight months. That we'd been together. Since Art moved in. And in that time I'd forgotten how to be alone for longer than the time it took to run to the store, or the length of a shift when they worked on a weekend day. Not that we did everything together, but there was always that certainty of seeing them, the certainty I'd missed after college when we were no longer roommates.

And now? It wasn't even back to the days when they were with Roman, the days when we messaged each other all the time with silly gifs and links to TikToks and random stuff we thought the other would like.

Now there was nothing at all. A vast, aching nothing.

They hadn't blocked me on all their social media accounts, so that seemed good? But they also hadn't been posting anything, so that seemed not-good. A measure of my desperation was how close I'd come to calling my mother and low-key hoping she'd sort the whole mess out for me somehow. She loved Art. She could explain to them that I hadn't meant to… to do whatever I'd done that ruined everything. I was only trying to, like, express my feelings in the only way I knew how, and maybe it wasn't *ideal*, but this seemed, y'know, like kind of an overreaction. All I'd really done was write them a book, right? Like, wasn't that at least kind of romantic? It was definitely the sort of thing their supposed book boyfriend would have done.

Not that I took advice from fictional people, I just mean that this was all super confusing because how could Art so desperately want that kind of thing and then freak out the second it happened?

Plus, would *Roman* write a book for them? No. Long answer the same as the short answer: nope.

So why did I feel so awful about it? Because I did. I regretted everything. Why had I written it? Why had I sent it to Maggie? Why had I agreed to let Adams publish it? Why had I planned this whole stupid dramatic reveal? I could have just *told* them and then we could have enjoyed the dramatic reveal together!

Except I couldn't just tell them. It's why I'd written *Peak Romance* in the first place. If I was the sort of person who could talk about my feelings I wouldn't have needed to write them into a novel, would I?

It was all circles and spirals of thoughts I couldn't control and I still had to get up in the morning and go to work, where everyone kept congratulating me and talking to me about the book, which, y'know, wasn't a *NYT* best seller ("yet" as Maggie kept reminding me) but for a debut book was doing... amazingly well? So well it felt a little weird that I'd written it, to be honest. I kept seeing it and thinking about it like I would any book we'd published, without remembering the extra added layer of *oh yeah I wrote this one, good on me.*

All of it would have been better with Art to share it with.

I'd fucked that up, though. Not just the chance we'd ever kiss (weep), share romantic candlelit dinners (sob), or lie in bed together with our fingers just slightly intertwined as we drifted off to sleep...

I had to stop having these horrible breakdowns where I

was crying so hard I could barely breathe. It was not a good look. Which I knew, but I couldn't help it. I was sad. So sad I couldn't remember what it felt like to not be sad.

More than that, I felt *lost*. Like without Art's anchoring presence I didn't know who I was anymore.

When I tried to describe it to Maggie she coughed "codependent" at me and pointedly went to get Puzo a frozen banana to chip away at.

I wasn't codependent! I was just… I just… Art saw me as the person I wanted to be (you know, when they weren't busy seeing me as the person I'd been freshman year of college). When I was with them, I could be better. Myself, but better. And when I wasn't with them I forgot who that was. Or could be. Or might be. Or whatever.

Basically without Art, there was no sparkle in the world, no shimmering, no color-shifting. Everything was just flat. And I missed the dimension and, uh, light refraction they brought to my life.

And their smile. Laugh. Eye roll. Everything.

Then one day I came home and found that they'd taken their computer. I got drunk like I hadn't been since college, the kind of self-destructive drunkenness that bypasses having a nice buzz and goes straight to puking your guts out and propping yourself up on the toilet while the bathroom spins around you and you wait for your body to start heaving again.

And even that was better than thinking about the big void on the table in Art's bedroom (the spare room) where their computer should have been.

I didn't get it. I didn't get any of it. I'd tried so hard to do all the right things. I mean, all the romantic things. They'd accused me of not being romantic, but wasn't this romantic AF? I'd declared my love for them! I'd written them a whole book! People everywhere could now read all about how much

I loved Art, how deeply I cared about them. How, *how*, was that not enough? What did they want from me? A skywriter? Actually, that wouldn't work that well on account of when you're downtown you can't really see sky all that well. Was I supposed to drop one of those massive banners from the side of a building that reads *I love Art* with little hearts all over it? What were the logistics of that?

And they hadn't even let me apologize! For whatever I'd done wrong! It wasn't fair. I knew that was a dumb, childish thing to say, but it really wasn't.

And then, oh god, my parents showed up.

I really do have affection for my parents. It might not be as cool and adult as being estranged from them, or merely tolerating them, but in reality, I just like my folks. Even when they're being sort of extra.

But not right now. Not when I was so messed up in the head.

Definitely not after an *Art took their computer they're really seriously gone now* one-night bender, which had ended with me in the bathroom making out with the toilet.

But of course that's when they showed up. I say "showed up" but they called first. From downstairs. Instead of just barging in, which they could have done, because they had keys. At least I was upright when they walked in the door.

"Preston—" My mom's voice started out cheerful as usual, then cut off as she looked around. At the kitchen, which had more than the usual debris around (and way more than the usual number of ramen wrappers). At the living room, littered with the Coke cans I was rumming until I ran out of rum, coffee table cluttered with a week's worth of mugs, floors unswept, various outdoor clothes and things in a pile in the entryway.

Then she looked at me. I'd had just enough time to dart to

the bathroom and fingercomb my hair with some tap water, but that didn't make up for the greasiness (maybe they'd think it was just water? did I maybe look like I'd just stepped out of the shower?), or the Art's-old-T-shirt I'd put on that first post-Art morning and just kept wearing when I wasn't at work. I was pretty sure the sweatpants were clean…oh. Except they'd been clean yesterday. Pre-puking. They were not clean now.

I was a wreck. Basically. And any instinct I may have had to hide that…well, to be honest, I didn't have an instinct to hide it. I had to hide it when I was nominally Doing A Job. I couldn't cry my way through Fairway. But I didn't have the energy to hide it here, in my own apartment.

"Son," my father said, his voice soft. I realized Mom was clutching his arm, fingers digging in. "Everything all right?"

"Art's gone." That was it. I fell apart.

I was not the man I'd been raised to be. I was a broken, screwed-up pseudo-man, who was crying in front of his parents over his best friend, who he loved, and lost, and oh god not again.

It didn't last long. It couldn't last long. I didn't cry in front of my folks. I knew the rules. You were allowed to cry if you were in deep physical pain (broken bone, severed limb) or if someone had just died. Otherwise: no crying.

But hearing the words *Art's gone* had hurt me so much I couldn't help it. And my parents? After they'd recovered from their bewilderment, they did what they always did: divided and conquered.

Dad started cleaning. That's how it had always been. Mom cooked, Dad cleaned. So off he went to the kitchen and we could hear him running water and merrily plunking dishes into it while Mom sat gravely next to me and—gasp—took my hand. Seriously like I was dying.

"Sorry," I mumbled, not looking at her. Vaguely wishing

I was a dirty dish my dad could just soak in the sink until I was ready to be scrubbed clean, good as new.

"Darling, why is Art staying with Wade and that nice young woman he's dating?"

I blinked. Stared at the tower of Coke cans I'd been building until I had to puke. Ran her words over again in my head before looking at her. "Wait, what? You talked to Art?"

"I didn't intend to, although if I had known…" Her words trailed off like she wasn't quite sure what she knew. Moving gamely on, she continued, "Well, I certainly would have been checking in on you boys before now if I had any inkling of what was happening."

"Art's not a boy. Art's just Art. They use they/them pronouns."

She blinked. "I…all right. All the same, Preston dear, why is Art living in the corner of Wade's very small apartment instead of in a bedroom here with you?"

What was I even supposed to say to that?

Feelings check: *Because I'm worthless and they hate me.*

Intelligence check: *Because they're so mad at me they moved out and didn't even tell me they were doing it.*

Logic check: *Because the world is a horrible place and Art thinks I'm a horrible person even though all I did was give them everything they said they wanted.*

"Because I wrote a book," I said.

My mother, incomprehension shifting quickly to concern, called, "George? I think we could use your input here."

She meant *I think our only son has lost his mind, can I get a second opinion?* I sighed and shoveled a pile of junk off the box of author copies I'd been sent, which had originally been stashed away in my room, but post-Art abandoning me I'd been sick of looking at them and had stashed it away under a bunch of crap in the living room instead.

I handed a book to my mother. Who stared at it. Then at me. Then back at the book. "You…"

"Wrote a book, yeah, I know."

My dad emerged from the kitchen with his shirtsleeves rolled up and his hands pink from being in water. "What's all this?"

Mom slowly passed him *Peak Romance*. "Look, dear. Preston…wrote a book. About…romance."

The expression on my dad's face could best be described as eye-bulging emoji. He took the book in slow motion and then looked at me, then the book, then me, then the book again. "We had no idea you'd written a book, son."

"No one did," I said miserably.

"It's a somewhat strange thing to keep a secret, dear." The reproach in Mom's voice had nothing to do with feeling personally betrayed and everything to do with all those missed opportunities to one-up her friends. Think of the months and months she'd missed of telling them all about my book coming out! How could I be so cruel as to deprive her of that pleasure?

"It wasn't really a secret. I just didn't tell anyone."

"But *why*?"

I didn't know how to explain it. How normal it had become to live a double life, how easy it had been to be evasive, even with Art. "It was just work. It was work to edit it and market it and do all the things you do, you know? It was just another part of my job. I wrote a book. Maggie thought it was good enough to publish. Adams edited it. And here we are. It came out last week."

The confusion on her face was almost hard to look at, as if I'd been speaking gibberish without realizing it. "Yes, but dear, I still don't understand what this has to do with Art."

"I might," said my father, who'd been paging through the

book. He looked up. No confusion there. "You didn't tell Art, did you, son?"

"It was a surprise," I mumbled. "Plus the big release reading was at the store, so I knew they'd find out when I walked in all like 'Hey, I'm the author.'" It sounded supremely stupid in retrospect. "I thought it would be... I thought they would like it. The excitement of it."

My dad came toward me and reached out, clamping a hand on my shoulder. "And then Art realized it was about him?"

"Them," I corrected automatically.

"Pronouns," my mom added.

Dad ignored both of us and squatted down beside me. "Pres, you didn't tell Art about your feelings?"

"I wrote a whole stupid book about them!" I shot back, avoiding his gaze by staring at the dark hairs on the backs of his fingers. I'd always thought I'd grow up and also have thick, dark hairs on the backs of my fingers, that it was a mark of manhood, but genetics or hormones or whatever had conspired and I'd never gotten much more than a sprinkling of not-that-thick hairs on my not-that-manly fingers.

"That's not the same and you know it."

I dumped my head into my hands. "What was I supposed to say? 'Oh by the way I might be in love with you also we're almost out of toilet paper?' This way was supposed to be better than that! I thought it was kind of romantic, you know? 'Surprise, I'm in love with you.'" And then I was crying again, but not as intensely as before. It was almost like self-defense crying, like I was crying in order to avoid looking at them. Or talking to them.

But I could still hear them.

Mom: "What on earth?"

Dad: "Look at the book, Cristine."

Mom: "What do you mean...oh. Oh dear. Oh no."

Dad: "Exactly."

Mom: "But I didn't realize he knew that he…"

Dad: "Apparently he did."

I raised my head. "I didn't know what? What didn't I know?"

They exchanged a glance, one of those thirty-years-of-marriage type glances.

"Darling, haven't you had feelings for Art…for a long time now?"

I frowned aggressively at her. "So what?"

"Well. Only that we didn't realize you fully understood what those feelings meant."

"Of course I understand what my own feelings mean! Why does no one think I can have feelings? Why does *everyone* think I don't understand what it's like to have feelings, when I have *a lot of feelings all the time!*"

She held up her hands. "Of course, dear."

"It's not *of course, dear*! It's my whole life! And I fucked it all up and I don't even get why when Art *loved* the stupid book, kept going on and on about the main character and how I was his book boyfriend and how great I was at romance and—"

I cut off.

Except obviously Art hadn't been talking about me. At least they didn't know they were. In retrospect that was more obvious than it had been at the time.

My dad's hand tightened on my shoulder. "Listen, boy, you two have been very close friends, and Art wouldn't throw that away. Have you tried talking to him?"

"Them," I said.

"Have you tried talking to *them*?"

"Yes! I called, I texted! They aren't on any of their socials! It's like they disappeared! Except *apparently* they're at *Wade's*." The idea of it stung all over again, like peroxide on an open wound. I glared at my mother. "How do *you* know they're at Wade's?"

"Oh, I happened to be in the neighborhood and thought I'd drop off that scarf he was admiring when we last saw him—not that all flamboyant young men wear scarves, but I have seen Wade in them before—"

"You happened to be 'in the neighborhood,'" I said flatly. "You happened to be in Manhattan. Randomly. For other reasons. So you stopped by Wade's apartment, which, how did you even know where he lived?"

"His mother told me, obviously. In fact"—here she paused as if something had just struck her—"in fact, I think Pam was the one who said, 'Oh, Wade lives right around there, you should stop by!'"

This seemed slightly far-fetched but not so incredible I could completely dismiss it. "So you stopped by."

"I did!"

"And you just happened to have a scarf with you that Wade admired at a party nine months ago."

"Well, it never hurts to be prepared, dear."

"Uh-huh. So you just showed up at Wade's. When was this?"

Her eyes slid away and she began fussing with the cans on the table, turning them upright with a determined look on her face. "Oh, who really keeps track? A few days ago."

I kept staring at her.

"Possibly yesterday. Was it yesterday, George?"

My dad, used to Mom's habit of never giving a straight answer to anything, said, "Why is Art at Wade's apartment? Is he moving out?" I opened my mouth and he shook his head. "Sorry, they. Are they moving out?"

"I don't know! How am I supposed to know when they won't even *talk to me*?"

Dad looked up at Mom. Then back at me. "You might have to give it a little time, son."

"It has been *fifteen days*, how much time can they possibly need before they *talk to me again*?"

He nodded seriously, not at all like I was a five-year-old having a meltdown at Costco. Then he patted my shoulder and said, "It might take more time than that. What you…what happened between you may take a little time to sort out for Art. But let us take you to lunch. Judging by the kitchen, you haven't had a square meal lately. Come on, Pres."

And since that was the same voice he used to use when I was sad about some minor life-ending thing that happened at school (getting picked third—THIRD—for basketball teams, or looking silly in front of a teacher I was crushing on), I responded automatically with a nod.

"Perhaps you should give your father and me time to finish tidying," my mom suggested. Then, as if it had just occurred to her, she said, "You could take a shower, if you liked! That should be perfect. Then we'll go to lunch, dear."

I nodded again, eyes still damp, and went to shower. I gave them all the time they needed and my folks did not disappoint; when I emerged from my shower Dad had finished the kitchen and living room, and Mom had done some kind of whirlwind cleaning in my bedroom, making it look like a human lived there instead of a grumpy bear getting its den ready for hibernation.

I was so pathetic I didn't even care that I was a grown man whose parents had just cleaned his apartment and were now taking him out to lunch. I just kind of leaned against my dad's arm in the elevator, wishing I was so little that I believed my folks could fix everything I'd broken.

Chapter Twenty-Three

Knowing that Art was with Wade and Ray was both good and also torturous like blades shoved under my fingernails. Or no. Maybe not that bad. Maybe just like having one of those low hangnails that rip off at the worst moment then get snagged on everything you touch, so even though the worst of the pain was over, you kept revisiting it again and again.

I kept revisiting it again and again.

My first instinct was to say goodbye to my parents after lunch, pretend I was going to be a totally normal, totally self-control-having human, and then immediately get a cab over to Wade's, where I would epically Grand Gesture at my beloved until they realized we were meant to be and surrendered to… wait, no, that sounded weird. They'd realize we'd loved each other all along in the kissing sense of the word and give into my…nope, off the rails again.

After a few more failed metaphors I figured out the reason none of them sounded right: boy fucks up, boy learns nothing, boy doubles down, persuasion check failed.

So I did not catch a cab, show up unannounced, and try to surprise my beloved into finding me charming.

Also, was it weird that in a way I felt almost reassured by my parents' initially unsettling "Oh, we totes always knew you were head over heels for Art, we just thought you were too dumb to notice" attitude toward the whole thing? Because on one hand: insulted. On the other: it was real. The way I felt. So real that even my parents knew about it. I was again happy they weren't like Wade's parents. Though oh my god, why had they acted like they were setting me up with Wade? That was so cruel! My mom even got Art involved, acting like she was…we were…

My mom got *Art* involved. In setting me up. With Wade. Who she knew I'd never even liked. Right. A little nudge for her dunce of a son, there.

Would I ever stop feeling stupid?

Probably not.

So I did not call a cab. I did not show up unannounced. I did not Grand Gesture (again). I did not make a fool of myself (again). I did not upset Art (again).

I stayed in the apartment with my feelings instead.

And over the next few days the ratio of time spent crying to time spent not crying began to shift in favor of time spent not crying. Which was probably a good thing, though part of me didn't want to let go of the crying. Being sad tied me to Art in some sense, as if my chest-tightening grief over losing them—not just the fantasy of us, but the reality of evenings spent watching TV together, of bringing them lunch at the store, of texting back and forth all day about work gossip or silly moments, of falling to sleep at night knowing they were just across the hall and then waking up in the morning hearing them hum as they got ready in the bathroom…

When I started thinking of those things and only crying a little, not losing myself completely, I realized that a truly terrible thing was occurring.

I was…well, maybe not *moving on*. That was a step too far. But I was coping. And coping seemed a lot closer to *moving on* than not coping. I wasn't regularly washing the dishes, but I was back to regularly washing myself. I wasn't eating home-made meals with multiple ingredients, but the kitchen wasn't littered with ramen wrappers and empty flavoring packets anymore.

Which was, in some ways, worse than anything else. If I was moving on, then Art was probably doing the same. And I couldn't stand it. I couldn't tolerate it. One night when I couldn't sleep, almost without thinking, I picked up my phone. *Please don't do this,* I typed, the words blurring. And send.

Nothing in reply.

Nothing the next morning.

Nothing the whole next day.

Until about ten p.m., at which time my phone rang and my heart stopped.

Except it was Wade. The traitor. The turncoat. He was supposed to be my friend—or at least—well, whatever he was, he should have been on my side.

I answered, heat rising beneath my skin, and snarled, "What?"

"Buzz me up, you incomparable dummy. Also next time you're drunk-texting you might check the recipient first, unless you're playing the home-wrecker and trying to get me to leave Ray. Which, I'm flattered, but no."

It took a really long stretch of time before I realized what he was saying. I hit the buzzer without a word and then scrambled to look at my sent texts.

Where.

Dammit.

I'd texted *Wade,* not Art. I'd texted Wade. At two in the morning. I'd texted him *Please don't do this.* Oh god. I hadn't even been drunk, though if you're accused of drunk-texting, the last thing you want to admit is that you were sober-texting instead. Better for him to believe I was under the influence of booze instead of melodramatic ennui.

I almost didn't buzz him up. It was so tempting to leave him down there, standing outside the door like a dumbass. Someone else should be powerless for once! Not just me.

Then I let him in. He'd probably knock until someone called security anyway.

"Shut up," I said preemptively. It seemed appropriate.

He whooshed in on a current of fresh air. Or at least hallway air, which was fresher than the air in the apartment. "But if I shut up, who's going to save you from yourself? Also, dear god, is this how you've been living?"

Wade stood in the entryway, kerchiefed and immaculate, holding a bowler hat in one hand with his other touching his throat, as if the sight of my place had disturbed him on a pearls-clutching level.

"Um. Fuck you?"

"Lord no, where would you even have sex in this apartment? Nowhere sanitary, I can tell that just by looking."

"It doesn't look that bad!" I managed to stop just short of adding, *My mommy and daddy cleaned it for me last week.*

"Mm-hmm. Would you please clear me off a spot on the couch? I could also use a cup of coffee." A glance at the kitchen. "On second thought, I'll have it delivered."

"I can make coffee," I said defensively.

"Of course you *can*, the question is will it be crawling with E. coli or mad cow or whatever."

"You can't get mad cow from coffee, that's why they call it mad *cow*."

He returned a dubious gaze to me. "If you say so."

I didn't realize until I was hitting the brew button that he'd basically manipulated me into making him coffee, which I never would have done if he'd just demanded it, but acting like I wasn't capable of producing coffee had made me want to prove him wrong.

The jerk.

I stayed in the kitchen until the coffee had brewed. At first I was determined not to clean anything because, y'know, screw that guy, right? But then I realized I had no clean mugs, so I had to wash some. And then I was sitting there with the hot water finally at the tap, and my hands soapy, so I kept going. I wasn't some kind of blink and it's clean miracle worker, but I had managed to more or less return it to the state my dad had left it in by the time the pot finished brewing.

If it was possible to make resentful coffee, that's what I did. Which I resentfully poured into a mug I'd resentfully cleaned, and then resentfully delivered to Wade, who was sitting primly on my rescue couch with his ankles crossed.

"I kind of hate you," I said as I handed him his coffee.

"In your position I would kind of hate me too," he replied.

"Um." What did that mean?

"After all, *I* didn't fuck everything up by being a fool, *I* live happily with a partner who has no reason to doubt either my commitment or my intelligence, and most of all, *I* get to see the person you think you're in love with every day." He waved an arm. His kerchief (or was it a scarf?) fluttered. "You should definitely kind of hate me, Preston. You self-absorbed ignoramus."

It was so completely unfair I couldn't even argue with him for the longest moment. I just stood there, breath caught in my lungs, trapped there like all the words I never said.

"Oh, stop being so hopeless. Get yourself a cup of coffee and sit down."

I stomped to the kitchen, got myself coffee, stomped back into the living room, and sat down.

"You texted me," he said dispassionately, surveying my hunched form like I was a distasteful relation he had no choice but to greet civilly.

"I didn't mean to."

"Oh, I'm aware. But I'm glad you did, because frankly Art doesn't need any more of your utter bullshit."

I gaped at him.

"You can't be this much of a fool. Did you really think they'd just forgive you after what you did?"

"I…what I… I *wrote them a whole book.*"

He waved this away, kerchief fluttering again. No, it was probably a scarf. Whatever it was, it fluttered. "You wrote *yourself* a book. And actually, darling, it's not a bad one. Ray loved it. I saw a lot of you in it, which ruined it for me, but aside from that it was surprisingly well written."

"Why does no one think I can write? I've been writing for years! Also, I can write romance, I *like* romance, rom-coms are easily my favorite movies!" When this failed to move him I added, injecting my words with so much sarcasm they were nearly unintelligible, "But thanks *so much* for your approval."

He shrugged like he didn't care, and the horrible thing about Wade was he genuinely didn't care. He'd never cared.

I flashed back to the night of his birthday party, the way the lights had hit his face as we were driven through the streets and he'd explained how little his parents meant to him. That was why he could be so detached: he had a lot of practice. I didn't have that kind of practice. I wasn't detached *at all.*

I slumped forward, landing my coffee cup on the table and my head in my hands. "Are they okay? They haven't answered any of my texts, it's killing me. It's been *three weeks* and they haven't said anything to me at all."

A loud sigh from beside me. "You are such a nincompoop sometimes. Of course they're not all right. They're devastated. Preston, do you get, at all, what you've done?"

"I wrote them a book! About how much I care about them! I didn't know how to say it, so I wrote it, and they loved it—

they told me all the time about how I was their book boyfriend and how I'd written everything right, that was exactly what they wanted, but then when they found out it was me—" I broke off. "I don't understand," I mumbled into my hands.

"That much, my friend, is perfectly clear." Another sigh. "Try to imagine it from their perspective. Imagine you'd been close to someone for years, lived together, drunkenly kissed this one time in college—"

"HOW DO YOU KNOW ABOUT THAT?" My guts felt like lead. Art had told Wade about that? How? In what context? WHY?

He waved me off. "Drunkenly kissed one time in college, turned to each other in times of crisis, thought you could wholly and completely trust this other person."

"They *can*! They can trust me!"

"And then, on a day you'd been looking forward to, anticipation you'd shared with the other person many times, it turned out that they'd been lying to you. For months. A lot of months."

"I wasn't lying! I wasn't. I mean. I didn't. I didn't mean to. That wasn't. I didn't. I thought…"

"Exactly, thank you. Imagine how betrayed you'd feel about the lying, and then imagine that in your workplace, surrounded by your coworkers, with an additional crowd of people, some of whom are your friends, this person proceeded to draw all the attention to you at the moment of unveiling his lie, which also had the added bonus of exposing both your gullibility—because how had you not known?—and also this very quiet, very private connection between you and the other person."

"I…" I frowned. "I didn't mean to… I mean…they weren't gullible? I thought… I kind of thought they'd figured it out.

You know? I thought it had become something... I don't know. Something we shared?"

"And yet, even if that had been true, do you really think that the bookstore in front of a room full of people was the best place to officially declare yourself?"

"But it was supposed to be romantic?" I cursed the question mark on the end of that sentence. "I mean it was just the type of thing that would have happened in the book, and they *loved* the book, they told me all the time how much they loved the book. Why did they talk about it so much if they didn't know I'd written it?"

"I haven't known Art that long but they do seem like the type to talk a lot about the things they love."

Some note in his voice made me look up. "What does that mean?"

"Oh, nothing. Only that I've heard endlessly about other things Art loves, but that's neither here nor there. Preston, you humiliated them, in public, at their job, and you acted like it was *romantic*."

"But it was! At least I thought it was. I mean." I hid in my coffee, drinking half the mug without tasting it, only slightly scalding my throat.

For once Wade did not speak. Mark this day on your calendar.

"I thought they had to know. I mean. It seemed so obvious it was about them. And they read it so many times. And talked about it..." Though now that I considered the matter, Art *was* the person who would fall in love with a thing and then tell you about every lovable aspect of that thing, which is how I know so much about *Game of Thrones* without ever watching more than the first two episodes.

I slumped again. "But...it was easier to write it down. Than it would have been to say it all."

"Be that as it may, you put them in a terrible position. In front of everyone they work with. At a job they have to continue going to, despite the fact that now everyone knows you think you're in love with them, and also that over the weeks they'd been talking up your book they either didn't know it was yours or pretended they didn't, which apparently people are somewhat split about."

"I thought it would be romantic. I thought…they were in on the joke, you know? I…bought champagne." It was such a stupid thing to cry over—again—but I did anyway. All my life I worked hard to never cry but in the last few weeks I felt like I'd cried entire oceans.

"Good god, you're a mess," Wade said softly. Then, featherlight, he laid a hand on my back. "There, there, you dunce. All is not lost." He didn't speak for a long moment, maybe waiting for me to get myself together, or maybe just for drama. "*Do* you understand, though? Because I don't think there's much to be done if you truly believe your behavior was justified, Preston."

I was too sad to bristle, though I wanted to. "Justified? How?"

"You nonconsensually dragged someone you claim to love into a very public scene that was, let's be clear, entirely about *you*."

It landed like a blow. I opened my mouth to argue, realized I didn't know what to say in my own defense, and shut it again.

"And while you can move on and you're still a published author, you're still the one who's written a book people are falling all over themselves to lavish praise upon, Art has to go to work every day and face the idea that they might be speaking to a customer who was there when you did what you did. They might be talking to someone who saw your wild, ludicrous gesture, who saw them crying as they left. Do you have any idea how awful it's been?"

"I made them cry?" God, I was as bad as fucking Roman. Worse, because I was trying to do something good and was too stupid to know it wasn't. "I never meant... I didn't think..."

"That's clear. But you did. So what now?"

I dragged myself upright and looked at him through watery eyes. "Do they hate me?"

"Don't be even more of a jackass, of course not. Or ask yourself why, of everyone Art could have gone to, they came to us. Not someone beyond your reach, but someone they know *because* of you. But Preston, you hurt them. A lot."

"I'm hurt too!" Which was, yes, the absolute worst possible thing to say, and I covered my mouth after saying it.

"Quite," Wade snapped.

"But how am I supposed to make it better if they won't talk to me?"

He looked expressively around at the apartment. "Is this what you're hoping to entice them back to?"

"It's not as bad as...um. It looks better. Than it did. For a while." I frowned. I hadn't exactly kept up my parents' hard work, and seeing the (new) pyramid of Coke cans and the stacks of mostly eaten TV dinner trays the way Wade was seeing them...okay, so, yeah. That wasn't a great look.

"I haven't been...well." Which was true, dammit.

"Yes, destroying years of trust with someone you love will do that to a person. Or so I'm told. Obviously I've never been so gauche as to fuck something up to this magnitude."

"Oh, well, good for you! Look, did you come over here just to mess with my head? Because it's a weirdly long ride for that and you probably could have done it by text message."

"If that's all I wanted, I could have." He sighed. "I never told you how Ray and I...became Ray and I."

Whoa. That was definitely not the direction I thought we were going in. I reined in my attention from the appalling state of the apartment and focused. "No. I guess I assumed…" What *had* I assumed? "That you charmed her by being obnoxious."

"I must have. It's one of my gifts. But no, she was TAing for this professor I needed to speak to for something I was researching, but the professor was exceptionally hard to pin down—would cancel meetings at the last minute, or not appear for scheduled office hours—and basically threw Ray to the wolves. She took a lot of shit off people who felt entitled to be angry at someone without risking their professional reputation, and one day I heard this prick call her a 'little bitch' as he was walking away, so I verbally eviscerated him. Like a hero."

"Oh my god. That's actually kind of adorable?"

He laughed. "Ray did not think so. She was livid. She told me if I ever interfered with her again I'd regret it, that no one needed to know how big my vocabulary was so I could keep it in my pants, and that she'd been planning to ask me out, but since I'd done that she wasn't going to, which should make me real fuckin' sad—that's how she said it: 'You should be real fuckin' sad about that'—because she was, in her words, a catch."

I covered my mouth with both hands, totally able to picture Ray saying all that, and super in awe of her. "That's so hot," I said through my hands.

"Yes. It was. And I was not immune to her before then." He waved a hand. "Not that I didn't think of myself as *mostly* gay. But it was easier in a lot of ways not to push outside of that, being as fabulous as I naturally am."

I rolled my eyes. "Blah blah, what happened with Ray?"

"I put my larger than average vocabulary to good use, apologized, clarified that I was not defending her so much as I was attacking him, acknowledged that I'd been wrong whatever my intentions, and begged her to reconsider."

"That is…the most you love story on earth," I said. "You and Ray hooked up because she told you she didn't want anything to do with you and you can't stand being told no."

He held up a finger. "You misunderstand. Ray and I hooked up because she told me she'd been planning to ask me out and I realized I was, in fact, real fuckin' sad when she said she wasn't going to. I didn't beg her for a date *that day*. I asked her to reconsider her stance and let me know the next time I saw her. Because I am a gentleman."

"Not much of one, since the whole thing went down while she was at work and forced to be polite."

"Yes, but I could hardly offer my phone number with impunity, since as you say, she was at work. Though not, I don't think, feeling any obligation to be polite. At least not to me. In any case, I didn't have to wait that long. I preferred to do a lot of my work at a café by the Cloisters and she tracked me down there the following day to ask me out." A dignified sniff. "She has since said that I was worth the trouble, though that was before a childhood friend's star-crossed lover moved into our living room."

"They didn't *move in*, most of their stuff is still here!" A fact I'd relied on to keep me from absolutely losing my mind.

"Preston, what do *you* think happened? In your dim-witted little brain, why do you think Art is upset?"

"I—"

"Really *think* about it," he insisted, as if he doubted my ability to think about anything.

I did think about it. That moment when Art froze, when they figured out I was the author of *Peak Romance*, when their face didn't break into the knowing smile I expected but did something else. "I thought they knew," I said meekly. "For the last couple of months at least. I thought they had figured it all out, that we were kind of in it together and when I got up to talk we'd...share this moment. Of knowing. Just us, no one else."

Wade exhaled a long breath. "Oh. That does sound like something you would invent to justify yourself."

"Hey. I mean. I didn't...think I needed to justify myself? I thought it was going to be wonderful. That finally everything would make sense."

"I can see that, in your head, what you were doing wasn't humiliating Art in front of their colleagues and customers. But do *you* see that, in reality, that's exactly what you did?"

Their face. That terrible, frozen moment when they said *You didn't*. Something broke open inside me and I began crying again, but this time it wasn't open sobs, like it had been before. It wasn't like childhood tears, all-out and uncontrolled.

This time my shoulders shook and my muscles contracted and I made hardly any sound. My entire body wept like a grown man who'd accidentally bumbled into breaking his best friend's heart.

Wade said nothing, but after a while he placed his hand in the center of my back and left it there while I cried.

Chapter Twenty-Four

There are seven stages of grief, right? Like. That's what the books say. I don't know if that's exactly what I was going through, but I do know that after Wade left I basically strapped into an emotional roller coaster and pulled the lever.

At first I was defensive. I got what he was saying, and I understood it. I could see how Art had been in a lousy position. I could see how they might have felt awkward in front of their coworkers. But what about me? What about how much I'd risked to stand there and say what I'd said? What about how much I'd risked to write the book in the first place?

Except…well, writing it hadn't really been that risky. Because I'd still been hiding behind a character, behind a wall of fiction, a structure I'd picked specifically because it had been less risky than the alternative, which was, y'know, talking to Art about how I, PK, felt.

Not that it hadn't *felt* risky to write it all out. Not that it hadn't *felt* vulnerable to let people read it. But there's feeling vulnerable and then there's… I guess I really had sort of put them in a bad position without considering how little say they had in it.

But it was supposed to be romantic! I thought they'd love it. A public declaration of my feelings! A grand gesture! I thought they knew what was coming—maybe not that I'd say all that, but definitely that it would be *me*. Was it really possible they had no idea? What about all those little signs I'd seen? What about the way they kept saying they were going to meet their book boyfriend?

What if I'd gotten it wrong?

The thought was almost too awful to consider. Those weeks, even months, when I thought that we were kind of... playing? And it was all in my head that whole time?

That was ugly. Not gonna lie. If what Wade said was true—and he was a lot of things, but he wasn't the kind of liar who enjoyed twisting people in knots and then stabbing them repeatedly right in the emotions—then I'd basically made it up. Those meaningful moments I thought Art and I might be having, where we were on the edge of acknowledging that both of us knew I'd written a book about how much I loved them? Were about as real as Donald Trump's integrity.

Maggie had been right all along. I'd been deluding myself. And the only reason I could come up with for it was that I thought it was, like, more romantic to keep my romantic feelings a secret than it was to admit to having them.

Which made no sense.

Seriously. How did that make any sense?

What would have happened if, at the very beginning, when I'd signed the contract and known the publication date, I'd come home from work with a bottle of champagne and said, "Hey, Arty. Guess what? I sold a book!" And we'd celebrated. And then I'd said, "Also, FYI, I'm super in love with you."

Right, okay, I couldn't have actually said that. But I could have definitely said the first part and put a pin in the second part. It would have changed everything, to have them with me through the whole process. To be able to talk to them about it, to share the weirdness, the ups and downs, the sense of unreality that came with realizing that I had a book, a real, literal book, coming out.

But I hadn't done that. And it was irretrievable now. For the rest of my life, my first book—which was also, like some sort of dream, my big break-out bestseller—would be associated with this whole mess.

And *I'd* done that. To myself. Because I had this dumb idea that not telling Art the truth for months on end would somehow be romantic. I'd convinced myself they knew, and I remembered that certainty the way you remember believing in Santa or the Tooth Fairy or the monster under your bed; I could still *feel* how real it had been, but with the benefit of time and clarity, that realness crumpled into dust.

They would have been so happy for me. With me. We would have celebrated. As friends, as lovers maybe, those were just details. But they would have been...proud. Of my accomplishments. Of my journey.

That was how we rolled. That was how we cared about each other. We'd shared our joys and fears and triumphs and setbacks. Until I manufactured this huge metanarrative and then used it to justify cutting myself off from my best friend in the world, while somehow also convincing myself that it was the only way for us to ever be together.

It was the kind of thought that a character would have in a movie while walking in the rain, getting splashed by taxis at street corners, losing a shoe, and then, like, having a raven swoop down and take off with their hat. Then you'd just have this character standing there, rain pounding down on them, water streaming down their shirt, one grimy bare foot on tiptoe, taxi flying by and spraying them right in the face with disgusting gutter water. And that's how you'd know they'd reached their lowest point.

I reached my lowest point sitting in my apartment, which I'd made some in-roads to cleaning, or at least the dishes had been washed and the garbage and recycling had been gathered up. I sat on the couch and cried, y'know, more, as if I hadn't cried enough. But it was different. Everything else was stripped away. Now I had nothing but sadness. Which I thought I'd had before, but I guess I hadn't fully. I'd still had anger and defensiveness and bargaining.

Everything else had broken up on the rocks. What I was left with was sadness and responsibility. I had done this. To both of us. And I had no idea if it could be fixed.

Hours on hours, days on days. It felt like an eternity was passing, one drop of water at a time, and all I had to show for it was an endless hole straight into my heart, which never stopped bleeding.

I finally, in a last desperate attempt, sent Art an email. I could have texted, but also, texts are so intrusive, and Art never left email notifications on, so I knew they wouldn't see it until they checked their inbox. It felt like I was respecting their space…while also needing to say one thing.

I'm sorry. I'm so, so sorry.

Yeah, no points for originality, but also, even after I stared at it for literally an entire hour, long enough for my screen to go dark, I couldn't think of anything else to say that wouldn't also be *seeking* something. Forgiveness. Understanding. Comfort. I wrote about six drafts before cutting everything that was in some way demanding a response or excusing myself.

And that's what I was left with.

I'm sorry. I'm so, so sorry.

That was the whole thing right there in black and white.

I hit send and vacuumed all the crumbs out of the couch. Didn't actually vacuum any of the rugs or anything, but the couch looked nicer than it had when we'd hauled it off the street.

Then I checked my email a hundred thousand times just in case Art had said something.

Not that I felt *entitled* to them saying something. I didn't.

But I hoped, oh god, I hoped so much. I held so much hope in my chest that sometimes it felt like it would explode inside me.

Or maybe that was just my heart, beating for Art whether they knew it or not.

A week passed. Another one.

And then.

And then.

It happened.

But not the way—any of the many ways—I'd pictured it. I thought I'd covered every possible scenario, every possible way for Art and I to see each other, from a tearful reunion in a meticulously clean apartment (for some reason in this one I'd also painted the walls and we had a forest green accent wall behind the couch, which, not gonna lie, looked really good), to encountering each other in the produce aisle when we were forty and realizing we'd been meant to be together all along.

It didn't happen that way. It happened this way.

I got a call from Joey Cagliari in the lobby, who said, in a whisper, "I think you should come down here, chief. Art's not looking so great." And then he hung up.

It was mysterious, and surprising, and every nerve in my body lit up like a pleasant electrical current had just whooshed through the room.

Art. In the lobby. Again.

I fumbled pulling shoes onto my bare feet and almost fell into the wall trying to get the door open. The elevator took eleventy-seven years to finally open on my floor. And then, omg, was it always this slow? Seven eternities passed as I rode it to the lobby, eternities in which Art might be crying or having a heart attack or god forbid *leaving*.

They didn't leave. They were there. Pacing in a corner. Well. At the end of the short hallway that had the elevator.

Art was *there*. Right in front of me.

Okay, Art was…not looking great. Could confirm. One of their hands was pressed against their mouth and the other was in a fist at their side.

I'd imagined so many different approaches, so many different first words I could say to them. But when it actually all went down?

"What's wrong? Did something happen to Rolf?"

They looked over. We stood there for a long moment. They'd been crying. I started walking forward without even thinking about it, because Art had been crying, and because this time I didn't need to hesitate, to wonder what was needed. Art had been crying and I was ready to be whatever they needed me to be.

Then we sort of collided and I banged my elbow on a decorative column but whatever, Art wrapped their arms around me and started crying into my chest. And said something that none of my imaginings had ever covered: "It's Ches. He's in the hospital."

Welp. So. This was an actual crisis. Not some made-up thing where I could play the hero. "Oh fuck," I said. Heroically.

Art's head grew heavier on my shoulder and I stood there, holding them, while they shuddered against me.

Chapter Twenty-Five

They didn't want to come up to the apartment. They kept alternately apologizing for being there and reassuring me that they were still mad at me, but in this breathless, teary way that made me want to comfort them.

We were beginning to get weird looks from people waiting for elevators, so finally I said, "Joey's gonna kick us out if we don't go upstairs. C'mon, Arty. We can decide what to do once we're sitting down."

They were still leaning into me. "Okay. But I'm not forgiving you."

"Noted."

And I respected that. I really did. I also relished holding them close as the elevator rose to our floor, and keeping one arm around them as we walked down the hall.

Never have I been so happy that I cleaned in my entire life. I hadn't even cleaned that well, in all honesty, but the place looked a thousand times better than it had when Wade had shown up. At least the dirty dishes were in the actual sink and the living room was perfectly presentable.

Not that Art seemed to notice. They sank down on the couch and grabbed the blanket we kept over the back to hide all the stains, pulling it around their shoulders.

"It's…" I was going to say *roughly a thousand degrees*, but I stopped myself in time. If Art wanted a blanket, they could have a blanket. "What happened?"

The story was halting and a little hard to track at first, but eventually I put the pieces together. Ches had gone back to their parents for a while, and Art had thought he was making good, finally getting his shit together. Well, maybe not all that, but at least for a moment Art had hoped that was what he was doing. (They were editing their own expectations as they spoke, as if they could revise disappointment and turn it into something less damaging.)

And it seemed to work at first. Like it always did. The heaviness in their voice reminded me of every other time Ches had seemed to be doing fine and then badly relapsed into drugs. I'd started out, back in college, pretty sympathetic toward him. Drugs were super hard to quit, right? That's why there were programs and stuff.

Fast-forward through years of watching the roller coaster Art hadn't consented to being on, the way that every upswing renewed hope, and every relapse seemed to wring their heart like a dirty rag, squeezing out every last drop. I wasn't angry at Ches exactly—I still thought he was in a tough position, and drugs *were* hard to quit—but I no longer had the energy for sympathy, because each time it happened Art struggled harder with their own feelings. Even talking about it, they'd say something, decide it was too harsh, mildly defend Ches, then kind of shake their head and try to pick up the thread of the story again.

It was hard to watch. Hard to hear.

And Art's eyes kept leaking tears the whole time, but they brushed the tears away like they barely noticed. "My dad called because Mom, like, couldn't. She just cried and cried in the background." They looked up at me, bloodshot eyes full of something like grief. "Do you think... I was so mad when he started taking these pills and acting like they weren't drugs, but I didn't…do you think he knows I love him? I just keep thinking about how mad I was, I *yelled* at him. I mean, I know things like this have happened before but this feels so much worse and—"

Then I had an armful of Art. This time they were sobbing these big heaving sobs, shoulders shaking, and the sound was terrible, like something was being torn from their throat.

I held them. I couldn't think of anything else to do. I said "It's okay" a couple of times before realizing that was a stupid thing to say since I had no idea if it was actually okay. So I stopped saying anything at all and just slowly rubbed my hand up and down their back as they began to calm down.

"What if he *dies* this time?" they finally whispered, which I knew had been a vague fear since Ches had almost overdosed the summer before Art and I met, but it hadn't happened in years.

Hard to know what to say. Like. The dude *was*, y'know, pretty seriously addicted to drugs in an all-encompassing way, but also, he hadn't died yet? I couldn't really say anything about Ches dying that wouldn't sound dumb. So instead I just kept rubbing their back and went with: "He knows you love him. He always knows you love him."

They started crying again, but this time it was a different sort of crying, and didn't last as long. It didn't feel like I'd said the wrong thing, though. Maybe not the right one—maybe there wasn't a right thing to say—but at least I didn't feel like I'd made things way, way worse.

As much as I dearly wanted to snuggle Art into bed and keep them there until morning, safe and sound, I knew that was probably more for me than them. They needed something else. So I shifted my body a little and surreptitiously slipped my phone off the table so I could scan for rental cars.

The position was awkward and I was using my left hand since my right one was back-rubbing, and when Art moved a little without me realizing they were going to, I accidentally dropped my phone.

Which hit the floor with a thump and didn't just lie there but kind of flopped over and skittered on its PopSocket.

Art pulled away. Their eyes went from the phone, to my hands, to the phone, to my eyes. "Seriously, PK?" It was meant to be their no-BS tone, except it was all tragic and watery, so it just sounded hurt. "My brother might be dying and you're on Twitter or something? What are you doing, talking to your adoring fans?"

Okay, *ouch*, but also. "Finding us a rental car. There's a place on the east side that's open until seven."

They blinked. "We can't. It's. I mean. We have work?"

I shrugged. "So we'll call in family emergency. But you need to be at the hospital and we're going."

"We're spontaneously driving to Pittsburgh?"

I moved to brush the tears from their cheek and then froze, my fingers right there, on Art's skin, like that was a thing I was allowed to do.

They froze.

We froze.

We stared at each other.

"Sorry," I mumbled and pulled quickly away. "Anyway, do you know what hospital?"

"Yeah."

"Okay then. I'll just get it from now through the weekend. We can always rent another one or extend the rental if we need to." Not gonna lie, it was a really truly horrible circumstance and everything, but also, I sounded like a *grown-up* right now, and it felt cool. To be the guy who could arrange for a rental car. Who could handle the details of, okay, a very minor thing like renting the car and getting his best-friend-slash-roommate-slash-unrequited-love to the hospital in a distant city so they could be with their family.

I was that guy in this one moment. And that part of it, the part where I was competent and trustworthy? That felt good.

The rest of it—the part where Ches was in the hospital, the part where Art had fought with him, the part where it almost felt inevitable but I still wasn't ready for it, the part where I couldn't *fix* any of the really important stuff? Yeah. That felt really freaking horrible.

None of this was about how I felt. I opened my arms, ready to be rejected, but Art leaned into them and started to cry again. This time I didn't mess with my phone, I just held them. It's easier to *do* something when someone you love is upset, but I could tell that I should probably just *be*. So that's what I did.

If you'd told me there would ever be a road trip with Arty that I wouldn't enjoy, I would have thought you were nuts. The wrong kind of nuts, not the crazy kind of nuts, because I am not a jerk who mocks mental illness. I'd coasted on that wave of grown-uppedness through renting the car, handing over my credit card and driver's license, taking the keys, and even pulling into traffic. Which was when I realized I had no idea how to get back to the apartment. I knew how to get there on the subway, and I could have walked it just fine, but the mental mapping it takes to walk a city is different than the way you map a place you're driving. I had no feel for one-way streets, or where there was construction taking up an entire lane. I didn't know how to get around the cabs and buses and trucks that seemed to be stopped in the street on every block, and I had no idea how everyone else was driving so freaking fast. How did anyone even *see* all the obstacles that quickly, let alone navigate them?

I pulled over to map the, like, seemingly obvious path home when it occurred to me: why bother? Art didn't have clothes there. I could buy a pair of jeans and a couple of T-shirts if I needed to. And what was I going to do when we got back to the apartment? *Park the car?* The idea was horrifying.

I mapped going to the hospital instead. Six and a half hours. That wasn't bad, was it? So that's…what we did. What I did. Art just went along with it, sitting silently beside me, nodding along when I asked them something.

Anyway, I wouldn't have thought it was possible to be locked up in a car with my best friend for hours and low-key hate it, but I did. Partially because of the way Art twitched and jerked in the light of passing traffic, checking their phone over and over again, the screen reflecting off the dark windshield. And partially because I hadn't eaten and we'd stopped for coffee, so of course I'd gotten a large, but over the course of the first two hours it started sloshing around in my stomach until I felt seasick.

I didn't want to put music on because Spotify doesn't have a playlist for "sorry your brother overdosed on drugs like you always said he would and the last time you talked you fought and he'll probably be okay but then again maybe he won't," so there was just car sounds and darkness and lights. Forever. For hours. Or, okay, for at least another half hour before I gave in, pulled into one of those travel centers as if we needed gas (we didn't), pumped the gas we didn't really need, and went to gather supplies, leaving Art in the car.

I needed the supplies. Much more than the gas. Chips of both potato and corn varieties, candies that could be popped in the mouth (of fruity, chewy, and chocolate varieties), candies in the form of bars, candies with nuts for protein. And five drinks that had caffeine. Five. I mapped again and there were still three hours left, so five drinks seemed perfectly reasonable.

Until I had to pee. A lot. Which, yes, in retrospect, was probably obvious, but by then it was one in the morning and I was running on Skittles, Mountain Dew, and one of those little shot-glass-sized energy drinks they keep right at the checkout counter in twenty-four-hour convenience stores. By the way: worst idea, should not have bought. It felt like my toes had each individually gotten super high and my blood cells were doing some kind of jig.

That's the kind of thing I would have said to Art, but when I opened my mouth to do so I remembered where we were going and why so I said nothing.

And also I remembered they were pissed at me and didn't want to remind them that I wasn't, in fact, a hero taking care of all the messed up things in the world, but that I was kind of also the cause of some of the messed up things in the world. I know this doesn't reflect well on me or whatever? But it's what I thought. Maybe it was the caffeine talking. Or maybe it was just me.

Probably Art's perfect book boyfriend would never have thoughts like that, but clearly I was really far from being anyone's perfect book boyfriend.

Then we hit roadwork. A road project. Some intense, detour-having, single-lane-driving works project, that I thought I could avoid by going around, except somehow I lost my sense of direction and it was so dark and also did I mention I hadn't slept and was high on caffeine and sugar? I finally had to pull over on a road that basically looked like it was a one-way trip to the suburbs. Plugged my dying phone into a charger cable, mapped our course again (I'd closed the map when it kept shouting at me to go back to the detour), finally got us back on track.

But the whole fiasco had blown out the very last remnants of any feelings of adultyness I'd clung to until then. Now I was just a supremely dumb twenty-six-year-old who impulse-rented a car, impulse-avoided a treacherous parking job, and impulse-drove through all of New Jersey and a lot of Pennsylvania to get to Pittsburgh at five a.m. with nowhere to go and no idea what to do next.

So, you know, I drove us to the hospital, where I finally stopped the car and sat there, tingling unpleasantly, my body still feeling the phantom vibrations of the road and jittering from the terrible food choices I'd made. And Art? Was asleep beside me, practically wedged against the door, hoodie pulled around their curved shoulders, face slack. They looked exhausted. I wished I could do something for them, but aside from trying not to make any noise so they could sleep, I couldn't think of anything.

And that's what we did until the sun came up. I sat there in a tense sort of guard duty, looking at stuff on my phone and sometimes nodding off until I jerked awake, while Art slept. I was just beginning to contemplate peeing into one of my empty bottles when they started to stir. Which was better than them waking up *as* I was peeing into a bottle, but I didn't think they'd rested nearly long enough.

I didn't have to propose they sleep more. I could tell they weren't going to by the set expression on their face.

"Thanks for driving."

So awkward. It wasn't like I'd done it with pure motives. "Anytime. I mean. Obviously not like I want this to happen anytime. Just that if you need me—I mean—if you need anything—anytime—" I swallowed. "Sorry. Should we go inside?"

They nodded. Which, thank god, because the peeing thing was getting urgent.

I found a bathroom. They went up to a desk-type thing. When I came out they were standing there, very still, waiting for me. Something about Art and stillness just seemed wrong. They weren't animated, the way they should have been, the way they always had been. Art sitting in class in college was this, like, kaleidoscope of fidgeting and shifting and fingers picking at cuticles and playing with their hair. Waiting for their nails to dry they'd be fingertip-tapping the surface of a book, or they'd have their legs propped up and their feet would be moving as if they were in silent conversation, pivoting at the ankle toward each other, then away again.

Not now. Now they just stood there, a pillar, attracting my attention because of how out of place it was to see someone who barely seemed to be breathing.

"We can go to the waiting area." They didn't move.

"Okay." I also didn't move.

"Maybe I shouldn't have come. I didn't think. Maybe… maybe I should have stayed home. This wasn't… I don't know."

My legs were still tingling from all the driving, but in that moment I would have gotten right back in the car and headed east if Art said we needed to do that. It was this frozen in time water droplet, like I knew it was going to fall, but I didn't know where it would land.

"No. No, we came all this way, all night, we should at least…we should at least try…"

Not gonna lie, shit was fraught, but words like "home" and "we" in this context weren't the worst thing to hear. "We'll do whatever you need us to do," I said, both because I meant it, and also because I couldn't make a decision about this. It wasn't my place, even if I did still have the grown-uppedness superhero glow, which I didn't.

They stood there; the only thing moving was their eyelashes as they blinked. Then they took a deep breath. "I guess it doesn't hurt to see my parents."

Which was about the least accurate statement ever. And

I didn't *dislike* Art's parents, but when it came to Ches, they had not made things easy for Art. If Art suggested that Ches didn't actually want to quit drugs, their parents would accuse them of being disloyal, as if stating the truth was a bridge too far over into realityland, where Ches would never get an office job and pay his taxes and adopt a three-legged Chihuahua he'd call Buddy and take with him everywhere.

My parents hadn't hurt me much, not even unintentionally. But Art's? Had made them bleed. Metaphorically. Not physically. Though I think that just messed Art up even more. You shouldn't hit your kids, for sure, but also you shouldn't treat them like they're only an afterthought, in second place forever to someone (or something) else. Those kinds of scars go deep.

I didn't know what to expect as we went to…wherever we were going. Would it be one of those massive waiting rooms like you see on TV? Would it just be an alcove on a busy ward? But it turned out the hospital wasn't that busy at this time of morning and the waiting area was just a smallish room with some chairs and a TV silently showing *Family Feud*.

And Art's mom in a chair. Just as still as Art was. Staring into space. She looked about twenty years older than she'd been at our graduation and I felt a rush of sympathy for her, even though I was still guarded on Art's behalf. What a horrible thing, fearing your son is dead, not totally sure he won't be dead soon.

Then she looked up and saw us there. It took a full ten seconds for her to click that Art was Art. They'd always played it a little masc with their folks—not like Wade's full-on performance of someone he wasn't, more like a low-key camouflage for who they were. But we hadn't stopped at the apartment and Art was wearing skinny jeans, a spaghetti strap top with a cute flowy shirt over it, and rainbow barrettes in their hair. They looked adorable. They looked *normal*.

And Art's mom, sounding gravelly and hoarse, stood and said, "What are you doing here?"

So yeah. That's about where we landed.

Chapter Twenty-Six

They did not wilt. They did not move. "I wanted to see if Ches was okay."

"They think...they think he will be. He took all of Rolf's medication. At the same time. Thank god it's nothing too toxic. But they're holding him because he's a 'danger to himself or others.'" Her tone made it clear she was quoting. "Though I don't know about that."

"He...did this on purpose?"

One of her eyelids twitched. "You know your brother. Can't live without a little excitement."

I almost opened my mouth. Almost.

Art's face was very frozen. "But the people here think he was trying to..." Their voice faded. They gave up. I watched it happen, the way I'd seen it happen over the years when they talked to their parents, like they were deciding that whatever the conversation was (Ches, a lot of the time, but not always), it wasn't worth getting into a debate. "Can I see him?"

"They said no one could see him, not now. They pumped his stomach and said he'll be all right, but then this fuss about the pills happened and now they tell me I have to wait until the psychiatrists get to him. It's absurd, but there you are. They're probably just trying to keep him long enough to charge for another day."

"But he's okay? I mean. In terms of the pills?"

She waved a hand, and even though the gesture was supposed to look casual, something about her exhaustion sent a totally different message. They'd been here before. All of them. And, not to shit on Ches, but they'd probably be here again. "Your brother will be *fine*. One thing I know about Chester is he's always fine in the end." Her eyes drifted, like she was seeing something other than this hospital room, like she was maybe seeing a time when Ches really *was* fine. Then she blinked a few times and settled her gaze on Art. "You shouldn't have come all this way, there was no need."

Art let out a shaky laugh. "I thought he was dying."

"It was just your brother being ridiculous, as usual."

"Where's Dad?"

This time she went slightly stiff. "Gone home. Said he needed to sleep."

Which seemed fair to me, but Art clearly understood the subtext better than I did. "Oh. All right. Well."

Then we all stood there for a long moment. I couldn't decide if this was when I was supposed to politely excuse myself to get coffee or something, but I instinctively didn't want to leave Art, so instead I just took a step closer to them and barely restrained myself from reaching for their hand.

"You could go by the house and see him if you like," she said unencouragingly.

"Maybe," they replied, equally noncommittal.

Which was when I figured out we weren't going to be seeing Ches.

Then Art and their mom hugged like relatives who didn't know each other that well and we walked out of the room, down the hall, got in the elevator, and stood there until it was time to get out of the elevator. Things continued in that vein until we were back in the rental car. Since I didn't know where we were going I put the keys in the ignition and stopped short of starting it.

Cue: silence. More silence. This one way less awkward. At least until I said, "So that was anticlimactic." Which upon point-two seconds of reflection I realized was definitely not the right thing to say.

Before I could take it back, Art laughed. "It really was. This is so Ches. Rolf *needs* those meds. And my parents will probably forget all about it." They glanced at me. "Tell me the truth: do you think he was actually trying to kill himself?"

"Uhhhh. I don't know. Maybe? But why didn't he take literally anything else?"

"Most of that stuff is in my parents' bathroom and I know they had a locking medicine cabinet installed a few years ago after a bad post-rehab relapse. So those could have been the only meds he had access to?"

I shrugged. "Maybe. But he could have gone to the store. I know you can reliably OD on, like, over the counter stuff, right? If you wanted to."

"And I guess if he was going out he could have just gotten real drugs…"

I couldn't tell what we were rooting for. A blatant suicide attempt would obviously be the worst, right? But, like…taking all the dog's medicines seemed pretty messed up regardless of intent. Except for how, y'know, Ches was still super not-dead, a thing I was strongly in favor of.

"The worst part, and I know this makes me a monster—"

I bit my tongue to keep from automatically arguing the point.

"—but for a second I almost kind of was okay with him dying? Then I realized how horrible that would be, how much I would miss him, and I felt really bad about it. But if it wasn't for Ches I'd probably never really have to talk to my folks, and that would be a relief." They sighed. "I guess I can do that anyway. I don't know. God, I'm so tired."

"Me too. Um. Sorry about saying it was anticlimactic."

"No, you're right. It was. I thought… I don't know what I thought. I thought something would have changed? But nothing has. And we came all this way." They leaned their head back. "You drove all night, PK. Sorry. Thank you. I mean. Not that it. Like, I'm not *not* still mad at you for all the other things, but. Yeah. Thank you."

I looked over, but Art was staring out the windshield at the hood of the car parked in front of our spot, on which a bird was sitting to wash its feathers. It was strangely soothing to watch, but I was more concerned about Art, whose eyes had filled with tears after they stopped speaking.

"I'm so happy he's not dead," they whispered, then leaned forward into their hands and started crying.

Not forgiven: check. Still the guy sitting here. "Me too." I hesitated before shifting over as well as I could and scooping them into a hug. We sat that way until they stopped crying but kept leaning on me and I risked asking, "Do you want to go to the house? See your dad?"

"No. They don't want me here. I guess we should just go home."

That word again.

"Okay." I started the car, backed out of the space, and got us back on the road.

Two hours later I half-deliriously pulled into the lot of a cheap-ish motel and begged for a room. It was way before check-in. It was way before even early check-in. It was almost check-out, actually.

Art took over negotiations and sweetly explained the situation. About five minutes later we were back on the road, this time with them in the driver's seat. I guess trying to check into a motel at like eight a.m. is not the best time unless you want to pay a bunch of money. Or maybe shop around. I was still contemplating whether we should have looked for another place when I fell asleep.

I woke up sometime later to the welcome sound of Art singing with the stereo. I snuggled into my hoodie, which I'd balled up against the car door, and went back to sleep.

I was so disoriented the next time I woke up that I actually thought we were back in the apartment and Art was humming along to Spotify as they washed dishes. It was such a good dream, or fantasy, or whatever it was. And then I realized I was drooling and that's when I opened my eyes to see the window beside my face, my reflection too bright, making me wince.

"Where are we?" I asked, but my voice was so low I barely heard it myself, mouth dry like I hadn't had a sip of water in months.

Which was when I heard Art speak, but not to me.

"Okay, good, at least you're… No, I can't. PK is sleeping. Well, he drove all night so I could see you so… Yeah, but Mom said… Okay. It's fine. No, I believe you, Ches, okay? All right… No, it's good. I'm tired, that's all it is… Fine. Yeah… Okay, I will… Yeah. Love you too. Bye." They sighed and fell silent.

I probably should have pretended I was still asleep, but I wanted them to know they weren't alone. I licked my lips and swallowed a few times to make sure this time I could actually make sounds. "You all right?"

"Oh. Hey. I should be asking you that." But they didn't look over, and when I did I saw tears on their cheeks.

"I'm good. I had a nap and everything." I tried to smile,

but despite the nap, my brain was still pretty scrambled and the smile didn't totally come off. "Ches is up and about?"

That same sigh again. "They're sending him home. I guess he charmed whoever talked to him and since the rest of the medicine in the house is locked up they decided he's safe? I don't know. He said it wasn't like he was trying to kill himself, he just thought the pills would help him sleep."

"Uh. All the pills?"

"Right? Like he thought that the exact human dose was exactly the number and combination of pills that happened to be in Rolf's supply? And people believe him? It makes no sense."

"So...we don't believe him, right?" I didn't want to leap to any conclusions.

"I'm not sure. I mean..." They trailed off and yeah, like, none of my ideas about what happened were great either. "I don't know. I don't *think* he was, like, for real trying to die. Or he would have done a better job. But on the other hand, he definitely wouldn't have taken a bunch of pills if he wasn't... pretty messed up."

"Yeah. Do you think he'll get...help for that?"

"Honestly I have no idea. Today he swears he will. But tomorrow? He'll probably be explaining why the edibles he's got aren't *really* drugs. I don't know. I just. I'm sorry we drove all that way for nothing."

"It wasn't for nothing, Arty."

"It really was. Unless you count talking to my mom, but it definitely wasn't worth going all that way for *that*."

"No, I mean." But I wasn't sure exactly sure what I meant except that I didn't feel like it had been a wasted trip.

"We haven't slept. We haven't eaten a single thing that wasn't created in a factory. We've wasted a ton of money."

"Yeah, but Ches was in the hospital. It's not like you could have slept anyway. And we would have ended up eating a bunch of like potato chips and ice cream."

"But for way less money."

I shook my head. "If we hadn't come, we'd probably wish we had. Like. We would have been sitting there all night thinking we should have gotten a car and started driving. I don't think there's a…correct way to respond to something like this. You know?"

They didn't speak immediately. The silence went on long enough for me to stop looking at them and waiting for a response. I shifted around in my seat, trying to get comfortable with a numb butt and pins and needles in one of my legs. Highway signs said we were in New Jersey, which meant we were almost home. Ish.

Home? Was it *our* home? Or just mine?

"I guess you're right."

It took me a long moment to remember what I'd even been right about. "It doesn't feel like it was a waste of money. And now you've talked to Ches, so that's good."

"He did sound kind of…impressed that we'd driven all that way. He said to thank you." They glanced my way. "Thank you, PK."

"Of course. Like. If you ever need anything. I mean that."

"I know you do. That's what makes it so much harder."

Gulp. "It seems like…it should be easier?"

Another long sigh. Had they always had a long sigh? Maybe. But not quite like this. Sighing can be punctuation to a sentence, the verbal version of that ellipsis-as-complete-message people do to indicate they have thoughts but aren't telling you what they are. But a sigh can also be a sentence, or no, like where someone in a novel wants to make a point about something and an entire chapter is just one sentence long? That's what Art's sigh was. A complete unit of thought. A conflict without resolution, presented in full.

A conflict I didn't totally understand, but thought I could begin to guess at now. "I'm really sorry about what I did. It…was a thing that I thought made sense. At the time. Based on a lot of…wishful thinking. Which isn't a defense, at all, please don't think I'm trying to justify it, but just…it wasn't heartless. It was…it was heart-full. Full of heart. I tried to do a thing that was all heart and I screwed it up really badly and I'm sorry. The word 'sorry' doesn't even scratch the surface of how sorry I am."

This time the wait for a reply was longer and I stared out the window at all the passing streets and houses and shopping centers. I vowed not to say anything else. I vowed not to dump all the things in my head onto Art's lap as if they owed me the space to make a case for what was actually, in hindsight, an indefensible thing.

I sat there next to them and every time I was tempted to say just one more thing I thought about what Wade had said, about how Art had gone into work after the reading, how they'd had to face all of those people who'd seen what I did, how they'd had to deal with the fallout in a way that I hadn't. And picturing that, the courage it would have taken to push open the door every day into a place where I'd shone an un-wanted spotlight on them in front of a bunch of strangers and customers and coworkers, made me bite my tongue.

After what felt like forever, Art spoke. It wasn't any of the things I thought they might say.

"You know how I have strong ethical objections to *The Bachelor* because it glorifies toxic heteronormativity?"

I parsed the question with care. "… Yes?"

"Let's go home and watch *The Bachelor* until our eyes bleed."

"Sounds good." I went on my phone and mapped the drive.

We'd get back to the city with enough time to return the car early, but we technically had it until Monday. And Art was driving. They were way less grumpyanxious about parking. Armed with a rough timeline with relatively few variables, I ordered groceries to be delivered later in the evening and made sure *The Bachelor* was on a streaming service we could access.

We stopped for gas, caffeine, and snacks one last time. And then we went home.

Chapter Twenty-Seven

Everything was awkward. So awkward. Art went to the bathroom while I brought in the groceries (turned out we ran into the guy as we were just coming up the block, so close shave there). Then they slowly sat down on the couch and didn't really move after that? I guess they were being a guest, which I wanted to respect, if that's what they wanted, but also I couldn't figure out how to say "So I support if *you* don't feel at home here right now, but you should know that *I* feel like you're at home here, but no pressure, but don't be stiff unless you need to be, but I don't know why you would need to be because this is your home, but no pressure!"

Basically we both pretended we didn't notice how terrible it was suddenly to occupy the same space, even though by the end of the car ride I thought we'd regained our old familiar comfort with each other. All that was gone. As if it had never existed. When in fact we'd lived together happily for almost a year.

Then *I* went pee and almost died because the bathroom had descended to pre-Art levels of, um, yuck. And I almost blacked out in shame and horror but fortunately (unfortunately?) I stayed conscious. I'd gotten my butt in gear for the rest of the apartment, started doing the dishes at night, even sweeping (except for under the couch). But I hadn't tackled the bathroom.

I did now. I bleached and scrubbed in a red-faced shame spiral, cursing myself for not getting to the bathroom before Art had. I shoved clothes into the hamper and swept and wiped down the toilet seat and the mirror (not in that order) and went on Amazon and ordered a new shower curtain, which okay, was a little late, but it would be there soon.

And Art would be back, right? They'd see the new, cute, sea creature themed and very much not mildew-stained shower curtain. When it arrived. In two days. I would hang it immediately, I swore to myself.

I washed up and went back out to the living room, where the first episode of *The Bachelor* was paused at the opening credits with the show title frozen on-screen.

"Did you just...clean the bathroom?" They craned their neck in my direction like it wasn't worth turning the rest of their body. Like I might disappoint them.

"Um. I mean." What was I supposed to say to that? "I failed cleaning the bathroom last time. This time I wanted to...make sure I did it."

"I wasn't about to. I don't live here anymore."

The words twisted around my heart like a boa constrictor, squeezing it so tightly I could hardly breathe.

"Right now, anyway," they added, and looked back at the TV.

While I stood there, chest aching, taking shallow breaths. "I didn't... I knew you weren't... I just wanted it to be clean for you." *Don't cry, don't be a baby, you're just tired, and probably hungry, do not cry.*

"I don't mind." They didn't look over. Or clarify. Did they mean they didn't mind it being dirty? They didn't mind me cleaning it? They didn't mind me thinking about it like they'd someday be in the bathroom again, and whenever that was, I wanted it to be clean for them? I had no idea. And I couldn't ask.

I escaped to the kitchen and started a pot of water boiling so I could make pasta. Pasta-time was enough for me to get myself together. When I brought out two bowls (with fresh parmesan on top and everything), Art was still sitting in the same spot.

They pressed play. We ate. *The Bachelor* was the exact perfect kind of terrible. And that's where we stayed for the entire first season. Then we got ice cream and started season two.

I don't know when I fell asleep, but I woke up with my face pressed against their arm and pretended I was still sleeping long enough to memorize the moment, in a totally non-creepy way. I just wanted to really dig that memory into my brain in case it never happened again because *I don't live here anymore* had cut me open and *right now, anyway* was only a Band-Aid over the wound. It still bled. It hadn't even begun to heal.

Somewhere in my pretending, the sleep became more than a doze, more than the hard-won naps in the car, but real, deep sleep. And in it I dreamed that we were in my childhood bedroom, that we were curled up together on my bed and I was brushing my fingers through Art's hair, but because it was a dream, I could feel that sensation on my own scalp. I was talking quietly in Art's voice, but I didn't know what I was saying, as if it was all through layers of cotton and echoes, like the old video tapes my parents have where they recorded over things they no longer needed but the quality gets sandy because the old stuff is still there underneath.

I just kept talking in Art's voice, my fingers their fingers, their hair my hair, and then, eventually, everything went quiet and soft and warm and the dream faded or ended or maybe just kept going into darkness but I swore I could still feel them at the edges of all of my limbs, that we could still feel each other.

★ ★ ★

Whew, I'd had some weird-ass dreams. I didn't remember all of them, not after that first one, but when I finally figured out I was really awake this time, I had the distinct impression I had been a lizard roughly five seconds ago.

I extracted myself from beneath my own duvet, now draped over me on the couch. Art was nowhere to be seen and my heart almost stopped before I thought to check their bedroom. The junk room. The junk room that had been their bedroom and then morphed back into being the junk room but with more Art.

They were there. Asleep on their bed. Okay. No problem. Not dying of loneliness.

Yet.

I took a shower, first off, and got into clean clothes. It was five thirteen a.m. and I doubted I was up for the day, but since I'd really drilled some holes into my sleep cycle over the last forty-eight hours, I figured I'd take advantage of the moment and make coffee.

It's always a little surreal being up that early if you aren't used to it, and I wasn't. It felt like stolen time, like I was a thief who'd snuck into a morning that wasn't rightly mine, but now I was inhabiting it with kettle noises and the crinkling of the French roast bag as I spooned coffee grounds into the coffee pot.

I grabbed my laptop and set it up in the kitchen while waiting for the coffee to brew. I didn't have a solid book pitch in mind, and I'd ignored Maggie bugging me for one, but I thought maybe I could write out something that might trigger an actual idea. So I started writing about the drive, about being up all night, about the way the road signs blur and the lights flicker. About how if you drive long enough your body becomes so attuned to the rumble of the road beneath you that your brain can't let go of it at first. The way it keeps jolting you as if you've fallen asleep, pinging your eyes to flick to the road and search for danger even when you're standing at a counter in a mini-mart somewhere in Pennsylvania, even when you're snuggled under your own duvet on your own couch in your own apartment.

Also we had to return the damn car. I sent myself an email and went back to what I was writing.

I played with ideas, characters, settings, just letting it all come tumbling out of my imagination until I unearthed some elements I liked. What if the person driving was going to a beloved grandparent instead of a brother? Or maybe not quite a grandparent—maybe a grandparent-like figure with a more complicated backstory? Was that too much? Make it a grandparent. But one the main character has conflict with, maybe is estranged from. Why are they driving through the night to get there? What are they thinking about on the way? Are they reflecting on the relationship or are they drowning everything out with loud music or podcasts with hundreds of episodes?

The coffee was decidedly cool by the time I ran out of words, and I found I didn't want it anymore. All I wanted was to fall into my bed (and plug in my laptop). But I had a pitch for Maggie, or at least the start of one. It'd be about memory and time and the complexity of caring about people, the impossibility of meeting them where they are when neither of you fully trust that you can share yourself with the other.

Maybe it'd be too convoluted. It was almost certainly not commercial enough. But at least I could rest knowing I'd done something with my stolen morning.

Then I turned toward the doorway and Art was standing there. Leaning against the wall. Watching me.

"Hey," I said, probably not exactly hiding my shock to find them in the kitchen.

"Hey."

"I was…" Why did I feel like I had to justify my presence there? Or justify my awakeness? Or just justify myself in some nebulous probably-related-to-having-been-crummy-to-them way.

"Working?" they suggested.

"No. Well. Actually kind of? Just playing with some new ideas."

"For your next book."

I swallowed. "I should have told you. Which Maggie definitely said. Over and over again."

"I get why you didn't."

Which was very much not the response I'd expected. "Um. You do? Because sometimes *I* don't know why I didn't tell you."

They offered me a look that managed to be annoyed and affectionate simultaneously. "Really, PK?"

"Really! I mean." I couldn't think of how to explain what I meant. "Okay, I know why I thought I wasn't telling you."

"Which was…?"

"I thought you knew the answer to that already."

"I have guesses. But you should probably tell me."

I wanted to whine a little at that even though I technically agreed. "It seemed like it would complicate everything. And maybe screw everything up."

"How? We've been friends for years. I don't understand how you could…" Their gaze landed on the floor and roamed around there, making me happy I'd swept. "Just, I thought we trusted each other? And then you kept this seriously massive secret from me. For *years*."

"It wasn't years! The book thing happened super fast, and it was totally Maggie's fault, because I let her read it and then she showed it to Adams and the team loved it and it was really less than a year because obviously it's not like I've been living a double life our whole friendship and you know, they didn't even believe I'd written it because they apparently didn't think I have the emotional capacity to write a book with feelings and actually it's kind of messed up that no one thinks I have feelings! I have feelings. I have all kinds of feelings, and it kind of hurts me *in my feelings* that everyone acts like I'm this shallow dimwit caveman."

"I don't think of you as a shallow dimwit caveman, PK. I think of you as someone with feelings who isn't comfortable with them. Which I think you might have proven through this whole fiasco." They slowly brought their eyes level with mine. "And that's not the secret I meant."

Welp. That shut me up. I opened my mouth, realized it was too dry to speak, closed it again.

"It was a long time. It must have been. That's...how you wrote it."

"Um. It's um... I mean...fiction?"

Their right eyebrow twitched. "Okay. So the thing where the main character lives in an apartment his parents gave him is fiction?"

"They didn't give it to him! He pays rent!"

"And the part where his college roommate shows up after leaving their girlfriend and moves in?"

"Okay, see, one, you weren't even using they/them back then, two, you left your boyfriend not your girlfriend, and three, it's a hot summer day in the book, not a rainy night! So it's *totally* different." I finished with the biggest verbal flourish I could manage, practically a *so there!*

"Mm-hmm," Art said, looking thoroughly unimpressed. "You changed just enough to make sure even random chance wouldn't coincidentally align real-life-me with your fictional love interest. You know that's completely impossible, right? If you'd tossed dice to pick personal traits, that character would have more in common with me than they do right now."

"Um."

"Because you had to work really hard to make us different."

"Um." That didn't sound quite right, did it?

"A thing you wouldn't have had to do unless there was a reason for it."

"I don't..." I made my voice dignified. "...think I grant your premise."

"PK." Something in their voice made me deflate. "Tell me the truth."

How could I? How could I tell them something I'd never told them in all the years since that drunken night when we kissed? I swallowed my fear and leaned back against the counter as if it could hold me up. "That night we kissed. Do you remember?"

They blinked. And blinked. And blinked again.

"It was finals and we'd gone to a dumb hall party but they had a lot of beer and we drank way too much. I'm sure you don't remember. It was just one dumb night—"

"Don't say that," they said sharply.

I froze.

"It wasn't a dumb night. And I wasn't as drunk as you thought I was. Of course I remember that night, you—you—" They broke off like they couldn't figure out what I was. "Of course I couldn't forget the night we kissed! I thought about it for weeks after that, but I figured you were probably horrified, or at least you never brought it up—"

"I couldn't! You acted like you forgot!"

"What else could I have done? Told you I waited for you to come back to bed after you were sick but I fell asleep accidentally and then I was too embarrassed to say anything?"

I just stared at them numbly. "Wait. You. You mean."

"We are both *jackasses*." They injected the word with as much venom as possible. "As Wade has mentioned to me no fewer than a dozen times."

"Yeah, about that, how could you talk to *Wade* about us? About me?"

"I didn't do it for fun!" They frowned. "But after you did the whole ridiculous thing you did I was so upset and Wade and Ray were so nice about it and I couldn't help telling them how completely messed up it all was, and how freaking angry I was at you, for screwing literally everything up. And lying to me. Forever."

"Hey, you can't blame me for lying if you were also lying!"

"I didn't write a book!"

"I didn't *lie* about that! I mean. Not exactly!"

"If you're about to tell me that secretly publishing a book that was secretly about how you secretly wanted to ask me out is somehow a defensible *untruth*, I'd really like to hear that argument, PK, because that's a whole lot of BS."

"I—I mean—" My mind latched on to the only thing it could. "I don't want to *ask you out*, I'm in love with you! Obviously! Didn't you even read the stupid book?"

"How dare you call it a stupid book!"

"I wrote it! I can call it whatever I want!"

All of a sudden we both realized we were like…having a ludicrous fight over insulting a book. And we stopped. Art sagged back against the wall. I swallowed and jumped up to sit on the counter beside my lukewarm press of coffee.

"Sorry," I mumbled.

"For what?"

"Everything." I was so tired I wanted to curl up like a cat right there where I was sitting. "I'm sorry about everything. All the things. If I'd known, if I'd thought for a second that you hadn't been grossed out by kissing me, I would have done something. Said something. Arty, I..." All the bricks and mortar I'd built up around my feelings seemed like a tower between us. I couldn't say—couldn't even figure out what I wanted to say.

Except I could see them standing there looking at me like they expected me to let them down. That guarded expression they wore when Ches had showed up, or when we'd gone looking for their mom in the hospital. That expression that said, *Go ahead and crush me again, I can take it.*

I didn't want to crush them. I wanted to stand with them for the rest of time. I hopped down and took a deep breath to gather myself. "I fucked up a lot of stuff. I get that. If I could do it all over again, I would do it so, so differently. I would do the thing I wanted to do back then and tell you how much I loved kissing you, how I'd wanted to keep doing it but you were so drunk it would be yucky."

"Also you were puking quite a lot."

"And there was that, yeah, true. I wanted to say something the next day but you acted like it was this huge mistake and I believed you."

"That was the point. You were supposed to believe me."

"But why? Why did we do this?" And how had I been so wrong about them knowing about *Peak Romance* but completely miss that they...what? They also had feelings for me? And had for years?

"Because we were both afraid. I get that part. But I figured...you know." They tucked their hair behind their ear. "That if it was meant to be then we'd eventually...get around to it. And then Roman happened and I thought maybe I'd been wrong because that seemed so good."

"Until you dumped him because he sucked so much."

"He *was* good at sucking," they mused.

My jaw snapped shut and I almost bit off the tip of my tongue.

They finally, finally smiled. "Kidding. Well, not really. But Roman's oral skills aside, then I came to stay with you and it was like, y'know, this was what I'd been waiting for. This was what would make it all make sense."

I just stared at them.

"And then we went to your folks' place for Christmas and I thought you were going to say something so I didn't, but then you didn't, so I thought I should, but what came out was always about Roman, so then I thought maybe I wasn't over him yet and I didn't want to start anything with you until I was—"

I don't know what came over me. I hopped down from the counter, crossed the kitchen, and took them in my arms, pulling them against me, kissing not their lips like a perfect movie moment, but this sort of jaw-slash-ear-slash-hairline area, my lips kind of dryly brushing across their skin, then hair, and managing only to be weird instead of romantic.

Art's arms came around me and we clung on to each other for a long moment.

"I'm sorry," I said again. "I should have told you. All of it."

"You should have told me about the book. You should definitely never ever have told me about the other thing in the middle of a reading in front of everyone I know."

I winced. "I know that now. I know how obvious it is. But at the time? I thought it would be sweet. I thought you knew already that I'd written it for you so it would just be this sort of...public declaration of something we already shared."

"Except we didn't share it. As evidenced by the lack of sharing."

"I thought we were *secretly* sharing it," I said. Meekly.

They thumped their head on my shoulder a few times before pulling away, backing up, resuming their wall stance.

While I stood there, much closer now, not moving at all. I had the distinct sensation they were sizing me up, evaluating me, trying to decide if I was worth it.

"I cleaned the bathroom," I said.

The barest hint of amusement shifted in their eyes. "I saw."

"Just, you know, I know that previously I was not the best at bathroom cleaning, but I've turned over a new leaf."

"Right when I happened to stop by? Funny timing."

"Aren't you…aren't you moving back in? I mean. Just. You called it 'home' last night. Or yesterday. Or whenever that was. Is it not…your home anymore?"

Another long moment of uncomfortable analysis, like a specimen being studied by a scientist. "I need some space."

"Okay." Because what else could I say? "Do you know how much?"

"No. Not right now. But I can say… I can say I care about you. Even though I hate what you did."

"Okay. That…yeah. I'm really, truly sorry. I've thought about it so many times, all the ways right up until the end I could have changed things. But I didn't."

"No. You didn't."

"So. All right then. Um. Okay." I swallowed, trying to be brave. "So I guess then just keep in touch? If you want to."

"I'm only going to Wade and Ray's, I'm not leaving the country."

"I know. It's good. At least, I'm glad you'll be close. And I hope you can…" Forgiveness seemed like an awful lot to ask. "I guess I hope you can kind of understand even if you can't forgive me. Because I never meant to hurt you. I have never meant to hurt you. Which isn't to say I'm not responsible for hurting you, I am, and I get that. I'm so sorry, Arty. I love you. I also hate what I did."

They nodded. "I should go."

No! You should stay! Stay forever!

I nodded but couldn't voice a word of support. It was almost beyond my abilities to not-say all the things I wanted to say.

"Well. I guess that means I'll just...go now."

"I love you," I said, not desperately, not like I was waiting for a response, not like I was begging them to stay. "That's what I should have said years ago. That's what I should have told you when you showed up here after Roman, like not that night, but at some point after it. Whatever else you think about me, just know I really love you."

They nodded, and it seemed like they were on the verge of saying something, then didn't.

And that was it. They backed out of the kitchen, unlocked all the locks, and went out the door.

Chapter Twenty-Eight

An agony of time passed. An unholy agony of minutes and hours and days and weeks and—

Okay, it was less than a week. But it passed *slowly*. Aching, dragging, endless hours in which I did not totally obsess about whether I'd ever see Art again (which was kind of silly, but every time I told myself it was silly I also remembered that I'd let them down in a different but related way to how Ches had always let them down and found myself rooting for them to never speak to me again like we were in one of those episodes of *The Bachelor* where you're desperate to see the bachelor pick the really cool woman but he inevitably picks someone the editors didn't even show being interesting).

Basically I had become the one the bachelor/ette *might* pick, but not the awesome one you really want them/him/her to pick.

Maggie eventually banned me from talking to her about it. She did volunteer Puzo, though, as she was leaving for a lunch meeting. I was so desperate that I sat there in Maggie's office and chatted to the bird for most of an hour. It was better than doing nothing. And the way Puzo tilted his head to the side really made me feel like he was listening to me.

Then, on a Monday, as I was getting ready to leave, I heard voices at the end of the hall. Voices I knew. Not just work voices, though Adams's low, no-nonsense school matron voice came through. But also?

Also Art's.

Art's voice.

In my building.

"I agree, but I would say that it was an authorial choice to diverge from what was expected in order to surprise the reader," Art was saying.

Adams laughed. "You call it 'authorial choice' but I suspect it was more down to authorial drunkenness."

The welcome sound of Art's laughter. "Are you saying that based on insider knowledge or assumption?"

"Let's just call it editor's intuition. You'll find Harrington in the far corner under the stairs."

Common misconception: I was under part of the roof, not a set of stairs. Not that it mattered. Probably not the time to—

"Actually it's the roof!" I called. Then, to Art, who was the only one paying attention, I added, "Maybe it's the eaves? I'm not sure. There's this dormer situation on this side of the building, the closets in all the offices are those slope-ceilinged things you can't get good shelving for. Um. So yeah. Now you…know about the architecture of this side of this floor of this building."

They lifted the bag they were holding. "I brought you lunch. Since you bring me food sometimes."

I had no idea what to say to that. They needed to think. They left. They didn't call or text or make any contact. And then they showed up with lunch.

"This might have been a bad idea. I hadn't taken into consideration the difference in workplaces and norms. I lucked out with Adams showing up when I was standing downstairs wondering how I'd find you." They glanced around. "This is your office, huh?"

The strangeness of it almost got the better of me, but I managed to say, "Yeah, totally," and do a swooping arm motion that knocked my wireless mouse to the floor.

I picked it up, dusted it, and settled it where I didn't think it could be easily knocked off again. "Um. Did you…want to eat?"

They shook their head. "I have to go. To work. Now-ish. But anyway, here's your half."

We somewhat awkwardly sorted out the selection of grocery store takeaway (cashew chicken for me, some kind of Asian fusion salad for Art, some eggrolls we split, and two kombuchas). Then we somewhat awkwardly said goodbye.

I realized as they rounded the far corner that I should have walked them out. Like a gentleman. But by the time I fast-walked down the hall, I'd lost them and had no idea if they were still wandering the building. They were probably fine. I mean. Find elevator, go to ground floor, right? Art could navigate an office building.

Still, it would have been nice to walk them down. Chivalrous. Or just. I mean. More time together.

I ate slowly, trying to understand what had just happened. But truthfully I had no idea.

Later that night they sent me a gif of an actor-type (or maybe a reality-show type?) pulling her hair out. *Customers driving me over the edge.*

Which. Was. Yeah. A text. That they would have sent me before. In the Before Times. Before I fucked everything up.

I sent back one of those two-animated-creatures-hugging gifs with *There, there. It'll be okay.* Which is a text I would have sent them in the Before Times.

It should have felt good, like we were getting back to normal. Except did we want to be getting back to normal? Yes? No? I didn't know?

The following day I contemplated getting them lunch and dropping it off, which if we were getting back to normal would have made sense, but in my current state of ambivalence about "normal" it didn't seem quite right. Which was confusing.

I'd been hoping for this since everything had changed, and now that it was here it didn't feel as good as I'd thought it would. What did that mean?

This may be dumb, but when I was sitting in the apartment later, trying unsuccessfully to distract myself with video games, I realized that the people I knew who had the most experience with like...relationships? Were my folks. The all-grown-up-don't-need-mommy-and-daddy's-help part of me had a brief skirmish with the any-port-in-a-omg-just-get-Art-back part of me, and you can probably guess which side won.

"Preston! Preston's on the phone!"

There was honestly something adorable about my parents. I'd found it embarrassing and kind of weird when I was a teenager that they seemed to like each other so much, but now that I was older, wiser, and also wanted Art to act like that when our kid called home someday in thirty years, I was inclined to find it charming.

"I'm having an issue," I said, before my mom could start in with any small talk, and after my dad said hello. "With Art. Or maybe me. Or maybe how we're...communicating? I don't know. But." I hesitated over the words. "I need help."

Dead air for five seconds.

"Why don't you tell us what's going on, dear?" Mom said.

Dad added, "We're happy to help in any way we can."

I took a deep breath. That was...yeah. Art's folks were like stick-your-head-in-the-sand and Wade's were super into appearances and everyone smiling, and mine? Were happy to help. And meant it. So I told them what had happened, about

Ches and driving through the night and coming home and having that conversation in the kitchen and apologizing and Art needing some space. And then how they'd dropped off lunch and we were texting again and it felt a lot like it had felt back before they moved in, when we saw each other, and talked to each other, and never really went deeper than that.

"But it doesn't feel like we've really...resolved anything? I mean, I said I was sorry, and I think they basically accepted my apology, and we fought a little bit over, like, details, but now we're just sort of..." I wasn't sure how to describe the sense of neutrality. "In a holding pattern, I guess."

My parents didn't speak immediately, but I figured they were probably having a silent conversation with each other, trying to decide how hopeless I was.

"And you don't like the holding pattern?" my dad asked.

"I mean. I don't want to be in it forever." Obviously.

"Because you have feelings for Art," my mom said. "Is that right?"

"Uh, yeah. I thought we already knew that."

"Some of us have known it longer than others," my dad mumbled. A movement sound and he cleared his throat. "Returning to the issue at hand, in what ways have you tried to address it so far?"

"Umm... I called you guys?"

"That's a start," my mom said soothingly. "Darling, I think it's clear that you and Art need to discuss this. With each other."

"Oh. Um." That probably made sense. "How...do we do that?"

"There's a new invention built to speak to people across distances," my dad began.

This time Mom for sure stepped on his foot. "You might

try calling? I know you kids think it's old-fashioned, but it can be helpful to hear someone's voice."

"I could Facetime them, I guess."

"Or see their face," she continued as if she'd meant that all along.

"Yeah, but then...what do I say?"

"Be honest with Art. That's all."

"And then be receptive with whatever Art says," my dad added, more serious this time. "Really listen, Pres. Talk about what each of you want."

"And don't want," Mom chimed in.

"Okay. Wait, I should write this down." I ignored their stifled near-laughs and grabbed a pen. "So I should be honest...and also...and also they should...be honest. And I should listen. And we should talk about what we want." The scrawl was basically illegible, but hopefully just writing it out would be good enough. "And what we don't want."

"That sounds good," my dad said.

"Okay. So like. You think I just. You think I just call them?"

"Or you ask them to meet up with you," Mom suggested. "Some conversations are best had in person."

"Face-to-face."

"Voice to voice."

I rolled my eyes. "Anyway, thanks, and also if this all goes horribly I'm totally blaming you guys."

"We are entirely all right with that, dear."

I said goodbye to the single parental unit occupied by both of my parents and hung up. I reviewed my notes. I deeply considered the many possible avenues of advance. I almost chickened out. Did I invite them over? But that made it seem like they no longer lived here. Did I suggest we meet up in public like internet strangers evaluating for serial killer tendencies?

But I didn't want to have this conversation in a café, or even in a park. Plus air-conditioning was a thing.

What was the best way to be respectful? To show I was paying attention?

I didn't actually know. But I had an idea. I texted Wade to see if I could maybe come over for a private conversation with Art on air-conditioned sorta neutral ground, but where they also were comfortable and felt safe. Pending their agreement, which I made clear I hadn't asked for yet, but I wanted to check it with the actual, like, people who lived there first.

Wade sent back, *Whatever Art decides. We can find alternative occupations if you'd like the place to yourself (and as long as you do not have sex on our bed; Ray is particular about linens).*

Which, like, peak Wade but also ahhh, why would anyone ever have sex on someone else's bed? The horror. I didn't bother typing back, but I did send a bunch of vomit emojis.

Then obviously, clearly, undeniably, it was time to talk to Art. Or at least message them.

I stared at the screen.

I washed the dishes I'd left in the sink.

I looked back through our recent, painfully casual messages.

I started typing, stopped typing, deleted.

I put water on to boil and wondered if there was such thing as eating too much pasta.

I went back to my phone and made a deal with myself that I'd have sent a message by the time the water boiled.

I ended up with *Was wondering if maybe I could come over to talk? (Cleared it with Wade, hope that's okay.)*

And then I waited. And waited. And wished I could take it back. And waited. And put the pasta on. And waited.

And then.

And then.

Sorry, closed tonight, yes. Okay. When?

In for a penny, right? *Is now too late?*

This time it took three minutes but felt like three hours for the next message to come through.

W&R said they'd go out for dinner. See you soon.

And that was that. I turned off the burner under the pasta, which was almost finished cooking, changed my clothes, returned to the kitchen to stare down into the pot. Pasta could travel, right? I dumped it into a plastic container, threw in some capers because Art liked them, and added some rosemary olive oil on top. Then into my bag.

And thus I transported pasta in a messenger bag on the subway to share with my bestie-slash-roommate-slash-person I was maybe in love with. Which is the grandest of gestures, if you squint a little.

Chapter Twenty-Nine

Wade, unfortunately, was still there when I arrived. If I'd thought about it I would have waited until he and Ray were safely out of range before opening my bag, but I didn't think about it (and I was also motivated by wanting to get the hot brick of pasta away from my body).

"And for the entrée tonight," he intoned to Ray, "we have the Please Don't Leave Me Fettuccini, which is a specialty of the house." Then, to me, he said, "Tell me you did not just pause to make pasta."

"I was already making pasta."

He crowed. "That's worse! That's absolutely worse."

"But you said—"

Ray shoved him toward the door. "I seem to remember you bringing me Please Don't Leave Me breath mints, which is even worse than pasta, mister. Bye, Preston!"

I waved and tried to ignore Wade's continued commentary, which was only cut short by the heavy door closing behind them. Feeling absurd now, I said, "I...tried to bring dinner. Sorry. I should have stopped for something."

Art shook their head and took the container. "Ooo, capers, yum."

"If you have parmesan or something, it would probably be better, but I thought if I put it on back at home it'd be all disappeared by the time I got here."

"It definitely would have been." They went into the kitchen. Kitchen noises commenced. Was I supposed to wait? Follow them? Do something else? I settled for meticulously removing my shoes and placing them just so on the little mat that lived in the entryway for shoe removal purposes.

"We can eat in here!" Art called.

The living room. The coffee table. The couch where we'd sat the last time I had been over, all of us crowding together to look at clips of *The Singer Not the Song*. When things had seemed so much better than they were now, except for the fact that I was kind of living a double life and also Art and I were both not telling the other some kind of important things.

Which. Well. Maybe that was where we started.

"I have an Important Thing to say," I announced.

"Did you just capitalize that in your head?"

"Maybe."

Art smiled and squared their shoulders. "I am ready to hear this Important Thing."

That was good. Um. So. Now I just had to say something. "We kissed one time in college and I have been hoping we would kiss again ever since," I said in a rush. "If you wanted to! I mean, I have been hoping you would want to. Not like I just wanted us to kiss if you didn't want to."

"I would not even consider that an option."

"Me neither!"

"No, I mean, I knew you wouldn't want us to kiss unless I also wanted to kiss." Art frowned. "I think that's what I mean."

"I am strongly pro-consent for kissing."

"We were pretty intoxicated last time, PK."

"We should not be intoxicated next time." I covered my mouth with the hand not (somewhat pointlessly) holding my fork. "Omahgud forget I shed dat."

They acted like they were thinking about it. "Nope, don't think I will. So you want to kiss me. Good to know."

I gulped and forced myself to breathe. "So um. So that's... that's a thing."

"Is it a thing or a *Thing*?"

"A *Thing*. Um. That is. That you. Uh. That you are now aware of."

"And that's why you brought me pasta?"

"Not exactly. More that...it seemed like we were going back to normal. Like. We were just going to...move on."

"I figured that's what you wanted." They speared a caper and ate it straight up, not even cringing at the salt. "I thought that would be exactly what you wanted. Pretend everything's back to normal. Pretend none of it happened."

"No! No, that's not what I want. At all. I mean. I wish I hadn't done it the way I did it, but also I don't want it to go back to the way it was before you knew."

"Before I knew you were a hotshot author, or the other thing?"

Which brought me up short. Because they felt like the same thing to me most of the time, but they weren't. "I should have told you about writing the book. I know that. I wish I had. There were so many times I wanted to share things with you. Or maybe whine about things with you. I had to whine at Maggie instead, but she's not a very gratifying whine partner."

"Is that wine in the—" they tipped their head back and mimed drinking "—sense of the word, or whine-with-an-h sense of the word?"

"The second one. Maggie's not a huge whine person. In any sense of the word, actually."

"You're saying you wanted to whine at me? That's what you wish you'd been able to do? *That's* why you regret keeping it a secret?"

But it wasn't. I put my fork down. "You're the person I want to share everything with. The day I signed the contract I got us takeaway and I almost told you right then. It was so exciting, you know? My first book sold! I wanted to celebrate it with you."

"So why didn't you? I just can't stop thinking about the many, many, *many* opportunities you had to tell me." They looked away. "Were you laughing at me all that time? When I talked about—when I said how much I liked the book? I went around like an idiot talking about my book boyfriend and the whole time you were, what? Giggling behind your hand?"

I wanted to jump on that and defend myself, but I couldn't totally get past the image. "Um, I don't think I was…giggling behind my hand? I'm not a cartoon, Arty."

"Oh my god, so not the point."

"I mean, no? But also, *giggling behind my hand*? I was definitely not doing that. I wasn't giggling at all. I was like…flattered that you loved the book, and stunned that I'd written something you cared so much about, and horrified that when I eventually told you about it you'd be pissed I hadn't told you immediately and it was all super complicated."

"It wasn't complicated! It was so simple. I say, 'I'm so dumb I'm in love with a fictional character.' You say, 'Actually FYI I wrote that book.' That's all you had to say!"

"In front of your friends? Because I wasn't even supposed to be telling people in the first place!"

They shook their head. "What friends? You could have just told *me*!"

"The first time I knew you'd read it was at your book club." I paused, stung all over again by the memory. "And you were *so* sneery. 'Oh, PK doesn't read books like this,' you said, to your friends, like I was some kind of oaf, like I was this—this—*buffoon*."

"I don't think of you like a buffoon!"

"You sure talked about me like one!"

"I didn't…" They set down their fork. "That's not what I meant. It's just. It's such a cliché to be in love with a romance novel hero. And my track record with actual people is so bad. I guess I thought *you* would be sneery, so I kind of got in first. Did it really… I didn't mean to hurt your feelings."

I bit back the automatic denial and shook my head when I couldn't think of what to really say to that. "It was really. Like. This thing I worked so hard on, that I emptied my whole heart into. And you were acting like I wasn't good enough to read it, let alone to write it. Like I was too dumb. Or not deep enough. Which kind of… I mean, I know I'm not a deep person? But it still stung." Which felt like such a stupid thing to say when I'd done such a hurtful, long-term, *public* thing to them and I was basically like *also this one time you said something insensitive.* I held my breath, hoping they would know I wasn't trying to say the scales were even or anything like that, just that…just that I had enough feelings that sometimes they also got hurt.

Art looked at me for a long time. Like an uncomfortable amount of time.

I didn't move.

"Sometimes it's still hard for me to believe you wrote it. But other times? Other times I hear entire passages in your voice." Pause. Fraught pause. "I *do* think of you as deep. Honestly. I know that you…that you feel things. It's just sometimes it seems like you want to be perceived as…maybe not shallow, but definitely not challenging. And when you feel things intensely, you can't help but be challenging to people, because not everyone wants to…put up with that. Which I know from painful experience."

"Oh my god, I never feel like I'm putting up with you! Who said that?"

They smiled weakly. "No one that explicitly. It's just an impression I get from people. That I'm a lot. And you're…not a lot. Not like that. You put people at ease, and I guess sometimes I forget that you do that as a way of sort of…not letting on that there's so much more going on beneath the surface."

"Ugh. That makes me sound like Wade."

That got a real smile. "Don't knock Wade. He knows you shockingly well."

I wrinkled my nose. "I doubt it."

"He really does, though. Because I'd talk about how angry I was, how horrible you were, and he'd go along with it—"

"I just bet he would," I muttered.

"—and then he'd remind me of some part of the book that sounded just like you, that was this barely there skin of fiction over what was just…you. Utterly and completely you. And even though I didn't stop being mad, I also kind of…remembered. That you weren't just the guy who made me look like a fool in front of, like, everyone. You were also the guy who brought me chicken soup that time I got food poisoning right before finals. And the guy who…took me in when I had nowhere else to go. *As well as* the guy who made me look like a fool in front of literally everyone."

I winced. "I know intention doesn't matter, but I never, ever meant to do that, and I'm so sorry that I did it anyway."

"I know you are. And mostly they don't think I'm a fool, they think I'm some kind of marketing mastermind. No one believed me when I said I had no idea. You'd think after the whole…after the whole scene…they'd know it was true, but a lot of them still think I was part of the big secret. I think they like that narrative more than, y'know, the truth."

"I'm so sorry," I said, pinned by their gaze. "I didn't think of it like that. And... *I* thought you knew too." They opened their mouth but I rushed on. "No, I don't mean that was like... an excuse. I think I just really *wanted* to believe it. The idea that it was this thing we were sharing even though I'd done basically everything possible to make sure that wouldn't happen."

"I wish we *had* been sharing it. Part of me is so mad at you for stealing that from us. From me. I could see what people meant when they teased me about how I'd known all along. They thought it was so sweet and romantic." Art's eyes filled. "You're such a jerk."

"I know." My own eyes filled. "I am. I'm the worst. I'm so sorry."

"You should be." They fell into my arms. "You really should be! We could have had so much fun, we could have had *everything*, but you messed it all up!"

"I know." Both of us were talking through tears. "I know I did. It's all my fault."

"You're the worst."

"I know! I know I am."

"But also." They hiccupped. "But also you're a little bit wrong."

"I am? Are you sure? Because I'm for it, but also I think it's definitely my fault."

"A lot of it is your fault," they conceded.

"I just...thought it was the kind of thing you would want. I thought there would be this beautiful moment when our eyes met because you knew all along. It just...seemed like that was part of our story. Which I know sounds so dumb, but—"

"It isn't. It doesn't sound dumb. I would have loved that. You were right. That just...wasn't real."

I gulped and scrubbed tears out of my eyes. "I know. That's why it's my fault."

"But not entirely. Because I wanted a fairy tale. Like, if it wasn't me, if it was someone else at work, if it was their...their whatever-person doing this big grand gesture, I can see how I would have thought it was kind of romantic and beautiful. Just like in a novel. And I never stopped to think that like... the perfect book boyfriend? Might not actually be a very good boyfriend. In real life."

"Uh..." I couldn't figure out what they meant. "No?"

"Well, think about it. Sure, that sounds like a great moment in a book or a movie? But in reality it's this kind of gross nonconsensual self-aggrandizing, like, performance piece."

I winced.

"I didn't mean that as an insult. I just think that's what it is, historically. It's almost always the straight white guy doing these borderline really fucked up things as grand gestures in movies, and the audience all goes *awwww* and the heroine cries and everyone lives happily ever after. But in real life that kind of thing wouldn't land you with a happy ending. It'd land you with a restraining order."

Which...they had a point. But also ow. "So you don't want a perfect book boyfriend?" Because I'd seriously have to go back to the drawing board and write a whole new book.

"No, PK." They took a deep breath. "I want a very, very imperfect book-*writer* boyfriend. Do you know anyone who might want the job?"

"I...um... I might know someone who fits that description." I held out my hand. "Will you do me the honor of, um, moving back in with me?"

They laughed. "I will."

"Oh good. Maggie will be thrilled. She's super sick of me crying."

"You were *crying*?"

"I mean. Maybe?" Since tears were still drying on my cheeks, the bravado was dumb. "Yeah. I cried in front of Maggie. I fought with you in my head. I cried in front of my parents. I fought with you in my head. I cried in front of Wade. I sort of…gave up fighting with you in my head. I cried a lot is what I'm saying."

"Me too. I'm sick of crying."

"Same."

"We should stop."

"I think…that's the opposite of what we should do. Probably we should just talk to each other more so we don't have to cry so much."

Their lips curled a little, the softest of smiles. "Seems wise. How'd you learn so much about romance?"

"I wrote a whole book about it."

"I had no idea."

We grinned at each other, the silliness rounding off the edges of everything we said.

"So you'll be my boyfriend?" they asked after a moment.

"I'd love that."

"Okay. Done deal." They held out their hand.

I grasped it.

Without any hesitation both of us leaned in and kissed. Again. Sober and adult and still smiling.

"It's better this time," I said.

"*We're* better this time."

"Very true. We should probably kiss again to make sure."

"Fair point."

We were *much* better this time.

Sometime later the front door opened and Wade called, "You two better not be boinking!"

Ray called, "You better be boinking but at your own place!"

We had our clothes mostly straightened by the time they entered the living room. "We're leaving," I said.

"Right now." Art gave them both hugs and cheek kisses. "I'll come get everything tomorrow."

Wade waved a hand. "Don't be so quick. Twenty-four hours is more than long enough for Preston to screw up again."

Ray elbowed him hard. "We love and support you, whatever you decide." She gave me a hug. "You too, Preston."

"Um, thanks."

Wade sighed and also hugged me. "You're a lucky bum, don't forget it."

"I won't," I said grumpily. Then Art took my hand and the grumpiness vanished. "I really won't." This was a promise for Art, not Wade.

"Awww, aren't they adorable?" Wade began making shooing motions. "Go home, lovebirds."

Which is what we did. We went home. Our home. Together.

★ ★ ★ ★ ★

Acknowledgments

As always, Alexis Hall and General Wendy are worth their weights in gold. Without Wendy's insightful (and generous) reading and AJH's ability to identify the soft spots, this book would not be nearly what it is now. I am forever in their debts.

BREAKING: Lost novel of Belle Époque Paris, The Throne, comes to the silver screen with an A-list cast. But will on-set drama doom the filming of this gay love story before it starts?

Read on for an excerpt from Eight Weeks in Paris *by S. R. Lane.*

10:44 a.m.

BREAKING: Nicholas Madden cast in live-action adaptation of LGBTQ masterpiece "The Throne"

Nicholas Madden was cast this morning as Frederick in period piece *The Throne*, confirming the rumors to that effect.

Cast alongside him are Sir Reginald Jarrett as Hubert, Andrée Belfond as Jehanne (it's been so long since the French *gamine* has been on our screens!), and Jason Kirkhall as Ambrose (an odd choice, as Kirkhall is best known for his superhero franchises, but he can be versatile…if one overlooks his long nights out).

We expect some drama out of so capricious a cast—lest we forget Kirkhall's flighty liaisons with starlets and K-pop singers, and Sir Reginald Jarrett's infinite on-demand supply of apricot tartlets. But even they are put to shame by Madden's legendary strops, his short-fuse temper, and his rank distaste for misbehaving costars. As the man critics have dubbed the Big Bad Wolf of Hollywood, Madden hits all the stops in the actor bingo, from "extraordinarily talented" to "a proper prick, actually."

Madden's fan base, trusting in their idol's penchant for dramatics, has set up an online clock ticking down to the first on-set breakdown (see it for yourself here).

Despite these apparent drawbacks, *The Throne*—with Priya Chaudhuri set to direct and the Henderson siblings producing—may well turn out a number of award-worthy performances. Chaudhuri, to whom official recognition is long overdue, is a hot bet for Best Director noms next year. *The Throne* might become her golden ticket into Hollywood history...if Kirkhall can keep it in his pants and Madden can keep it together.

Set in turn-of-the-century Paris, *The Throne* was for decades a lost novel. Rediscovered in the early nineties, it was heralded as a masterpiece of LGBTQ literature. The love story at its core is frequently cited by modern critics as a rare early portrayal of a non-tragic gay relationship—though its depiction of bohemian queerness during the Belle Époque is not without its flaws and prejudices.

With Madden cast as one of the two mains, only Angelo, the novel's most complex and controversial figure, is left to cast.

While Madden will have his work cut out for him as dark, brooding Frederick, Angelo may prove a challenge for the most seasoned actor (as the disastrous stage adaptation from the early aughts has eloquently shown). Whoever bears the brunt of that role and shares the stage with Madden—a man unaccustomed to sharing the spotlight—will have to be an egoistic diva in his own right, or risk being utterly outperformed. With how many times *The Throne* has been in and out of production, those who claim the novel incompatible with the silver screen may well be proven right...

14:01

UPDATE: Cast! In a strange turn of events, *The Throne*'s Angelo will be played by Christian Lavalle, better known for his

Calvin Klein and Armani campaigns and his 1.5M Instagram followers than for his acting history. Lavalle, 25, became a Dior mainstay at the tender age of sixteen and has been steadily acquiring modeling gigs ever since, but his experience as an actor is limited to a few appearances in French soaps, television gigs, and international ads.

Casting a newbie to act opposite Nicholas Madden is certainly an odd choice. Can he strike up the right kind of chemistry with the Big Bad Wolf, or will Madden have to carry the movie's huge emotional arc on his shoulders? Will *The Throne* crumple under its own weight?

At least he's French.

Filming is set to begin in June.

June 2024. Paris.

Christian Lavalle was one of two things: a vapid boy-king without the skill and understanding to rival his good looks, or a *devastatingly* talented actor.

Nicholas very much doubted he was the latter.

The Parisian sun in June, warm and soft, spilled like liquid gold over the cobblestones of the Place Colette, the butter-soft columns of the Comédie-Française, and the polished red tables of the café terrace. It was a gorgeous day in Paris. On a late afternoon like this, all one wanted to do was relax in the sun, wear a cool suit of clothes and sip a cocktail.

Nicholas mostly felt hot and overdressed. The sparkling water he had ordered had done nothing to cool him down. It had scattered strange butterflies in his stomach.

He and Lavalle had arrived within minutes of each other to their nonofficial meet and greet. Lavalle had immediately been waylaid by a horde of fans, and did not seem inclined to put a stop to their fawning.

Nicholas was not a patient man.

But the lean young man who held court in the middle of the Place Colette, surrounded by the gaggle of his devotees, drew his gaze and attracted his attention, inescapably.

Because Christian Lavalle *demanded* attention. His beauty was compelling and undeniable. In a lily-white shirt and black jeans he looked infernally cool; the heat seemed to be beneath his notice. In his ad campaigns he had been merely exquisite; in motion he was...*distracting*. His hair, made golden by the sun, just touched the corners of his smiling eyes. He was laughing.

"Don't look so offended, Madden," said Madalena, slipping into the seat next to his. She stretched out her arm along the back of his chair and crossed her long legs. "The boy's done nothing to deserve your wrath except land the job. This is a very good look on him. Very *chic*."

"He's twenty-five years old," said Nicholas. "Hardly a boy."

"Then *you* are positively ancient."

Madalena grinned at him. In the Parisian sunshine, she, too, was even more beautiful than usual. Her dyed hair was burnished to an auburn sheen; with her white skirt splayed over her crossed legs, her sweetheart neckline betraying a fair amount of brown-skinned cleavage, she looked like an actress right out of the nineteen forties. A shame she had never shown any penchant toward the vocation. She was content to be his PA, to haul him out of bed in the mornings and drink his expensive coffee. Nicholas dreaded the day when she grew tired of him and went off to ru(i)n someone else's life. He suspected her exorbitant pay had something to do with how long she'd stuck by him.

But she *was* beautiful, and he was—even an ocean away from home—famous, and people looked at them, attracted as moths to the flame of recognition and notoriety. The rare few who could tear themselves away from Christian Lavalle were already turning their smartphones on them, daring to take candids and tapping away. He could imagine the tweetstorm.

@somenosyfucker y'all nicholas madden is in paris and hes not lookin happy about it

@noprivacy someone dare me i'll totally ask for a selfie

@celebsenlive c'est qui elle??? depuis quand il a une copine?

@unautreconnard Nicholas Madden est à Paris? Il tourner-ait pas un film? 😲

Pictured: a scowling man, hands stuffed in his pockets, glaring at his prospective costar.

It didn't matter. He was in Paris for *The Throne*. The table read was scheduled in less than two days, provided Lavalle could shake off his fans for long enough to make it. Nicholas found the prospect sadly uninspiring. The thrill he'd felt when the script had finally, *finally* landed in his lap had now all but faded. *The Throne* was something real, a period piece with modern sensibilities, a project he could back without feeling that he was giving in to mediocrity. He was an ardent lover of the novel. He'd been waiting for that opportunity for… years. Years. He had made *damn* sure he'd be getting the role.

And then the Henderson siblings, or some inept casting assistant, had chosen Christian fucking Lavalle, prima donna sublime, to play his Angelo. He was a *fashion model*, for god's sake, an Instagram *influencer* with a reputation for flightiness and barely any acting experience; and nepotism, or beauty, for all Nicholas knew, had landed him the role. It was sacrificing quality to sell tickets. No doubt production had meant to appeal to twin demographics: those who were young and online and celebrity-hungry, and those who were easily distracted by a pretty face. Nicholas had no patience for it.

Madalena tsked at him. "Keep making that face and it'll stick that way. Wind's a-blowing."

"We're supposed to have a—" Nicholas's voice lowered into scorn. "A *meet and greet*. Basic courtesy; the regular fare. I've been here half an hour. He lacks even the professionalism to know when to put away his fans."

Madalena shrugged a smooth shoulder, and produced a tablet from somewhere. "He posted a picture of the Comédie-Française on his Instagram account. Fans flock to him like bees to honey."

Nicholas closed his eyes briefly. "Of course he did."

She turned the tablet. Lavalle's Instagram account was a steady, pastel-colored stream of pictures of Paris, himself, himself and dogs, himself and fans, promo shoots for ad campaigns he was plugging, more dogs, and more Paris. *Amélie*, times ten thousand.

"A disaster," Nicholas said shortly. He doubted Lavalle had even noticed him. Smiling for the cameras must take up the entirety of his cranial activity.

Madalena hummed, scrolling through pictures of honey-gold buildings and bright sun. "Chaudhuri called."

"Pardon me?" Madalena's job was to field his calls and deflect the loonies from his path, not to hit voice mail on the fucking director of the fucking movie.

"Calm down," Madalena said, still not looking at him. "She wanted me to pass on a word, that's all."

Nicholas was only mildly appeased. "Anytime you feel willing to share, Madalena—"

"They've chosen a location for the café. There's a neat little underground bar near Bastille they can convert to Belle

Époque aesthetics, whatever that means. She wants you to drop in tonight, get a feel for the place. Food looks good. Very classic. The menu boasts touches of, I quote, 'bistro avant-garde'—whatever *that* means."

Avant-garde food tended to be jelly-colored foam on foal-liver crostini: the sort of thing that was both inedible on the tongue and offensive to good taste. Not a single good medium-rare steak in sight. "Fine." Nicholas glanced away. The gardens of the Palais-Royal glimmered across a plaza of black-and-white marble columns. It was tempting to escape there for a few hours—to stretch out his legs on one of those green iron chairs between the trees, take in the sun, turn off his phone. *Rest.*

"She wants you to bring Lavalle along. Have a private dinner. Get to know the guy."

Hell. Well, there went that fucking idea. Nicholas cast her a dark look. "Say that again."

She lifted her eyebrows at him. "Dinner with Chris Lavalle." She pointed, helpfully.

"Thank you, Madalena, I know where my damn costar is." So did the rest of the world, apparently. Regrettably.

"And here you are: glaring exquisitely at him, in full sight of every Parisian in the neighborhood, which is doing no good whatsoever for your optics—I say this out of love, not just because your job is also my job. You haven't exchanged a word with the man. Give him a chance," she coaxed, as gentle as with a lion. "Talk to him. He might turn out to be a kinder soul than you think."

Nicholas didn't need a kind soul. He needed a costar—an equal, a partner, a man he could respect. "He's a diva. An influencer. He isn't an actor. His English is atrocious."

"His accent is lovely. And you barely speak French."

"I know enough." He could say *bonjour, merci,* and *sortez de mon chemin, bordel de merde*, which was usually enough for his purposes.

Madalena brushed sun dust off her skirt. "You keep looking at him."

"The entire blasted world is looking at him. He's making damn sure of it."

"The entire blasted world isn't about to play his lover. And you've been furiously eye-fucking him for half an hour. People are bound to notice." She wriggled her smartphone at him. "I noticed."

"You had better," Nicholas growled, "not be looking up pictures of your employer on that thing."

"I don't need to look you up. You're trending."

"For fuck's sake, Madalena!"

Laughing, she swiped to show him. And there he was—in his expensive sweater, in profile; his elbow was resting on the table next to his coffee cup, one hand covering his mouth. Half in shadow. He looked pensive. Absorbed. Odds were, any one of the morons pointing their expensive smartphones in his direction had caught *who* he was looking at, too. *Goddamn it.*

What the hell *was* wrong with him? Was he a green boy, untrained and inexperienced, so easily distracted by a pretty face and a lithe body that looked as though it had been made for—

He stopped that thought right the fuck there. And handed the phone back, grimacing. "I've been...preoccupied."

"He *is* gorgeous," said Madalena.

"His job description is to look handsome and wear shiny things. Of course he's beautiful."

But Nicholas thought it a weakness. Beauty of that kind meant men like Chris Lavalle could coast by in the world, safe in the knowledge that they would always be loved. Beauty of that kind was too great for this life. Nicholas had worked with good-looking men and women in the past, but never before had it got so much…under his skin. It was an irritant. He disliked it.

"You put too much pressure on yourself, Nicholas." Madalena sighed. "Get a good look at him now; everybody does. He expects it, I suspect. You're gonna get closer to him than anyone else around here ever will," she added. And wasn't that the root of the problem, Nicholas thought, somberly. "Better get over it now, while you're still at arm's length. He might lose some of that attitude once he's in the water with you."

The script had several nude scenes. Nicholas had dismissed them as a regular day's work. Then he had learned whose mouth he would kiss, and who would touch him—so intimately. And things inside his head had gotten a hell of a lot messier.

Theoretically, sex scenes were about the least *sexy* scenes one could film. Nicholas had shot plenty of them in the past. Nudity did not trouble him; he'd kissed enough people on-screen to shrug off the intimacy of it. The technique—the skill—was in looking believably sensual while fighting off the intense foolishness of gooseflesh and wearing a skin-colored sleeve over one's cock. The best way to achieve this, he had found, was to hold himself at a distance from his costar, and manage, however awkwardly, to laugh with them: make the whole thing a day's trip down insanity lane.

He doubted he could laugh with Chris Lavalle.

He was a young Apollo, too lovely and too magnetic to be real. You couldn't laugh with someone like that: you could only worship them or scorn them.

As though summoned by the thought, Lavalle turned across the Place Colette and met his gaze, despite the sunshine in his eyes, despite the distance between them. Nicholas's hand stilled around his coffee cup.

He had remarkable grey eyes. He was a cliché of a Frenchman, charming and remote.

"He's coming over," Madalena observed, chin upon her hand.

"No; is he?" Nicholas muttered.

Christian Lavalle, having at last shaken off his posse—who remained hovering, though thankfully distant—came to a stop beside their table. He gave them a smile: cordial, diplomatic. He met Nicholas's eyes for a moment, then moved on to Madalena with a polite confusion that soon melted into polite disinterest.

"Hello," he said, in a soft voice. "Shall we get on?"

His English was stilted, as with non-native speakers who learned it early on but never fully grasped the measure of the language. His voice was overly formal, and oddly accented, a little deferential.

"Get...on," Nicholas repeated.

Lavalle shrugged. "They have told me to meet Priya at *Le Renard d'Or.*"

Priya, Nicholas thought, with vague disbelief. Priya Chaudhuri. Their *director*. He glanced at Madalena, who helpfully said, "The Golden Fox. The bar I told you about."

"We are to have dinner." Lavalle widened his eyes a fraction, smiling. It was a fantastic smile. Nicholas had given the press many a fake, charming grin in the past; this was the best of them all combined. The simmering hatred of them, streamlined, brutally tailored down to an art.

He realized abruptly that Lavalle had no better an opinion of him than *he* had of Lavalle. Hands in his pockets, rocking slightly upon his heels, he looked entirely at ease.

This was his city. His ground.

"Dinner," Nicholas said softly.

Lavalle glanced down, then up again. His lashes were long and fair against his cheeks. "*Mais bien sûr.* I have made a booking for eight."

Nicholas had assumed Chaudhuri meant for them merely to

look about the place. Eight was late for dinner—though not so late for Parisians, who enjoyed eating late into the night; give them a bottle of Beaujolais and a platter of charcuterie, and they would cheerfully wait out the sunrise over the Seine. Lavalle seemed intent on fitting himself to the stereotype as closely as possible. He now turned his lovely smile on Madalena, who—to her credit—neither blinked nor blushed against that frontal attack. "A table only for two, I'm afraid. Although... I am sure I could call..."

"Oh, no." Her voice was amused. "You two will want to get to know each other." She extended a hand. "I'm Madalena Torres. The PA. Get him home before midnight, yeah?"

Lavalle ducked his head, his smile fading; a flush was just touching his cheekbones. What measure of *control* could the man have on his facial expressions? It was insanity.

"We should go then," said Nicholas shortly, standing. Somewhere to the left of them, someone was snapping pictures. It was grating; yet Lavalle seemed content to linger, presenting his best profile. He was used to it. His job was to look his best for photographs—candids and otherwise.

Nicholas hated amateur paparazzi with the same fervor he hated professional ones. He always visualized the headlines, the tweets, the bloody BuzzFeed captions. "Traffic'll be hell," he grunted, to speed things along. Madalena held his phone hostage on most occasions, or he'd have called his chauffeur.

Lavalle blinked at him. "Traffic? Nobody drives in Paris."

Nicholas looked at the endless flood of cars exiting the arches of the Palais du Louvre, streaming toward the Opéra Garnier.

"Nobody from Paris drives in Paris," Lavalle amended. *"Ah, mais, mes Américains!"* He sounded amused. "We will take the bus. If we walk to the Seine we will find one going directly to Bastille, alongside the river. It will be much more pleasant. Being stuck in traffic is a...a pain in the ass. *Non*?"

Nicholas couldn't remember the last time he'd taken public transportation. His chauffeur would think he'd been kidnapped.

Nevertheless, with Madalena's generous blessing and her kiss burning upon his cheek—a little teaser for the cameras—they found themselves no later than a quarter hour later in one of Paris's green, foul-smelling buses. No seats; these had been optioned by what looked like half the little old lady population in the city. Instead they stood, and swayed.

Lavalle curled both hands around the metal railing, balancing himself with familiar ease, and stared out the window with distinct interest, as though there was something captivating about the view. In profile, he looked abstracted and sad. Did he sweat, or was he utterly unaffected by the heat? Nicholas was mildly impressed. If this was a character he was playing, Lavalle had gone full method.

What the fuck was Chaudhuri thinking? Casting a model who'd never acted in anything much bigger than a late-night soap was courting misery. For a movie that was already heating up next year's award season talk, of all things. Angelo ought to be played by a Frenchman—or at least someone who could speak the language well enough to bluff international audiences—but he was a baroque, interesting character, full of contradictions. He required *talent*. To have him played by a wannabe comedian with his sights on another Dior campaign was nothing short of an imposture.

Lavalle looked the part, at least. In a silken waistcoat, he would be the perfect Belle Époque debauchee. His proud manner, and the haughty curl of his mouth, would suit Angelo's cynical nature to a fault. And he was deeply, notably beautiful—the kind of beauty that was not easily overlooked, not even in Hollywood. His eyes, most remarkably, were grey and clear as still water. All-seeing. Nicholas thought of classical statues, marble-white and merciless and blind.

But Nicholas knew *The Throne* inside and out, and he would not be fooled by appearances.

Angelo was no indifferent torso of Apollo, listless and diffident. He was a man who had been betrayed often, who had loved and who had lost. He did not show emotion easily. He kept his cards close to his chest, an act Nicholas doubted that Lavalle—who did not so much wear his heart on his sleeve as display it prominently on every social media platform known to man—could achieve with any kind of subtlety.

"I don't get tired of it."

"What?" Nicholas, torn from his preoccupations, was brusque. Lavalle didn't seem offended.

He pointed at the view. The bus was coming up to the unmistakable arches of the Pont Neuf, and beyond it were the tall, dark spires and pale beige buildings of the Conciergerie, holding court above the brown, rushing river. The sun beat down hard, and the sky was a pale, Venetian blue. White slips of cloud were streaming away to the east, toward the hidden towers of Notre-Dame. It was only just the beginning of summer, the longest hours of sunlight in the year, and the days ran long and luminous.

"I've been here a thousand times," said Lavalle. His glance at Nicholas faltered just on the side of charming, as though sharing an intimate moment with a near-stranger was something he wasn't used to; as though he didn't invite intimacy with every picture, every selfie, every #nofilter #homesweethome #liveyourbestlife he posted a couple times an hour. "But I've never grown tired of the view."

Nicholas stared at him. Lavalle held his gaze for a moment, then glanced away. His hair fell softly into his eyes. He'd have to cut it, for the role.

He *had* to be a con. No one was this…this naturally unaffected, to the point that artlessness itself became an affectation. Nicholas could barely figure him out; every second he spent in Lavalle's company troubled him the more.

Lavalle was disconcerting. He kept reinventing himself. He was no longer the elegant, charismatic young man from the Place Colette, who had posed and smiled and allowed his congregation to take an endless stream of selfies. Nicholas had no idea who *this* man was, with that shy smile, those pale sleepy eyes. He only knew that his body was responding in kind—was roused as though from deep slumber into some new state of being, more febrile and more real.

The bus lurched to a stop at a red light—Place du Châtelet, a green plaque said—and with a startled noise Lavalle stumbled against him. He was a sudden, warm weight against Nicholas, who, having wisely braced himself against the railing, captured his elbow in his hand. Muscle and tendon and sheer vitality. Lavalle's eyes lifted to meet his.

They were almost the same height. Nicholas was a touch taller, and broader about the shoulders. He had the sudden urge to slip one arm firmly around Lavalle's waist. Lavalle's hand had landed on his chest, and as the bus resumed its course it remained there, his fingertips tangled in the wool of Nicholas's sweater.

"Pardon," he said. The *n* was softened in his accent, barely there.

"Sure," said Nicholas. His own voice, he realized, was hoarse.

Don't miss Eight Weeks in Paris *by S. R. Lane,*
available wherever Carina Adores books are sold.

www.CarinaPress.com

Fail Seven Times *by Kris Ripper*

Justin Simos knows a few things for sure: he's gay, he's an unrepentant jerk, and he's in love with his best friend—and his best friend's girlfriend.

Alex and Jamie aren't like other people. They aren't fazed by his moods. They laugh at his critical analysis of nineties cinema. They definitely want to have sex with him (…again), and Jamie wants a go at him with her favorite flogger. Despite the fact that they're already perfect together, they want him to join them.

Justin doesn't have words for this thing between the three of them, but he knows romance isn't supposed to be part of it. As long as he ignores his feelings, maybe they can have fun. Keep it simple. Don't fail.

Except Justin's not great at simple, and real damn good at failing. He's not brave enough to be with them, and trying might destroy everything. It's too big a risk. He can't be this strong, passionate person they see him as…unless maybe he already is.

Discover another romantic love story from Carina Adores.

Will on-set drama doom the filming of this gay love story before it starts?

Nicholas Madden is one of the best actors of his generation. His personal life is consistently a shambles, but he'll always have his art.

Chris Lavalle is out, gorgeous and totally green. He has thousands of Instagram followers, a string of gorgeous exes and more ad campaigns to his name than one can count. But he's more than just a pretty face, and this role is his chance to prove it.

Eight weeks of filming, eight weeks of 24/7 togetherness bring Nicholas and Chris closer than the producers had dared to dream. Chemistry? So very much not a problem. But as filming gets set to wrap and real life comes calling, they'll have to rewrite the ending of another love story: their own.

Don't miss
Eight Weeks in Paris by S.R. Lane,
available wherever Carina Adores books are sold.

CarinaAdores.com

IF YOU ENJOYED THIS BOOK WE THINK YOU WILL ALSO LOVE

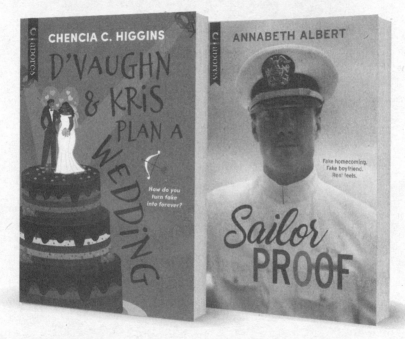

Carina Adores is home to romantic love stories where LGBTQ+ characters find their happily-ever-afters.

Discover more at
CarinaAdores.com